W9-BXQ-517

EVIL UNDER THE TUSCAN SUN

STEPHANIE COLE

BERKLEY PRIME CRIME
New York

BERKLEY PRIME CRIME
Published by Berkley
An imprint of Penguin Random House LLC
penguinrandomhouse.com

Copyright © 2022 by Shelley C. Bloomfield

ISBN: 9780593097830

First Edition: February 2022

Printed in the United States of America
1   3   5   7   9   10   8   6   4   2

Book design by George Towne

In loving memory of my mother,
Fran Costa—
poet, actress, genealogist,
English teacher, art lover,
homemaker, and friend

1

By the middle of November at the Villa Orlandini, I couldn't remember what seventy degrees and sunny looked like. Anywhere. It was as if there were some meteorological dial that fluctuated between Mist and Drizzle and back again. Since Mist became my preferred setting, I started fine-tuning it. There was blanket mist that seemed to hang, pinging mist that had an edge, spritzer mist that was kind of a refreshing aerosol.

I found myself longing for late autumn back in what I increasingly began to refer to as my native land—even though I knew full well that Weehawken, New Jersey, was completely capable of leaving Cortona, Italy, in the mud when it came to the soul-sucking weather of November. At least Cortona, where I had been working for two months designing a cooking school, had inhabitants who either commented cheerfully on the daily drenching or acted like it didn't even register in what was a fatalistic worldview in the first place.

In the last month, certain things had happened at the

Villa Orlandini. The final build-out of the commercial kitchen. The decamping of Annamaria Bari, the sous chef and very former love of Chef Orlandini. Annamaria was the sixty-year-old stalwart who kept the villa running both in and out of the kitchen, which was her throne room, until two months ago. Her throwing in the cheesecloth after four decades of assistance would have left a big enough hole even in what had been the old villa kitchen, let alone the new, expanded, fully outfitted, and glorious kitchen I had designed and finally brought to completion. Now it echoed. Every footfall clattered in the sheer absence of Annamaria. Can a thing of beauty be an empty joy forever? What if Michelangelo had painted a chapel ceiling, and nobody came?

Although her absence was keenly felt, nobody mentioned her. Not, at least, in front of Chef. He was pained, he was betrayed, he was off his game on the bocce court. He appeared close to committing the Italian version of *harakiri*, namely, drinking box wine. Personally, I didn't waste any sympathy on him since he had pretty much brought on the decamping of Annamaria Bari himself, what with casting her aside in the kitchen to ingratiate himself with one of our students, who was busy ingratiating herself with him. With all that reckless ingratiating going on, something was about to blow.

It did.

It was Annamaria.

Bad enough she had been charged with murder—somehow, the victim hadn't even been her kitchen rival—that, she could stand. But after forty years as Chef Claudio Orlandini's sous chef, she had some reason to expect it was turning out to be a life appointment. So, when it was all cleared up, she was released from a murder charge, and the clearing up included her own vision on the matter of Chef. Annamaria Bari wasted no time taking herself off to New York to visit her aged mother for an unspecified amount of time.

If Chef had simply broken some pots to vent his simmering feelings of betrayal, I wouldn't have minded. I had a job to do. But what I didn't see coming was just how the absence of Annamaria was bound to come down on my own unsuspecting head. The final stages of the kitchen build-out meant I, Nell Valenti, was on hand a lot. In the kitchen. Riding shotgun on the contractor, making last minute changes, solving a whole crop of unforeseen problems, stepping up my meal prep game for the villa "staff," just to exercise the kind of control I like during that process when things are disturbingly disorganized.

In the four weeks since Annamaria had left, what Chef discovered—and truly, I didn't see it coming, but then I found the man unpredictable—was that he liked having me around. I became his surrogate Annamaria. When I found new ways to hang cookware, he made the kinds of jokes he always made with Annamaria. When I jazzed up leftover dinners, he nearly genuflected the way he did with Annamaria. When I spied this particular train, finally, roaring toward me where I stood quaking on the track, Pete dismissed my concern.

"He'll get over it. He's just enjoying the return of his routine, that's all."

This attitude goes to show you just how dangerously ignorant a child can be about his parent. But Pete had received a boost in the ignorance department: toward the end of October, Pete's picture had made the November cover of the slick bimonthly magazine *Bellissimo!*, whose target readership is "For Those Who Celebrate Life Arts." By

"Life Arts," they mean food, drink, adornment, travel, and transportation. In the three weeks since the magazine hit high-end hair salons the world over, Pierfranco Orlandini had become a celebrity.

He hit every demographic in *Bellissimo!*'s readership. The cover photo showed him standing just inside the olive grove, leaning against the little Ape, his arms crossed, one hand holding a glass of red wine tantalizingly askew, and travel (not to mention female fantasies) was hinted at in the title of the cover article inside: "Under the Tuscan Son." As for adornment, look no further than the man himself in his tight-fitting jeans and work shirt, squinting sexily into the bright daylight. Behind Pete, the villa property laid out the rest of this *Bellissimo!* environment, what with the charming tumble-down fountain sporting the seventeenth-century Veronica of the Veil statue, plus the stonework of the looming villa buildings. Lesser and greater splashes of sunlight made what could be viewed by any rational human as shameful decrepitude into, instead, an invitation into a mysterious Tuscan past.

Pete was so busy being Pete in the weeks leading up to Ziti Variations that I was a bit relieved when he announced his manager Vivi had set up business meetings in Rome. This was the first I had heard of his manager Vivi.

"Why do you need a manager, Pete?" I asked him as I towel-dried my hair. "You're an olive grower." I managed a smile all on my own, with no help from a Vivi. "You're not a performer."

Nodding absently, he said with a faraway voice, "You never know."

As I sat down next to him on the bed, I heard the mattress creak. I realized it might have been creaking for days or weeks, maybe even longer, but at that moment, I was hearing it for the very first time. I searched Pete's face, and he slipped an arm over my shoulder.

"Look at your father."

"My father?" Dr. Val Valenti, half shrinkster, half huckster, with a cable TV show for what he himself called "the worried well."

Pete made his case. "He's a psychologist, like I'm an olive grower"—as I listened, I was thinking of how it happens that the term "significant other" can suddenly feel like it's shifting away from the "significant" zone and landing more in the "other" territory. Pete had dreams, it turns out, that had nothing to do with expanding his olive oil production—"first and foremost," he asserted.

"I see." If you're saying the same thing twice, like "first and foremost," then you're really not saying anything at all.

"But look how television has acted like a handmaiden to him, to getting his message across."

"My father has no message"—as he started to interrupt, I lifted my hand—"although his show has plenty." I gave a halfhearted little laugh, and Pete drew me in, but not before I saw on his face a look that made me think—unbelievably—he felt a little sorry for me. My heart flopped. The mattress creaked. In that moment, I decided to stay cheerful and to trust that he'd see through all the nonsense. After all, he had seen through Chef Claudio Orlandini's nonsense years ago.

A dazzling momentary light will find other patsies who celebrate "life arts," and Pete would be back designing the expansion of his olive oil production space. I would ignore my concerns that the article "Under the Tuscan Son" barely mentioned the Villa Orlandini Cooking School, and no mention of girlfriend Nell Valenti.

The night before Pete left for his business meetings in

Rome, Chef closed himself in the kitchen, where he spent two hours clattering around, all alone, preparing a special meal for Rosa, Sofia, Pete, and me. Of the four of us, only Rosa viewed this activity as suspicious. She was fond of Chef, but had well-developed crap antennae that, I noticed, mostly twitched when he was within a mile of the rest of us.

It wasn't until he escorted me to my new seat—my heart sank when it turned out to be Annamaria's—at the villa dining table in the chapel of the Veronicans, the medieval order of nuns whose convent the building used to be. Pete, Sofia, and Rosa all sat as Chef poured wine, a lovely and pricey "super Tuscan" he kept for special occasions, and announced the menu.

Beef carpaccio, beef braciole, beef bollito misto . . .

Down the line he went. And I knew we were sunk. I had only been at the villa for two months, but that was long enough to know that when a meal prepared by Chef ran heavy on the beef, he was absolutely *up to something.* And he was, but he made us wait, there in the plentiful candle-light, lulled by an endless loop of the Three Tenors softly in the background, through the carpaccio course, which I found overseasoned with thyme. When Chef is in the grip of what he believes is a great idea, he loses track of herbs and spices. It was when we were forking a sensational beef braciole that he came out with it.

"Ecco la Bella Nella," he intoned, grabbing my fork hand to his breast as though we were in a death scene, *"la mia nuova* sous chef*!"* Spoken with all the weightiness of white smoke drifting upward from the Vatican chimney.

His new sous chef? I choked on my braciole.

He didn't notice.

Pete's eyes widened in alarm, but I couldn't tell whether it was Chef's announcement or my gasping for air, but he probably figured I was a goner either way. Sofia looked pleased for me, murmuring something in Italian along the lines of an employment opportunity of a lifetime. Rosa's eyes narrowed, thinking no doubt of her dethroned sister Annamaria, who might want to resume her role at the villa, and although I wasn't entirely sure of the windup to a lusty *malocchio*—the dreaded Italian curse—I had seen that same look on Annamaria when a curse was about five minutes away. I managed to catch Rosa's eye as I chugged my wine, conveying my horror at my fate. Rosa knew me well enough to know my look did not refer to detouring a bit of savory rolled beef down my windpipe.

As I caught my breath, I surveyed the table.

Pete's knife and fork were poised midair.

Rosa gripped the edges of the eighteen-foot dining table. *Malocchio* averted.

Sofia looked like she was picturing Plácido Domingo in his dressing room.

Only Chef himself flounced back into his seat, smacked his lips, flung his napkin onto his lap, and dug in, having solved the problem of the kitchen vacancy in one grand unilateral announcement, shocking in its tone deafness. Had he run the harebrained idea by me? No. Had he consulted the rest of us, a pretty competent and well-meaning group of villa denizens, as to how to remedy the absence of Annamaria? No. His Bella Nella, as he called me, had one foot out of Cortona already, thinking ahead to stateside jobs in cooking school design.

I had already turned down the same offer of a sous chef job from Stealth Chef, who had attended a four-day marinara workshop last month. And the only reason my other foot was still on villa grounds was Pete. The timing was awkward. I could see I needed a job if I stayed on past the completion of the cooking school, but playing sous chef to the mercurial Chef was not what I wanted. But nothing else was being offered, we were nearing the booking for a four-day private party, and there was a gaping absence of kitchen help.

At that moment, I realized a truth about cooking school design. When, exactly, the project ended was really rather up for discussion. Was it officially ended when the space itself was ready? Or was it ended when the program was up and running? If that, then for how long? Two workshops? Three months? Day one, when the first student alighted from the Cucinavan delivering the group to our doorstep? When it came right down to it, just how responsible was the designer—in this case, me—for dragging the school into the zone of established success? Could that possibly be my responsibility? It hadn't been with my other two school designs, so why was it feeling like an issue here at the Villa Orlandini?

Was I taking a more mature view toward the scope of my career?

Or was it just a blind for not wanting to leave Pete?

I said the only sensible thing in the circumstances. I said yes. For me, this felt like conceding a limb or an eye, but Chef nodded, paying me hardly any attention, and asked Pete to pass the bread. So I actually flung my napkin down on the table, rose, and voiced my stipulation in Italian: Chef must actively interview for Annamaria's replacement (here he snorted, Rosa's nostrils flared, and Pete lifted an eyebrow), for which I would give him one month. At that, everyone rolled their eyes. Including me. With a sigh, I knew I'd have to find the replacement myself. Before going to bed, I'd advertise the job on a few online culinary job boards.

While Chef hummed his way back into the kitchen, promising tarts upon his return, Pete moved closer to Rosa and Sofia, and went over the plans for the four-day private party we were calling Ziti Variations, arriving in two days. I stared at the play of candlelight on my wine. Almost enough light, almost enough wine. Since Pete had assumed (I would say "seized," but no matter) control of the day-to-day operations of Villa Orlandini Cooking School, I had stepped back, which pretty much meant I didn't weigh in on anything short of total incineration. But when I heard a lively discussion kick up between Pete and Rosa, not even the promise of a beef tart from Chef could pull me away.

The issue was the sleeping arrangements for Copeland Party of Three turning up by car for Ziti Variations. New York billionaire philanthropist Philip Copeland was treating his eighty-year-old mother, Mimi, and her best friend, Muffy Onderdonk, to the four-day luxury trip to the villa. When I heard him use the word "luxury," I felt the tectonic plates of my internal organs rumble and shift. No good could come of it. The perception was all a matter of where you stood. We were a cooking school with excellent pedigree and adequate accommodations, not a high-end villa hotel with some amusing cooking classes thrown in instead of snorkeling or golf.

Until that call from Copeland on November 1, we had been registering students for that same weekend midmonth for Advanced Sauce Techniques for Professionals—Pete's idea—with a targeted enrollment of ten. We were well on our way to filling the spots (much to my alarm) when Philip Copeland intervened and made the extravagant gesture of offering to buy out the entire course, Advanced Sauce Techniques for Professionals, and renaming it Ziti Variations (much to my alarm). In honor of his beloved, zitiobsessed mom, who resided in a memory care unit of 305 West End, a swank assisted living establishment on the Upper West Side of New York.

That weekend in November was the only one that would work. It was Mom's birthday, Philip's only free time in the next four months, and Muffy's—well, Muffy was always available, he tossed off dismissively. Chef and Pete deliberated for a full five minutes before taking Copeland up on his "generous and intriguing" offer. I shrugged philosophically. Maybe it was coming at a good time: three guests rather than ten, a senior citizen Ziti Fest instead of the intense and annoying challenges voiced by professional sauce makers. And because Pete was busy off being the Tuscan son of *Bellissimo!* fame, we were a man down.

It was clear that Muffy and Mimi would share the rather nice barn apartment, renovated with a couple in mind—any couple willing to pay much higher fees. So Mimi and Muffy would buddy up—although those old girlhood friends had buddied up again at the assisted living establishment—in the barn, where we'd exchanged a queen-sized bed for two twins. The question, though, was where to put Philip Copeland himself. All that was left were the Dante, Da Vinci, Michelangelo, and Raphael rooms on the second floor of the old dormitory. Still the size of nuns' cells, but clean, freshly painted by local ace painter Hera Neri, and decorated with wall art the same the world over—easy cheesy images of leaves, birds, cityscapes, and words like *Family* with the *i* dotted by a heart—ordered from Amazon.

Rosa had assumed Signor Copeland would be billeted in one of those rooms.

Pete, working the problem out differently, had proposed my doubling up with him in his cottage, which would free up the abbess's room, my digs since my arrival two months ago. A bad precedent, I told him vaguely, even though that particular bad precedent had already occurred two months ago, when I was made to give up my own space to accommodate a villa guest. Never again. The next time I walk away from the charming, fully outfitted abbess's room, it would be with my suitcase in one hand and my train ticket in the other. Finally, Pete demurred.

It was Chef who made the final determination, although I had forgotten about the matter of where to sleep Signor Copeland, and it only arose after that dinner when Chef announced my new role. Pete and Rosa were at an impasse, and Chef, surprisingly quick to pick up on the problem, set ceramic ramekins containing fig galette down at our places. One glance at the mysterious brown hue to the fig filling made me realize that Chef had substituted the dark rum with beef bouillon. Was there no end to what this man was up to?

"Signor Copeland," he decreed, "has room *vicino al mio*"—the room near his own on the first floor of the dormitory, which used to be occupied by *"quella donna cattiva"*—that bad woman. That bad woman? What bad woman? What century was he reaching back to? Some naughty nun kept locked in an Orlandini mental closet where the things they'd rather not think or talk about were tossed?

Rosa, always quick to sense a dastardly insult, erupted. I couldn't follow her. But her uncharacteristically shrill voice sounded just the way I imagined the crowd did at the spectacular and violent end of Benito Mussolini. And then I knew. When Chef chuffed and snarled and spat his response at her in chilling Italian, I realized he was referring to Annamaria. That bad woman. Pete stepped in, manly unto death. "Pop," he shouted, "that's completely unfair to Annamaria, who's only ever been—"

Chef was having none of it. He flung a couple of expressive, if obscene, gestures in his son's direction. Sofia, dabbling in the fig tart, gasped. When Rosa, ordinarily the most even-tempered of the multitudinous Bari family, couldn't take it anymore, she let loose with a lusty *malocchio*, her two fingers jabbed in the direction of Chef, lest the curse go astray. I was reminded of Zeus delivering thunderbolts to unsuspecting mortal offenders. Chef, struck suddenly with the kind of dread I experience when I hear my parents are coming for a visit, staggered backward against the table, and when he clutched at the tablecloth to steady himself, he overturned the cruet of olive oil.

At that, even Pete gasped.

Everyone froze.

With shaking hands, Chef dipped his fingers in the overturned extra virgin olive oil and hastily dabbed behind his ears. Witnessing what Pete later told me is a well-accepted antidote to the bad luck of spilling olive oil, I thought Chef had finally lost his mind. Rosa noisily sucked in enough air for all five of us, and with a triumphant "Ha!" launched another *malocchio*. Haggard and quaking from the effects of grief, temper, and supersonic curses, Chef smeared his palms in the spilled oil and proceeded to smack himself on his neck and cheeks like the spilled oil was *eau de cologne*.

"*Silenzio!*" bellowed Pete. My boyfriend. Oh, so proud. He was grand, every bit Plácido Domingo, only without the vocal range. Then the best he could follow up with was "Shame on you!"

When he appeared to need a GPS to get his clenched fists out of his hair, I stepped up. "Sofia"—I turned first to the noncombatant in the room, who was smiling at me with trust—*"per favore servi l'espresso."* This was formal Italian for something more along the lines of *"For the love of God, bring the damn coffee."* To Chef and Rosa, I said, *"Non c'é altra scelta."* There is no other choice. "Signor Copeland will have Annamaria's room. Hera Neri will paint it." I'd pull the paint wizard Hera off what remained undone on the job in the dormitory cell rooms and put her swiftly on Annamaria's room, soon to be filled by a New York billionaire who brings his mommy all this way for a ziti treat.

Chef lunged toward Rosa. "Ha!"

Rosa glowered, able to discern I had not finished. "But"—I raised my voice at him, gesturing at Pete to translate what I barely had enough words in English to get across—"I never want to hear you call Annamaria Bari a bad woman. Ever again. Do you understand? You have no right to breathe the same air as that woman—"

"Ha!" shouted Rosa, who somehow sensed it was the moment for a "Ha."

I was winding up, aloft in my frustrations with this bald-headed, brilliant, culinary miscreant in front of me. "Yes, she left you—"

This wound he understood, no translator necessary. "She leave villa! She no leave me!" He thumped his chest so hard he coughed.

"Yes," I overrode him, "she left the villa—"

"Ha!" crowed Chef.

"—in order to leave you—"

"Ha!" crowed Rosa.

"You selfish, blind, insensitive—"

Pete split his time between lobbing these words in Italian at his father and muttering to me not to overdo it. At which both Rosa and Chef crowed, "Ha!"

I stood up as regally as I could, considering a piece of braciole was clinging to my chest, and fixed him with a cold eye. "Beef bouillon? Really, Chef? Where"—I mused, flinging down my napkin, which landed on the fig tart—"did you learn to cook?" I asked one of the top five living gods on the culinary world stage. Since the Orlandinis and Baris were looking at me with dazed expressions, I strode from the table and right out the door.

I headed straight to the abbess's room to draft the job description for a sous chef. In me, fury works as a kind of acetone for the wiles the soul can occasionally practice. Strips them right off. I wanted something frank and accurate with no attempt to soft-pedal. Unlike what had been my own experience at the Villa Orlandini, I wanted potential applicants to get concussed with the truth. No faint of heart need apply. After all, a position working as a sous chef under Claudio Orlandini was some lesser-known circle of hell reserved for manufacturers of hard-shell plastic packaging.

Still, it had to be done. And before I went to bed. Done and posted to a culinary job board. Although I was hoping for a gender-nonspecific bruiser, preferably from a work-release program at a Sicilian prison, I believed an intimidated Chef would not lead to fame and fortune for the Villa Orlandini School of Cooking. So my first attempts ran along these lines:

WANTED: Sous Chef

Villa Orlandini Cooking School, Cortona, Italy
No experience necessary—will train the willing and reasonably able
No application too preposterous!

Under Knowledge and Special Skills for qualified applicants, I included:

- Strong communication skills, particularly in any of the 6,500 world languages unknown to Chef (may sometimes include Italian)
- Strong attention to detail, because someone should have this
- Ability to work independently during bossy harangues (personal sound-canceling equipment recommended but not required)
- Good organizational skills that permit bathroom breaks during 24/7 work week
- Willingness to do whatever necessary (ask about recent homicides)

At that point in the effort, I felt my heart sink. What if nobody applied? How could I ever work as that man's sous chef? After my tirade in the chapel, how could he ever want me to? If I was suddenly homeless, I was fine with it.

I had stood up for Annamaria. At least I could face her—that is, if I ever saw her again.

2

Two days later, there she was.

Annamaria herself.

When Rosa and Sofia enticed me out of the office for *"una sorpresa,"* I couldn't tell whether the mist I was experiencing came from the sky or their lips. Succumbing to their tugs, I got pulled away from Hera Neri, a fifty-year-old lifelong Cortonan who always needed work and happened to paint walls and woodwork very well.

"First apartment on the left, first floor of the dormitory, it's open. A rush job."

"Color?" was all she asked in her pretty decent English.

"How about lavender?"

To that, I got a nearly imperceptible shake of her head. "I see no lavender in bedrooms since I was a nanny."

"Well, then, what have you got the most of?" I put it to her sensibly.

She was a petite woman whose early wrinkles always seemed to me like the hieroglyphics of disappointment. Taut skin, lips thin with worry, only her gray eyes lively.

"Insane asylum green," she blurted, *"cos'altro?"* What else?

Losing sight of her, I shouted, "Insane asylum green it is, then. Goes with anything. Oh"—I went on—"after that, how about the oil production space? Big job."

"Color?"

I slowed down to get the picture. "Something along the lines of old food co-op beige."

"Sì, sì, capisco, Nell. *Grazie."*

Clutching me by my forearms, Rosa and Sofia led me outside in the pinging Tuscan mist and through the courtyard. Once I could tell the Copeland Party of Three for Ziti Fest hadn't turned up early, I was game. Just outside the stone archway to the villa grounds, there she was. Only I didn't recognize her at first, with the Mondrian umbrella from the Museum of Modern Art angled over her face. When Rosa and Sofia ducked under it amid much laughter and audible smooches, I felt my heart lift. The shoes were stylish, the legs shapely. Standing next to a used Fiat Panda, the newcomer slowly lowered the umbrella and pulled it shut despite the mist.

Annamaria Bari smiled hard and bright at me, and all I felt was joy. In the month she was gone to New York, to look in on the Bari mother, she'd had her salt-and-pepper hair cut chin length and side parted, and her fashion sense brought forward out of the early sixties. I threw my arms around her and hugged the breath right out of the two of us, wondering where on earth we were going to put Philip Copeland after all.

"Annamaria, you're back!"

Whenever I'm truly happy, I don't care if I state the obvious. Rosa and Sofia were leaping like they had just seen Chef lose big-time in a bocce tournament. I craned my neck to glance into the Fiat. "Where is your suitcase?" A creeping alarm left no room for Italian. I was remembering the green plaid valise with a red yarn pom-pom she had carried away with her the morning she left—what I thought was for good.

"Ah, *tu non capisci*, Nell." She brushed back some misty hair from my face.

"*Cosa intendi*, Annamaria?" What do you mean? Even though I suddenly sensed something was up, this woman would never resort to harebrained infusions of beef into something only ever meant to be sweet. Rosa's lips were pressed together, and poor Sofia gnawed at her knuckles.

"Come with me," she said in beautifully accented English, gesturing toward the Fiat.

No questions asked, we all climbed in, willing to go anywhere with her. It was a short trip. Annamaria did a one-handed turn into the courtyard, where she eased the car into a small space next to the Ape, our blue farm truck. As we alighted, she rested her forearms, just for a moment, on the roof of the car and gazed inscrutably at the dormitory, where she—*that bad woman*—had lived for decades.

There on the first floor in a larger room, with a connecting door into a shared bathroom, up the corridor from Chef's digs. Now repainted insane asylum green by Hera Neri, who was putting finishing touches on the woodwork. Through the vicissitudes of villa life—in other words, what was on or off about Annamaria's peculiar relationship with Chef Claudio Orlandini—she had set apart her private space, like a priest hole, away from the unpredictable swirl of Orlandini life.

Preceded by Rosa and Sofia, who were bounding toward the main building, shaking off the mist with helpless laughter, Annamaria and I followed slowly. As she unfurled the umbrella and lifted it over both our heads, she explained in broken English that she had taken an apartment in Cortona over the jeweler's shop. Tomorrow she started a job cooking half-time for the Veronicans at the new (well, just a hundred years old) convent, which was all they could afford—at that, she shot me a lifted eyebrow and wise grin—and she bought a car for *"la libertà."*

Without missing a step, we hugged each other, and I filled her in on Pete's new career as culinary hottie and how he blithely assumed others in his world would make themselves uncomplicated during the run of his fame. The way it stood, I told her, was that he had interviews, personal appearances, and business meetings that did not include anyone actually at the villa. Annamaria took in the Pete report without comment. She was withholding judgment.

I linked arms with her. "How's your mother?"

Bria Bari, her mother in Bay Ridge, Brooklyn, was as well as could be expected, considering she was ninety and couldn't remember where she had placed her gnocchi board or the hairbrush someone named Benito had given her oh so many years ago. At the door to the kitchen, Annamaria set a hand on my cold, wet sleeve. "And," she said in a low voice, "I believe I start dating nice man from Siena." As my eyes widened at this piece of information, she let out a merry little laugh, and pushed open the kitchen door.

We stepped inside. At the sight of her, Chef, who was sitting at the utility table in a wilderness of cookbooks, nearly fell off his chair. Annamaria was not looking at him, though. She clapped her hands together once in real delight at the final build-out of the commercial kitchen. "Oh, Nell," she cried, as Chef tried to control his face, "is magnificent." In a rush, she turned and declared other things in Italian that I could hardly keep up with, but seemed to include something along the lines of "I always knew you could. I always knew you would. I always—"

It was Chef who interrupted, slamming cookbook on top of cookbook in an effort to appear nonchalant. "So," he uttered with a stony look, "you are back." His hands were shaking.

"Only," she said, unperturbed, "to cook. I will help you three half days."

"Is no good." In an instant, his forearm had scattered the pile of cookbooks. "I need all the time."

Annamaria and I exchanged a look.

This was true, but not in the way he meant it.

"No. Three half days—you need more, you try something new, you do it yourself." When he sputtered, because he had to sputter about something, she added, "Three half days, and for twice as much money."

He didn't quite get it. "Eh?"

"Oh"—she smiled in a pitying way—"I forget you no speak *inglese. Il doppio dei soldi.*"

He glared. Then waved her off with a low, cunning look. "I no need at all. I have Nella."

"I quit." It was just that easy. Turning on my heel, I left Chef scowling and Annamaria slipping out of her jacket.

In the last day and a half of performing as sous chef, I oozed out of Chef's kitchen as often as I humanly could, dashing to the office and checking for any applications from the job posting. Zero. Never anything other than zero. I was agog. Could all these faceless job hunters be just that smart? Was nobody at all jazzed by what I had clearly put out there as a challenge? Was I swimming in the wrong applicant pool? Maybe I should ditch the culinary crowd and see whether there was an online job board for masochistic celebrity groupies . . .

No denying, when Annamaria showed up, my relief was as big as one of her light, moist, candied fruit–heavy *panettones*. I was plucked from the gladiatorial arena of playing sous chef to my employer, whose kitchen on any given day was beginning to look like a lost scene from the movie *Gaslight*. On a whim, the man could change the day's menu, and as you stand there blithering because you're grating the wrong cheese, chopping the wrong vegetables, and pounding into submission the entirely wrong cut of meat, he would somehow make it your fault. Bullet dodged. But the save by Annamaria's return still left the question of how I could justify my presence at the Villa Orlandini once the kitchen expansion opened up to the first set of students. Presumably, now Philip Copeland; his mama, Mimi; and her old bestie, Muffy.

Swinging by the school office, I grabbed the three welcome packets Rosa had compiled just that morning and headed for the door to the courtyard. As I tugged my hood up to cover my head, and tucking the slick packets under my jacket, I stepped out into the Tuscan morning mist and made a welcome discovery. The sun. Admittedly, a little bland and uncommitted, like it was having misgivings about the whole gig, pretty much like me on every date I had agreed to in the last fourteen years. At that moment, though, all I had on my mind was a tiny quality assurance task I could take off Pete's shoulders since he was in Rome at his business meetings. The final check before Copeland Party of Three showed up tomorrow.

First, I hurried over to the pricier barn room, where Mimi and Muffy would be the very next people to set foot. Since Rosa had prepped the place, I knew it would sparkle. In a copper bowl on the small table in front of the side windows, she had set an array of pomegranates and persimmons on a bed of fallen, brown oak leaves. The large, cheerful room—more like an apartment, really—had the unmistakable smell of fall, and for a minute, I felt homesick. Slowly, I set down two of the packets, one on each of the beds. Rosa had mopped the plank floor, but I had nixed the idea of waxing it, what with visions of Mimi and Muffy breaking their necks.

I wanted no accidents, no guilty patient care, no impending lawsuits.

The bathroom was spotless, the limpid sunlight found its way across the main room, and the renovated barn met our two Orlandini criteria for quality assurance: (1) Does it still smell like goats? (2) Does it still bear any evidence of last month's crime?

No, it was pristine.

So I headed out the back door to check out the small patio we had just contracted a stone mason to put in as a perk for our barn-room guests, when something caught my eye. From where I stood, I could see past the rear of the two-story dormitory and clear down to Pete's Silver Wind Olive Grove. A man and a woman were walking the perimeter of the olive trees clearly locked in an animated conversation. In a fleecy, rust-colored swing coat, the woman was making broad, sweeping gestures, frowning at her high heels squelching in the soft ooze.

The guy—tall, hunched, and moussed—was wearing a belted brown wool trench coat that Ralph Lauren sold back in the eighties, when he was still just starting out. Not a good look for tall, hunched, and moussed—let's face it, there are belts that never look good on anybody, including the skinny, and this one resembled what sailors use to secure battleships—but he was earnestly snapping off pictures with his phone.

I didn't recognize either of them.

What were these two doing on villa property without either Pete or Chef in tow?

I watched as the lady in rust plucked an olive on a low-hanging branch that had missed the harvesting hands of Pete's little crew. Holding it up, she leaned toward the guy, and just when I thought she was going to pop the beauty in her mouth and discover just how many tastes a Moraiolo olive can have, she flicked it away. As if all that was left of the olive was the pit. She wasn't here for the olives, that much was clear. Then what? As the guy held the phone motionless, she lifted her elbows and swung her forearms wide. It was a clearing kind of gesture, like a pioneer encountering Nebraska for the very first time. The wool coat guy just nodded his head tensely a few times.

When I had just about decided I'd had enough of these two, I tapped the one remaining welcome packet on the palm of my hand and started in their direction, waving quickly at Hera, who was pulling a drop cloth from the back of her orange Ape. Without stopping, I strode toward the trespassers. True, Pete could have hired them . . . to do what exactly? Appraise Silver Wind Olive Grove? But why would he need an appraisal? Not for an instant could I imagine him selling the grove, not when matters like his life's work, his heart's passion, and his daily dream-making were all caught up with the olives.

Still, there was an air of business, a whiff of no-damn-nonsense about these two, especially the woman. Anyone who wears high heels overland during the rainy season doesn't grow anything except possibly richer, in the first place, and in the second place, anyone who dislodges her feet from the sucking mud with what I can only describe as manic relish can only be distracted by a higher—or maybe a lower, yes, maybe a lower—purpose.

If Pete hadn't okayed their presence without him to escort them, then what were they after? Had they somehow made sure he wasn't at the villa before they made free with his olives? I'd find some kind words when I got right up alongside them, that I knew, possibly something that did not begin with "Who the hell" or "What the hell." I'd work hard to eliminate any question that included some hells. But when I was within eighty feet of the two of them, they saw me and took off through the trees. The two of them were doing that kind of stiff-legged run that kids try out when the lifeguard booms at them that there's no running on the pool deck.

The whole scene brought me up short, mystified by their presence, surprised at their getaway—but not for long. I hadn't seen anything in their hands that rightly belonged to the Orlandinis, and when the guy fumbled his phone like he was flipping pancakes, I watched him scoop it up and stiff-leg it after his companion. Was trespassing, I wondered, a matter of degree? If nothing is injured or removed, is it kind of like no-trace camping, only against the law? What were the trespassing laws here in Tuscany? I don't think I had ever seen a posted sign about it since I'd come to Italy. No part of the Orlandini property was fenced, no warning signage was posted, even the stone, gated entrance archway was purely decorative.

Still, I watched.

I had to give that wild-haired woman credit: she was heroic in heels.

Of the three of us, though, I, Nell Valenti, known for sensible footwear (well, strappy flats), had the edge: I dashed back across the lawn, rounded the barn, and made it to the vintage T-Bird. Since (a) it's never locked, and (b) I always carry the ignition key on my sizeable key ring that reminds me of a movie prop, I flung the packet on the seat, jumped in beside it, and cranked the engine.

As I backed out of the parking spot, in the rearview mirror, I saw Rosa running toward me, arms and legs pumping. "Nella! Nella! *Dove stai andando?*" Where are you going? She threw in something about Signor Copeland on the villa phone, but I waved her off, shifting into drive. *"Prendi nota, Rosa!"* Take a message. *"Ciao!"*

Nothing Philip Copeland could possibly have to tell me mattered more than collaring our trespassers. Had they let me join them and come across in any way as plausible people—out for a stroll, even—they might have put me off. But that wild-haired lady in muddy high heels and the assistant who made the rookie error of thinking anything retro is stylish triggered my internal alarm system. If I couldn't follow them, maybe at least I'd get a gander at the license plate for future reference.

After all, we might be a cooking school open to anyone in the well-to-do public who could pay our fees, but beyond that, nothing about the Orlandini property was open to the public. No public paths, trails, tours, playgrounds, or picnic grounds.

Pete might give me a hard time about my suspicious nature, but my publicity-loving boyfriend wasn't here. And, aside from the Copelands, no one was expected. Those two strangers in the olive grove were up to something. And I was going to get to the bottom of it.

At the entrance to the Villa Orlandini, I slowed to a stop, where I idled. In the distance, I could swear I heard a car engine rev up. Where had those two parked? The car sounded outside the property, sitting—I was guessing—on the narrow shoulder of the road that ran by the front entrance. As I heard the other car approach, I slipped down behind the wheel, popping up just enough of me—Nell Valenti as prairie dog—to catch sight of a red Jeep Renegade. I gave the trespassers just enough of a head start so I could pull out without drawing their attention to the ocean blue '57 T-Bird following them that always reminded me of a bird of paradise in mating plumage.

Quite the smart disguise.

As they sped along the curving road into the town of Cortona, I became aware of the noise coming from the T-Bird's exhaust system. A tinny, holey rumble of a blown muffler. Gritting my teeth, I dropped back. Had the Jeep slowed up, too? Coming into town, I hoped I'd just blend in with all the other city sounds while I tooled around looking for a red Jeep. Which is pretty much what happened. No Jeep in sight, but blaring motorcycles, raucous café patrons, the nasal singsong of Italian sirens, and—bless my good luck—the growl of construction vehicles cloaked my ailing muffler's presence.

I cruised Via Santa Margherita, one of the main thoroughfares in Cortona, eyeing the traffic. Nothing. Choosing some random side streets, I swung down the lanes, passing Bar Dell'Accademia and Tempero, two of my favorite restaurants. In November, tourism slackens, which was tough on the local merchants, but it made my tailing job more possible. As if I knew what I supposed to be doing. I braked, cursing myself for losing them, when suddenly, on one of the side streets just off the piazza, I spotted the Jeep jammed into a tight spot, its occupants gone.

I eased the T-Bird slowly past the rear of the car so I could memorize the license plate. I've got to hand it to Italy when it comes to the legibility of their license plates. Big black letters on a large white background with friendly blue borders. Telling Siri to make a reminder, I dictated the plate number and drove around until I found a parking spot for the Orlandinis' car. Unless I missed my guess, the Cortona version of a Chamber of Commerce was around the corner and halfway down this small block of buildings.

At least I knew the director, Benedetto Ricci, whose English was good, from several phone conversations over the last two months about how we could work together to bring more local attention to the Villa Orlandini Cooking School. Now I was taking a chance he'd noticed the wild-haired woman in heroic heels and her tall, faux-retro assistant. Maybe he could point me in the direction where they were last seen. Maybe he had gotten wind of why these two had come to town and what, for that matter, their business was. Since Benedetto Ricci's gig had everything to do with promoting Cortona business, the man was a good resource for me.

I barreled around the corner and slammed into a dark-haired man, early forties, sweeping the leaves from the sidewalk in front of Forno di Carlo, a bakery next door to the Chamber of Commerce. After an exchange of *scusis*, the man's big dark eyes shot me a look, and we stepped away from each other.

When he'd made a safe, leafless path across the front of the bakery, he gave me another look, and waved me aside. I stepped back, and the guy started clearing the sidewalk in front of the Chamber of Commerce. *"Grazie!"* I called. I don't know why I yelled, since at that moment he was about three feet away from me. My mother tells me I have a bad habit of trying to make nervous conversation at moments of extreme attention in someone else's life. "Do you work for the bakery?" I yelled, thinking perhaps in all those wrappings this guy was as good as deaf.

"Potestri dirlo"—You might say that—was all I got in return.

I'd never met the bakery staff, mainly because Chef was irrationally jealous of the baker, Carlo, and refused to patronize the store. That, of course, meant no Forno baked goods for the students coming to the Villa Orlandini School of Cooking. Although Chef acted like the best bakery in Cortona was a den of unspecified iniquity, we all knew he couldn't produce a loaf of *pane rustica* anywhere near as superb as Forno di Carlo's.

"I'm Nell Valenti," I said, thrusting out a hand. "From the villa." He stared. I bungled ahead. "The cooking school." And the final lameness. "Up the hill."

He briefly shook hands. *"Ti lo visto."* I've seen you.

Since he made the comment in a tone I couldn't quite make out, I stiffened. He sounded like he was pretty sure I was the one who personally boycotted the bakery. Then he bent back over the broom. And didn't speak. I jumped into the silence, defaulting into haughty. If I managed to collapse my nostrils any tighter, I couldn't breathe. "Forno di Carlo makes very nice little Ricciarelli, Signor . . ." The soft, traditional Tuscan cookie I had experienced at meals here in town, where the best restaurants serve the soft marzipan-loaded delight from Forno.

"Giannini." Then he added: "Carlo Giannini. Thanks."

"Oh"—I suddenly understood—"are you the baker?" The Carlo of Forno di Carlo.

"Sono io," he said—That's me—scraping a wet, matted pile of leaves off the curb. "The nice little Ricciarelli are mine."

"Very nice." I held up a finger. "I said very nice."

He went quite still. "It's still just a cookie."

At that, I heaved a sigh. "Okay, see you later."

"Eh, Nell Valenti," he said, catching my arm. *"Che cosa c'è?"* What's the matter?

"Too early in the day for existential despair." I gave it to him in English, not really caring whether he kept up. "I haven't had my coffee yet."

"Existential despair?" His skeptical look made me think his English was better than I'd first thought.

"All I did was make a remark—"

"Sí, è vero. You made a remark."

"And you made a big deal out of it."

He jerked his chin at me. "You sounded like a cookie reviewer."

"I was being neighborly," I hissed. How we could go so quickly from to-die-for Ricciarellis to the kind of bad-tempered stuff that usually takes months to discover truly mystified me.

All of a sudden, Carlo the baker staggered backward a step, one hand covering his heart protectively. "Huh," he gargled. I'll never understand these hypersensitive people who can't even navigate a spirited disagreement about cookies. Then he topped it with a nearly inaudible *"Ho visto un fantasma."* I have seen a ghost . . .

I have observed that people who claim to see ghosts are generally more than happy to talk about them. So for a moment, I felt Carlo and I found some nice common ground that did not involve sweets. Since his brown-eyed gaze looked off into the distance, I squared my shoulders and turned around. And there she was, clear across the piazza, the wild-haired brunette in the rust-colored swing coat, only now without her companion. As we watched the woman lightly dash up the steps to the Hotel Italia, still in those heels, the man beside me was murmuring a doom song with no lyrics.

Un fantasma, the baker had whispered. Someone from a long time ago. From Cortona? Or somewhere else. And what had brought her back? Collaring her inside the hotel, where apparently she was staying, was unlikely. "Someone you know?" I tried on him. Nell Valenti, always dazzling with the obvious. When he snorted, I took that for a yes, and as he started peeling strips of wood from the poor broom, I asked, "Why don't you go after her?"

The plan was sudden and half-baked, but I figured I could follow him and wrangle an introduction to the woman trespasser. On a deep sigh, Carlo said, less to me than to himself, "The *fantasma* will find me." And as he turned toward the front door of his shop, he went on quietly: *"Lo fanno sempre."* They always do.

Suddenly, Carlo whirled to look at me, and he raised an arm and beckoned. *"Vieni,"* he said. Tipping his head toward the bright entrance to Forno di Carlo, holding the door open for a mother in a paisley headscarf and bangle bracelets pushing a stroller, he went on: "Fresh batch of my *pane rustica.*" He twirled the broom. "Bread that make Claudio Orlandini *pazzo.*" He made a crazy face. Then I followed him inside, taking in the fine flour dust that reflected the sunlight in the yeasty air. "I give you one." He shot me a crooked smile. "Make up for cookie fight. *Sta bene?*"

3

✤

Forno di Carlo was lively inside, between the chatty counter help and the customers peering into the display cases at the technicolor, paper doily–lined pans crowded with Tuscan baked goods emitting the aromas of candied orange peel, anisette, sweet almonds, and toasted walnuts. Another case held the rounded boules of *pane rustica* and the familiar long loaves of ciabatta. An assistant with her hair held back from her face with a stretchy leopard-print headband was holding out a samples tray to a shy three-year-old girl. Urging me to follow him into the back, Carlo windmilled his arm. And I followed.

Over against the wall was a row of glass-door convection ovens, where the pleasing smell of fresh bread scented the kitchen air. On a baker's table near the ovens I spied a round workmanlike stone grinder and, alongside that, a clear plastic ten-pound bag of what looked like grains of wheat. I turned to the baker, who had set the broom next to the back door and was slipping out of his blue hoodie. "You grind your own wheat, Carlo?"

"Eh?"

I mimed turning the grinder handle.

He smiled and reached into a chest-level metal bin and drew out a loaf of his *pane rustica*, which he quickly wrapped up in a white paper bag printed with Forno di Carlo. "Only," he shot me a devilish smile, "for the special, ah, stuff. *Capisce?*" He presented me with a fresh loaf of stone-ground-by-hand rustic bread.

I couldn't imagine how good this special bread must be compared to the regular "stuff" sold out front to the public. And then it hit me. "Carlo," I put it to him, "would you show three Americans how to grind the wheat?" Last-minute addition to the schedule for Ziti Fest. But I already liked the idea of bringing the threesome into downtown Cortona for an on-site demonstration by this artisan baker. Maybe they could grind their own flour that they then turn around and make into handmade ziti shells. I spitballed some ideas about the demo lesson with Carlo, who seemed agreeable.

Tomorrow, late afternoon. Best time for him. Just as he was seeing me out of the kitchen into the busy front of the house, explaining his work schedule, I caught my breath at the sight of the woman on the threshold of Forno di Carlo. The mass of hair was held back with random clips, and she had changed out of the swing coat and heels. Crowding her was her tall, moussed companion. Behind me, Carlo Giannini drew in his breath. We watched as she stepped inside and pretty much repeated the act I had witnessed in Pete's olive grove.

It was a wide-angled, appraising look she made of the place, going so far as to tap on the walls, which she scraped with manicured fingernails, dictating to the companion. The woman wasn't in the least bit interested in the wholesome smells of fresh baked goods or being seduced by the samples tray or the squeals of the kids getting to choose. Forno was a community gathering spot, I could tell, where tourists got quick lessons in Italian sweets, where *nonnas* brought the counter help up to date on the antics of the *bambini*, where young men pointed to each exact cookie they wanted to have boxed up for their dates.

None of this even registered with Carlo's *fantasma*.

He was moving in her direction on uncooperative legs like a man suddenly twenty years older than the one who had just been sweeping the wet, matted leaves out in front of his shop. Before I could even decide on an approach, I stopped right in front the woman, noted we were the same height, and gave her a quick nod. I could tell she didn't recognize me, but I started to think she didn't pay much attention to people. *"Parla inglese?"* I asked her pleasantly.

Her eyes, the color of cognac, but not one of the very best brands, settled on me. "Yes." Perfect English, whoever she was. The companion, not quite knowing how protective he should be, stepped closer. "Why?"

I didn't want to make a scene in Carlo's lovely bakery. In truth, I had no idea whether a scene was something appropriate. Anywhere. So I led with something simple. "I noticed you in Silver Wind Olive Grove earlier."

"Ah," she said, giving me a long look, "so that was you."

"I was coming over to see if I could help you when you scampered off." Still smiling. "Scampered" wasn't quite the *mot juste*. What the two of them had done was more along the lines of a stiff-legged retreat. Still, I gave her an out and waited to see whether she'd take it. What she didn't do was show any interest in who I was or why I had some reason—unlike her—for being on the grounds of the Villa Orlandini.

Her look was sharp. And her words had a strange, menacing quality. "We needed no help."

"Were you sightseeing?" I said pleasantly.

At that, the woman gave a short laugh. "Even in Cortona, there are better sights than an olive grove."

Behind me came a low voice. "Ciao, Renata." Carlo.

Barely an acknowledgment of him. "Another time, Carlo. You'll come to a meeting." The whole time she was speaking to him, her cognac-colored eyes were on me. The bakery lady in the leopard print was offering samples to Renata's assistant. When he hesitated, Renata told him, "Go on, Jason. It's a start." Then she narrowed her eyes at me. "Is there something else?"

"The Villa Orlandini is private property." Then, "If you have legitimate business with"—here I hesitated—"us, we'd be happy to show you around if you make an appointment."

"Really?"

If there's one thing I hate, it's sarcasm when it isn't my own. The mother with a stroller pushed gently by us on her way out, a filled bakery bag lodged in the basket.

"That won't be necessary. I know the Orlandini property"— she inhaled, then gave me a riveting look with an ambiguous smile that instantly lowered my body temperature—"as if it were my own."

The Copeland Party of Three arrived midafternoon the next day. If I hadn't been crossing the courtyard, I never would have heard the white Rolls-Royce Phantom ease noiselessly up the driveway, turn, and purr to a stop about two feet away from my left leg. It made an entrance like an A-list movie star. It drew to a stop like a champion racehorse. It was ostentatious but completely unshowy. Despite myself, I was smitten. The only other Phantom I had ever seen was John Lennon's bright, floral 1965 art-on-wheels when it was on display a year ago in Vancouver, when I was toying with the idea of getting far away from my parents.

The doors opened, and out stepped the driver, Philip Copeland. Since Ziti Variations had happened to us on the villa end so quickly, we cut down on all the required paperwork until the only thing left was a liability waiver. But I had done my research since I liked knowing who was entering Orlandini world. Copeland was fifty-two, never married, owned a penthouse on Central Park South, inherited some dough, made the rest in real estate, and contributed generously to New York City nonprofits. He belonged to the Yale Club, drank single malt scotch, was good to his aged mother, went to great lengths to keep whatever vices he might enjoy well out of sight, and was believed to head to Europe to keep up with whatever those may be.

As two Copelands and one Onderdonk unfolded themselves from the black interior of the Phantom, then stood looking around at the Villa Orlandini as they stretched discreetly, I knew I was looking at some fine flesh straight out of the New York *Social Register*. If we were at the Westminster Dog Show, these would be the composed and leggy Afghan hounds. Copeland was bald by choice, with a straight nose, golden brown eyes, and a mouth that looked like it could mince words faster than Chef could mince onions.

The man, dressed in a fashionable patchwork shirt and off-white wool suit, gave me a smile. "Nell Valenti?" It was a nice voice, so soft and laconic I could have mistaken him for Southern if it hadn't been for the total lack of drawl.

"That's right," I said, shaking his hand. "Mr. Copeland?"

"Three," he said with some energy, "here for Ziti Variations." At that, he indicated first his mother, Mimi, who stood awash in a sudden sliver of Tuscan sunshine. Her medium-length softly waving hair was a white that had no sheen, like a seagull. She crossed her thin arms over an alpaca coat, and she was careful to plant her feet comfortably apart for stability. She had been taller at some point in her eighty years, and her shoulders looked like they had lost some natural padding. Her glistening eyes were remarkably blue. An attempt at lipstick had gone a bit awry, but it was her breathy laugh that made me take to her right away. And then she spoke. "And . . . where are we, Philip, darling?"

Philip and I took turns. I started. "Welcome to the Villa Orlandini."

"Cortona, Mom. This is Cortona."

"In Tuscany."

Mimi lifted her head, interested, and glanced around. "A villa." When she suddenly pulled her alpaca coat tight, she looked a little worried. "You say this is Monaco?"

At that, the final member of the Copeland Party of Three hurried around the front of the Phantom, giving the winged ornament a fond pat and rubbing her friend's shoulders. Muffy Onderdonk was shorter than Mimi, but not by a lot, and she wore a crushed velvet purple hat over her razor-cut blond hair. Her eyes were green, her nose was snub, and her lips were what in her debutante days must have been described as rosebud. She moved quickly, stood straight, and looked like she had dressed for a long flight. Loose pants, loose long-sleeved top, and a gray fleece vest. This was a woman who could meander the aisles at Zabar's without anyone ever knowing how rich she was.

"Meems?" She clasped her old friend. Her voice was a

surprising, sonorous alto. "We're in Italy. You remember our junior year abroad?"

Apparently, Mimi Copeland did, and her eyes widened as she clapped a long-fingered hand over her mouth. "I'll say I do! We made the *Wellesley News*." Her beautiful face grew serious, and she whispered, "But not in a good way."

Muffy laughed heartily. "That was Rome, Meems. This is Tuscany, about two hours"—she shot me a questioning look, and when I nodded, added—"and a half." She went on: "Two and a half hours from Rome."

Somehow, the information steadied Mimi Copeland, who drew in a breath and linked arms with her son as she took in the setting. "Delightful!" she declared.

And I could tell Philip, Muffy, and I exhaled. I wasn't sure the drive time between Rome and Cortona had made much sense to her, but she liked what she saw from where she stood in the villa courtyard, and she was game. As Rosa and Sofia hurried toward us to help with the luggage, Philip pulled his black leather messenger bag from the front.

I stepped closer, getting a whiff of a raw, spicy Tom Ford cologne that was being spritzed on men walking through the section at Saks. "I'll show Mrs. Copeland and Ms. Onderdonk to their room."

Slinging the strap of the bag over his shoulder, Philip Copeland shot his cuffs. I hadn't seen a man shoot his cuffs since, well, possibly in a Cary Grant movie from the forties. A little sartorial detail that maybe males on the *Social Register* receive when they're sixteen. Any sixteen-year-old boys I ever knew would have fallen down laughing if someone tried to explain how exquisitely important it is to straighten out one's cuffs. Philip Copeland inclined his head. "I appreciate it. Thanks. Mom, Muffy, don't wait for me."

"Rosa and Sofia," I pointed them out to him, "will take good care of you." While those two villa mainstays stood beaming at him, I asked them in Italian if they could please bring the ladies' gear to the barn room. "And," since at that precise moment I couldn't remember if it had uttered these words, I repeated to Copeland, "welcome." Twice never hurts.

The niceties descended. "It's good to be here." He smiled.

I tipped my head. "We want you to feel at home."

He tipped his head. "We already do."

"Your welcome packet is on your bed." I smiled. This could go on for quite some time. Still, it felt like something was getting established.

"I'm sure it has everything I need."

"For one, a map of the grounds." I found myself making a vast gesture across the Orlandini property as though I was a real estate agent showing Moses the promised land.

"Lovely. May I?"

"Look around? Of course."

Muffy and Mimi were gazing at me expectantly. I spoke to them, "Let's head toward the barn just behind you." Taking her bestie's alpaca-clothed elbow, Muffy got the plan right away, and together, they took a few steps in the right direction.

"What are we doing here?" I heard Mimi whisper tensely to her old friend.

"Ziti Variations, Meems. It's a cooking school."

"Oh." A single word, drawn out until she ran out of breath. Then, with finality, "Cooking." It was as if it was a novel idea to her, like bungee jumping.

"Yes. It's your birthday tomorrow."

Mimi shook her head vigorously, sure of her ground.

"No, no, no," she lifted a long finger. "My birthday is in November," she corrected her friend.

"It is November, sweetie." I heard the catch in Muffy's throat. "We'll have fun."

"When I'm with you, Muffaletta," said Mimi linking arms with her friend, "it's always fun." And with that the two women were out of earshot.

I turned back to the man who had bought out an entire ten-student advanced sauce workshop just so his eighty-year-old mother could enjoy some ziti four thousand miles from the memory care unit at her assisted living facility. "You and I"—I made a gesture between us, as though there could be any confusion about who exactly was meant by "you and I"—"need to meet to discuss the schedule."

A thoughtful nod. Then Philip Copeland narrowed his eyes at a bird near the top of our tallest tree in the line of Tuscan cypresses that always remind me of the spindle in *Sleeping Beauty*. "And I can fill you in on my mother's condition. This will no doubt be her last trip abroad, and—"

"You'd like it to be perfect."

Although his lips hardly moved, there was a hint of a smile. "As close to it as we can get."

For some odd reason—and when it came to Chef, odd reasons sprang up like the targets in Whack-a-Mole—Chef declined to deck himself out in full chef regalia when it came to meeting the Copelands or giving them the kitchen tour. Annamaria was gone by the time I got back from town, just to prove the point of her new unavailability, but not before she made a *ragù* for the Copelands' first dinner and deputized Rosa to serve it later. A good choice for anything that involved either major logistical endeavors for, oh, the 101st Airborne Division or cannoli. Rosa was your woman. So within the first couple of hours since Chef and Annamaria were brought back into each other's sphere (I hesitate to say "reunited"), I could tell something was already afoot.

Anamaria had left work hours earlier than she used to.

Chef had donned dress pants, a teal Hawaiian print shirt, and a collarless navy blue leather jacket.

Unless I was mistaken, we had a mutiny by the captain and first officer on our quaking hands. We'd see how it played out over the next four days, but I had the strong impression Chef and Annamaria were vying for which one of them would win the prize for indifference. My sigh was monumental. That kind of behavior had implications for me as the cooking school designer and free-ranging factotum.

If certain expectations weren't met along, say, the lines of how close the realities of Ziti Fest matched up with the photos I had clapped up on the school website, I, Nell Valenti, would be the lightning rod for complaints. I had the sort of face that was apparently the flesh-and-blood version of a survey seeking to get to the nub of customer satisfaction. My worried creases, occasional hand-wringing, and tepid smile seemed to signal to cooking school customers that I was a one-woman complaint department.

Bad enough when the workshop participants had coughed up our usual fees.

But the Copeland Party of Three was another matter. By buying out the Advanced Sauces Workshop for Professionals for Mama Mimi's eightieth birthday bash with ziti, Philip Copeland was basically forking over seventy-five grand for four days of baked tubular macaroni—or, when it came right down to it, a whopping twenty-five thousand dollars for each Copeland partygoer. Not including airfare. Not including the rental of a Rolls-Royce Phantom. Not including extras, like rounds of drinks for us here at Sotto-voce, right on Piazza della Repubblica, the best cocktail bar in Cortona.

I took in Hera Neri, sitting alone at the bar, still in her work clothes, cradling a beer and checking out the other customers. And there was Benedetto Ricci, standing avun-cularly behind a table of Australian tourists, tossing me a snappy salute. I winked. And there we were, as well, Philip, Mimi, Muffy, Chef, and I. Hardly slumming. But just to glance at our little group, no one would be able to pick out the philanthropist, the socialite, the world-renowned chef, or someone with the name Muffy.

I felt strange being in a quickly intimate little cocktail party that seemed to cross some lines that made me uneasy, but not so uneasy I couldn't down my favorite cocktail, just a G&T and not so much ice, as it would dilute the liquid festivity. While I sipped, I kept silently drilling myself to maintain decorum. After all, I represented the Villa Orlan-dini Cooking School. I wore pearls. You can't get sloppy with someone wearing pearls. And you certainly can't *be* sloppy if you're the one wearing the pearls in the first place.

One would think Chef Claudio Orlandini himself would be representing the cooking school that bore his name, but no.

He hadn't shaved either his face or his head for the bar hop.

He was listening—as he stroked her arm—to Mimi tell a dim tale about dressage.

He was rattling off answers in unintelligible Italian to the others' questions about his scorching hot lost love, Ital-ian movie star Dalia di Bello.

He was working a trapped modicum of clam from between his fake incisor and canine teeth.

He was downing what had to be his third mai tai, in some unspoken pissing contest between him and our host, Philip.

As for myself, I was down to the ice cubes in my G&T, trying to identify the piped-in music that featured a fabulous trumpet, wondering how we'd ever be able to restore whatever decorum we were giving the old heave-ho. Just then, I caught the eye of Muffy Onderdonk, who gave me a surprisingly savvy look of understanding. We exchanged the sort of glance you share back during a college midterm when you and that other person know damn well you're the only ones who have studied the stuff. I felt heartened. I sat up straighter. She pushed the remains of Mimi's drink far away from her. I straightened my pearls. She glanced at her cool Shinola wristwatch to get a peek at the time.

At least the little gathering seemed undramatic. The event, I was beginning to appreciate, was proving uneventful. Scratching my chin, I was debating whether to order another G&T. Maybe I could let down my hair. Take off my pearls, even.

And then, of course, it happened. Chef lunged at a passing bocce team member, and the noise level tripled. Muffy went off in search of the restroom with an anxious backward glance at Mimi. Both Philip and I responded to that look by scooting our chairs a few inches closer to his mother.

Waving her arm like she was signaling a rescue plane— and maybe she was—Mimi hailed a waiter. *"Cameriere!"* At that, with a wide, beautiful smile, she stretched out toward her drink, snagged it, and held her empty glass aloft.

In that moment, I recognized the fabulous trumpet was

Wynton Marsalis, and the song was the dreamy "Where or When."

So I jumped when a hand clamped me on the shoulder, and I turned to see Carlo the baker. Our *buona seras* to each other got lost in the crush of clinking glasses and soft jazz and chairs scraping. With him was the woman Renata. Were they on their way to a table? Or out the door to the piazza? His *fantasma* had collared him, and although I didn't see any dread, I did see anger in his flushed cheeks.

Renata, clad in a swirl of a dress like an artist's palette after a painting frenzy, let one side of a vermilion-and-white beaded shawl droop provocatively off her shoulder. While Carlo was muttering, confirming the stone-ground wheat plan with me for tomorrow, I was tuning in on Renata, who was striking up a conversation in her perfect English to the ones closest to her—Philip Copeland and his mother.

"Haven't we met?" she said to Philip with lifted brows.

His eyes swept her. "I would have remembered." A nice cross between gracious and sexy.

Renata pressed. "New Yorkers?"

Mimi seemed delighted by the mysterious wild-haired woman. "Is it so obvious?" She let out a breathy laugh. "I'm Mimi . . . Copeland," she finished, "and this"—her left hand drifted back to touch Philip's face—"is my son, William."

With a quick look of pain flashing across his interesting face, he corrected her by addressing Renata directly. "Philip Copeland, actually."

"Philip Copeland," agreed Renata, now alert to the wealthiest guy in the room. "Of course!" Then she tipped her head consolingly. "William was—" And suddenly she had overstepped.

He managed a little smile, glancing at his mother. "William was my brother."

"Dead, of course," added Mimi, her face blank, her eyes at some space further back than the past. At that, the table collectively held its breath.

Muffy, who had returned and was slinking into her seat, seized the opportunity to change the subject. She turned to Renata. "Where do you live?"

Renata beamed. "Weekdays, Gramercy Park." She licked her rosy lips by way of explanation. "Weekends, I've rented a cottage near Pirate's Cove on Long Island for a few years. I've been lucky in business."

"What's your business?" That was Philip.

"Managing a nice inheritance from my father," she said, offering no details. "Plus an eye for the occasional start-up. Think *Shark Tank*," she said, "only without the other sharks."

Although Mimi laughed a gay laugh, Philip was scrutinizing the mysterious newcomer in the heels and drooping shawl as though he was doing a head count of all the sharks in the tank. "What brings you to Cortona?" he asked her.

Edgy and flushed, Carlo started off. "Hell is empty."

Unfazed, Renata answered with a general look around the table. "Developing some properties. Looking for some potential investors." From a slim blue leather bag slung across her neck, she drew out a couple of business cards and set them down on the table.

Muffy gazed at Renata's card. "Art for Heart's Sake," she read. "You're on the board."

"So true," she splayed fingers across her chest. "Such important work." Her voice dropped. "We provide art school scholarships for talented disadvantaged youth in the metro New York area." They were words she had spoken many times before, I could tell, but there was something fast and mechanical in the way she spoke them. Just some kind of lip service, I decided.

Mimi was caught up being vacant and gracious, her beautiful long fingers wrapped around her second cosmopolitan, smiling softly through a sad dreaminess. "Philip," she announced, "will send you a check."

And the chatter became general. Renata recalled having met Philip at the By the Sea fundraiser for Art for Heart's Sake out on the island maybe a year ago. Chef came back crowing about a *bellissimo* play by one of his teammates in the last bocce tournament. Raising his hand for another single-malt, Philip said he couldn't recall any fundraiser out on the island. Mimi wondered if one ziti was actually— properly speaking—a zito. And the blessed Muffy asked me out of the corner of her mouth just how soon I thought we could leave.

Dealing out a half-dozen more business cards, Renata wished us a *buona notte* and set off after Carlo, in no hurry at all.

4

*A*s we piled into the Rolls, Chef shotgunned the front passenger seat, which left Muffy, Mimi, and me on the swank leather bench in the back. While Mimi quizzed Chef rather unsuccessfully about his bocce prowess, I turned to the bright-eyed, snub-nosed Muffy and asked her something polite about her line of work. It was a new era of delicate questions, and I had long ago decided to set myself apart from my mother, Ardis Wentworth Valenti, whose blunt probings of strangers and acquaintances ran along these lines: *Well, you must be retired by now, eh?* or *Just how much longer do you expect it will take before you 'find yourself'?* or *Do you do anything interesting outside the—* here grasping for the concept—*home?*

"Oh," said Muffy, folding her arms in a cheerful way, "I retired a few years ago from the Department of Commerce." At that revelation, I was surprised, for one, that this wealthy woman—whose ancestor Onderdonk probably hailed from the New Amsterdam days on Manhattan

Island—worked a job-job for a government agency up until retirement. Her eyes twinkled. "Yes, I was a bureaucrat."

"And—?" All I could do was prompt her lamely.

"I was single and I had money, so I could please myself." She lifted her shoulders in a happy shrug. "So I did. I liked office work. Hunting down lost cargo, sniffing out any funny business with bills of lading. That sort of thing." As we turned in through the stone archway, I admired the road studs we had just installed to light the courtyard, when Muffy added, "I felt like I was doing my bit." Wrinkling her nose at me, she lowered her voice. "Hokey, I know."

"Not at all," I told her, as Philip brought the Phantom to a diaphanous stop a foot from the stone walls of the dormitory. Mimi pushed open the door and sprang out, delighted all over again to be here, wherever that was exactly, to do what exactly—don't tell her don't tell her, it was on the tip of her tongue—and how exquisite it all was and how lucky we all were. "I like your friend Mimi," I said softly, not caring whether I had just slipped out of bounds into the nonprofessional zone.

By the side of the Rolls, Philip stood quietly. But Chef, who views stillness as the anteroom of death, beetled off toward the main building, tossing back the invitation to dine.

"So do I," said Muffy, with a catch in her voice. "In a way, I had it easier than Mimi."

"How so?"

"Her big decision," said Muffy, as we walked together around to the others, "was which china to use at dinner." We watched as Mimi actually sprang after Chef, and Philip followed slowly. Alone, Muffy Onderdonk and I shook our heads at the descending nightfall. Something unspoken shot between us about how lives get lived, regardless of the prospects. Lifting her hand, Muffy watched the cool mist land in the failing light.

"It was a different time," I said. When Muffy nodded, I went on. "But you made it out."

"Oh, yes, but for me it was different. My parents didn't give a good goddam about any of that stuff. Pop was a rich socialist who kept looking for places to get rid of all his 'blood money,' as he called it. Mom was an elementary school teacher for years at PS 154 in Harlem. Believe me"—she laughed lightly—"if anything, they were slightly disappointed when I went to work for the Man."

As we entered the main villa building, greeted by the aroma of a veal ragù, we slowed.

Muffy's lips were pressed tight. "For Mimi Atwill, daughter of Clement Atwill, it was cotillion. Wellesley. Marriage straight out of the *Social Register*. Junior League. All the boxes got checked. But none of it ever amounted to more than just—"

I saw it. "Checked boxes."

With a small nod, Muffy said slowly, "She did every- thing expected of her."

I thought about my own upbringing in the Valenti home. Ours was new money, and Dr. Val and my mother, Ardis, viewed it as a kind of anointing. All that delicious new money was some kind of grace of God, no denying, and only child Ornella was the heiress apparent. Carefully, they attached the strings to the little marionette who liked to cook from the age of three and, wherever possible, used their liquid gold to slick her way.

It had nothing to do with cotillion or the *Social Register*. Those were the traditional hallmarks of old money, and all the responsibilities and avenues that rode sidecar. Dr. Val and Ardis Valenti understood that wasn't their world. And they liked their world better because it was a matter of demonstration. Demonstrate the money you've made because you're brilliant and tough. And all their anointed only child had to do was sign on with the empire. Was that so unreasonable?

In the corridor leading to the chapel, Rosa and Sofia passed us, bearing bowls of tagliatelle and what bore a strong resemblance to Annamaria's excellent Bolognese veal ragù.

Muffy smiled sadly. "Mimi Atwill and I lost contact for nearly a lifetime." She lifted her shoulders in a slight shrug. "Who can say why. I never knew her husband, I never knew her sons, and one even died. I never knew the Atwill home on the Upper East Side had burned down. Or that she had a cancer scare. And then a while back, we ran into each other at the Delacroix exhibition at the Met, just after her son had drowned, and we were both devastated by all the years we had lost."

Together, we stood on the threshold of the original Veronican chapel, now the villa dining room. Muffy lowered her voice. "And what with the dementia, Mimi loses more of her past all the time—years, even, that didn't include me."

Chef, Philip, and Mimi were finding their seats at the indestructible old dining table that seated eighteen. Rosa was lighting the four-feet-tall Gothic Advent candelabras she had arranged around the room, and we all—all except Chef, that is—murmured at the glow reflected in the two remaining stained glass windows. It was beautiful. Mimi half rose, half twirled, half spoke in sheer delight at the scene. Philip was gazing up at the vaulted ceiling, and Muffy found her place next to me and began unfolding her blue linen napkin one corner at a time. I knew the glossary of Chef Claudio Orlandini's facial expressions well enough to know it was smart to tune in to what he and Rosa were muttering about in rapid-fire Italian.

From him, a hand gesture like a door swinging open. *What is this?*

Annamaria's dinner for us. Brandishing her tongs, Rosa started to plate the tagliatelle into graceful little pasta towers, then signaled to Sofia to ladle the robust meat sauce.

This—this is tagliatelle. It should be ziti. He slapped his palm. *This weekend is ziti. All ziti. Ziti until we choke.* And he widened his eyes in the direction of the Copeland Party of Three. When he caught sight of Muffy's serene smile, he returned it. I strongly suspected she was fluent in Italian.

Rosa was unmoved. *You know perfectly well Annamaria makes tagliatelle for the veal ragù.*

His nostrils flared. *The veal ragù is Bolognese.*

Yes. Sofia smiled broadly at him, a star pupil. *This time she used our best Moscato wine.*

Chef jerked his head toward the Copeland party and, through gritted teeth, insisted, *They pay for Toscano. They want Bolognese; they can go to Olive Garden.*

Rosa clicked her tongue at him.

Sofia tapped the air between them with good-natured little shushes.

His eyes were slits, and not even the candlelight all around us could penetrate. "That woman," he growled, which instantly put Rosa, Sofia, and me on high alert. If I heard anything along the lines of *That bad woman* again, I was worried about what I would do, so without drawing too much attention to myself, I sat on my hands. Rosa was building up a thunderhead, the Copelands were passing the salad, and it was Sofia who made a very astute point.

With her sweet expression in place, she blinked, and while uncorking a bottle of Moscato, asked Chef, still in

Italian, *Would you care for another helping of malocchio? Or are you still dreading the first one?*

For my own part, I quietly set the cruet of Pete's extra virgin olive oil right next to Chef's wineglass and then, with a flourish, removed the stopper.

"Problem?" asked Philip Copeland.

I jumped in. "Chef just wants everything to be perfect."

Mimi pulled in her shoulder blades and rhapsodized. "It already is," she announced, and nodded like a little girl offered a sweet when Sofia materialized alongside her with a Parmesan grater. "Care for sahm chis?"

Muffy raised her loaded fork, easing it back and forth just below her snub nose for a quick, heady scent. Giving Mimi the fond side-eye, she whispered, "I agree. It already is."

Once Chef gave up and sank into his chair, he grew quiet and picked at his meal. The Bolognese veal ragù was simple and superb.

It was Mimi who took a breath from chewing just long enough to direct a question at Chef. "Can this scrumptious sauce"—she put it to him like she was thirteen and getting to pick out her birthday pony—"be used with"—she chewed her lip in gleeful anticipation—"ziti?"

Philip shot her a fond look. "Mom," he said in the tone he might use if she had gone over her credit limit at Bloomingdale's, "all of your meals are prepared in 305 West End's kitchens. Don't even bother your head about it." As soon as he said it, I could tell Philip Copeland could hear how it sounded.

Muffy winced at him just as Mimi responded, "I'm not bothering my head," she said, her bright blue eyes roving his face, "Philip dear." She sat up straighter, lifting her pasta-loaded fork as though she were making a champagne toast at a wedding. "I am treating my head, you know." She went on with enormous grace, "I don't have to—" Suddenly, her face fell apart when it became clear she was stumped how to express what she meant and then turned with frightened eyes to her best friend.

Muffy raised her wineglass and finished Mimi's point. "You, darling, don't have to make the dish yourself"—she tilted the glass in Mimi's direction—"to want to know how it's made by others."

"Precisely!" cried Mimi Copeland, who sat back and enjoyed the moment. "Muffaletta always knows." In Chef's face, I saw a new mix of feelings—a flash of compassion, a dose of fear. Dimly, aside from language lapses, he knew he wasn't that much younger than the two octogenarians at the table. They were more his peers than Philip or Rosa or Sofia were.

In that moment, as a chastened Philip brushed his mother's hair with his lips, and she smiled the smile she must have had all of her long adult life now, I saw Chef brace his forearms against the table, and I believed he was running the same scene, but with himself in the role of Mimi, watching ideas disappear halfway through even a short explanation. Right now, Chef could rail against anything Bolognese—mainly because it had been Annamaria's independent choice—or dazzle audiences with stories from his restaurant years. But how long would it be before some impatient or kindly or patronizing youngster would tell him not to bother his head about it? How long?

Chef Claudio Orlandini rose to his feet. "Yes to ziti," he replied at long last to Mimi's question. "But!" he proclaimed, gazing past us all, past the blazing candelabras, through the stained glass windows, and into the night he could still navigate. "Tagliatelle is best. Annamaria"—his voice softened—"give us all the best." For him, it was a big statement, and in his dark eyes was some murky understanding that made him a little uncomfortable. With simple charm, he looked at Rosa and Sofia standing off to the side of the group, their sharp eyes on the boss. Very simply, he said to them in Italian, "When you see your sister, tell her I say *'brava.'*"

Rosa wasn't entirely ready to relent. She found a speck of sauce on her wrist. "Of course *'brava,'*" she murmured as she flicked it away with a single stroke.

Wanting to prolong the time at the table, I ditched what would have been a discussion of the schedule for the next four days in the school office down the corridor from the kitchen. Instead, it felt infinitely better to keep it casual, and I realized I had been forgetting my own advice: *At the Villa Orlandini Cooking School, we are selling an experience.* Four pricey days with a world-renowned chef as tutor.

How many American gastrotourists who dip into their kids' college funds to land here for a workshop will actually return to Scranton and reproduce, garlic clove by peeled shallot, what they were taught? As I gazed at our tight little group of Copelands, I raised my glass and my voice. "To the Copeland Party of Three."

Philip chuckled and tapped his glass with his knife. "Go on." He flashed me a smile.

"Here's what lies ahead," was how I put it. Out of the corner of my eyes, I saw Chef set his elbows on the table and fold his hands. Interested. I gave him three seconds to overrun me, and when he didn't (fretting still about his own aging), I plunged ahead. Tomorrow, I rolled out for the Copelands' pleasure, we would be experiencing firsthand stone grinding of the hard wheat that yields the very durum semolina flour that will become our ziti.

At that, Mimi clapped. Chef poured more wine. Rosa blew her nose.

"Here"—my voice rose—I swear it was either the sweet and thick Moscato wine or the candles—"in the villa's own newly expanded and outfitted kitchen, we will make our pasta dough, and then with the help of a state-of-the-art"— I felt like I was talking about robotic surgery—"extruder, we will produce our ziti for the dishes of the next day."

Mimi, smitten, touched a graceful finger to her bottom lip. "Too wonderful," she murmured.

I kept spinning straw into gold as Philip pushed back his chair, crossing his legs at the ankles, and Muffy unobtrusively snapped a couple of Mimi photos with her iPhone. I pitched a few possibilities for field trips. Into the woods for truffles with Stella, our next-door Lagotto Romagnolo, aka truffle-hunting pooch extraordinaire. Into Cortona for an afternoon at the Etruscan Museum to enjoy the ancient beginnings of Tuscan kitchen and cuisine. To Arezzo for a tour, plus firsthand field experience at our cousin Oswaldo Orlandini's farm, where we can pick our own veggie needs for our ziti dishes.

At this point, Philip Copeland, his hands in his pockets, was nodding as though he had just learned the market was up three percent. Or he'd been named the Yale Club's Wiffenpoof of the year. His eyes were on me as I continued to extemporize my way through the Orlandini Experience this rich philanthropist had forked over upward of seventy-five grand to buy.

Raising one finger, I intoned, "Ziti alla Genovese," and a second finger, "ziti lardiati." I finished up, pulling my fingers together as though I were going to end with *na-*

maste. I promised them a discovery of the persuasive flavors of pig back fat and Montoro onions. "And on our final day, *bellissimi americani*," I effused, and Sofia hadn't even handed me her ladle, "we enter the new territory of"—I heard Mimi Copeland catch her breath—"dessert ziti."

Philip Copeland sat up straight and shot me a smile. "Ziti!" he proclaimed. "It isn't just for dinner anymore."

"So true," I agreed as the others laughed.

"Nell"—he studied me—"this is a beautiful room. The original chapel. Built when?"

I squinted at him, then said, "I'm pretty sure it was 1573."

"Thanks to your map of the grounds, I've been making my way around."

I helped myself to more salad, always happy to have students show some initiative. "Great!"

"I believe there have been . . . changes to this property, which are very suggestive."

I'm not sure he was using the word "suggestive" properly. But for that moment, he looked congested with excitement, so maybe he was. Takes all kinds. "Ah," was my response.

"I'm . . . helping"—he gestured dismissively with his wine glass, which for some reason I took to mean that "helping" in this context meant "bankrolling"—"with an upcoming exhibition at the Met on historic architectural drawings. Early stages. You can check it out online."

"Very interesting," I said, hoping it would get to be.

He got to the point, including a bemused Chef in his glance. "Would you be willing to lend us the architectural drawings of the Villa Orlandini for the show? I'll take care of shipping and insuring them, naturally."

Mimi's mouth made a charming O, and her face told me this was an offer that warranted enormous respect. That may be so, but all I could say was, "I don't know anything about villa drawings, Philip. If there are any, I don't know where they'd be."

Philip, I could see, was making allowances. "The library?" He spread his hands as though it was a wacky idea, and I cursed myself for not knowing without asking whether he meant the public library in town . . . or a villa library right here on the spot, with club chairs and an antique globe.

So, with what I hoped was a winning smile that covered every conceivable meaning, I said, "I'll ask."

His golden brown eyes crinkled warmly at me, so I figured all was still in play while I looked into this matter of libraries and what, after almost five hundred years, could only be architectural drawings crumbling to brown dust.

After a G&T earlier at Sottovoce, I sipped in a miserly way my half glass of Moscato and left it at that. Rosa had chosen my playlist for the meal, and Charlie Parker's "Loverman" seemed downright conversational in that setting. At the tender age of thirty, I was beginning to understand that there were, in life, these flashes of happiness, arranged almost randomly out of unexpected things. I let my eyes settle on Mimi, at peace in a ziti dream; on Philip, whose eyes were closed in order to make room for the saxophone; on Muffy, whose skin just below her eyes was twitching with busy thoughts she was keeping to herself.

"You always loved jazz, darling," murmured Mimi, leaning toward her son.

"That was William," he corrected her gently.

Chef was sighing just to take in more of the veal ragù, Rosa slipped out to locate dessert, and Sofia lit the wall sconces. Even without Pete there, I was happy. There was just something about Charlie Parker and a rare stained glass scene from the childhood of Jesus and the last drops of Moscato lingering on my tongue.

There was a sharp and ephemeral beauty about the table.

Here's what lies ahead, I had told them.

But it wasn't until two days later that I'd realize I had left something out.

Murder.

5

During the night, I had visitors.

Rosa knocked on my door at 11:20 to tell me that we were out of porcini mushrooms for the *ziti Neapolitana* we were preparing the day after tomorrow.

"Call Oswaldo," I directed.

I had a flutter of guilt that I had already been asleep for half an hour, and poor Rosa was still in her work clothes, neat gray pants topped with a white sweater that strained across her chest. On that November night, she had added a plaid Russian aviator hat with ear flaps. Tuscan born and bred, the woman still had an affinity for what I thought of as frozen tundra chic.

"Righty hey," she clipped off at me in one of her attempts at idiomatic English and, with a salute, disappeared into the dark.

Chef knocked on my door at 12:06, in his black silk pajamas and an indigo blue leather steampunk coat with enough metal on it that he could dislocate a shoulder just trying to slip the damn thing on. While I wondered where on earth he had scored this questionable outerwear, Chef was waving his phone right in front of my face. The yammering in Italian and some other tongue I couldn't identify affected my ability to know just what he was talking about, but it was utterly clear that he was falling somewhere on the continuum between normal excitement and outright mania.

I could tell he wanted me to look at his phone, but he couldn't let go of it. I bit my lip and waited, my shoulder sagging more with each passing minute. Finally, the man sucked in enough air to power a transatlantic crossing in a hot air balloon. "Is chance of a life!" He dribbled at me. Chance of a lifetime? Something that didn't include his lost love movie star Dalia di Bello, or a bocce world championship, or a diabolical plan to get back at Annamaria Bari for throwing him over?

"Che cos'è?" I yawned in his face.

"Hot Chef: Stile Italiano!"

I had no idea what he was talking about. Exuding enough sweat and saliva to put him right out of the running for *Hot Chef*, he managed to convey finally that he has been invited to compete for a spot on the new season of *Hot Chef* by submitting an audition video in the next seven days. When a passing breeze was just a little too cold to enjoy, I pulled Chef just far enough into my room to shut the door. Hands on the cold dead flesh of my hips, I leaned closer to him. "So what you want is television?" After all the work on this pie-in-the-sky cooking school at his very own villa? Suddenly that was too shabby?

His steampunk-clad arms shot up over his gleaming head. Was La Bella Nella really this obtuse? "Is gelato *sopravvalutato*?" he shouted. Is gelato overrated?

"I take it that's a yes." And all I wanted was to get my eight hours sleep before tearing over the town and countryside with the Copelands tomorrow. And then, enraptured, Chef let slip what I finally understood was behind it all. A spot on *Hot Chef: Italian Style* was better than Pete on the cover of *Bellissimo!* Ah. The old boy was envious. *"Domani!"* Tomorrow.

And as he turned to go, he quickly sketched in slower Italian the plan for the video. Pete was still in Rome, so we'd show the great Chef Claudio Orlandini in nature—very hot in nature—in the olive grove. Nella will be in charge, Rosa will make video, Chef will star. And pitch the charm. Big hit. When I put my naked foot down, I reminded him we had Copelands on hand. These Americans are our first responsibility. We bickered as he charged out into the night, and I yelled after him, "After they leave!" and he yelled back at me, *"Domani.* No other time!"

By the time he disappeared in the direction of the dormitory, I couldn't for the life of me tell what had been decided. Shutting the door firmly, locking it ferociously, I stood in a state of dark wonderment. Would joining the Dr. Val Valenti empire really be so bad? Was my father, when it came right down to it, any more difficult than Chef? Would he not, my dad, actually try harder to please me? To keep me home? To keep me under his domineering eye? To help me wheel around my own personal tank when he sucks the oxygen out of every room? No, between Chef and Dr. Val, it was truly a toss-up.

Ah, there was the true competition. Forget *Hot Chef.* Although—for all its madcap messiness—I felt an attachment to this villa and its denizens. Here I had freedom. And my talents were truly valued.

At least not much time had elapsed—and not much sleep had descended—before the third visitor knocked on my door. I had spoken to Pete by phone hours earlier and knew he was still in Rome, so it wasn't him. Who was left? I let out a little snort as I strode to the door, shrugging into my fleecy red robe. Sofia, perhaps? Here to deliver the news that the last of our Roma tomatoes had gone bad.

Philip Copeland, perhaps? Here to register a request for new digs because the new paint smell in Annamaria's old room was too strong for him to sleep? Even if it were true, I couldn't imagine the man descending on the privacy of a villa staff member. It just wasn't done. Maybe it wasn't a knock at all. Maybe it was just Stella the truffle hunter stropping her tail against the door, no harm intended.

Gnashing my teeth, I exhaled and flung open my front door.

To my surprise, it was Muffy Onderdonk standing there in her understated way. "It's Mimi," she told me quietly. "She's missing."

6

With my insides undergoing the first stage of cryonics, I staggered back from the threshold of my beloved abbess's room, my hallowed sanctuary, and croaked at the woman. "What do you mean missing?" Maybe Chef was right. Maybe La Bella Nella actually was that obtuse. Muffy didn't waste time wringing her hands since that was a job that required only one of us, and I had jumped in. Under the fleece vest she had worn when she arrived at the villa, her purple hat pulled down to her eyebrows, she was wearing white silk pajamas. In her oddly still hand, she held a pack of Lucky Strikes. The other hand held a Bic lighter.

As I started to sink down onto my bed, she approached. Without any drama, she added, "We must find her." Then Muffy filled me in on just the essentials. The two of them had turned in just about ten o'clock, Mimi waxing lyrical on how happy she was to be there. They reminisced about the Wellesley Class Council retreat out in the sticks at Camp Caribou, Maine, when they were juniors and went out to smoke and drink with three other girls late one night and got lost in the godforsaken woods. Laughing, Mimi settled down and fell asleep, Muffy noted, by 10:30. After glancing through the email on her own phone, Muffy turned out the light and fell asleep. Sometime after midnight, shouting from somewhere nearby woke her up.

"Chef," was all I said, with no explanation.

"And that's when I realized Mimi was gone." As I started to quiz her on the obvious points, she held up a patient hand. "Yes, I've checked. The bathroom, the courtyard." She fell silent then, just blinking and shaking her poor head. "I couldn't get into the main building. Or the dormitory."

"It's on a timed lock."

"It never even occurred to me she'd wander." Angry with herself, Muffy turned in a flash and pounded the doorframe with her fist.

I wanted to sound reasonable. "Why would it?" I asked as I struggled into a pair of jeans I had flung over a chair. "Mimi seems a little forgetful—"

At that, Muffy let out a hollow laugh. "Nell, you don't have the whole picture. Back home at 305 West End?"

"Yes?" It wasn't going to be good news.

"She's in the memory care unit."

"I know that."

"It's kept locked."

While this sank in, I felt a spasm of disbelief that Philip Copeland hadn't mentioned this fact about his mother. No time to waste on recriminations. I threw one of Pete's wool jackets over my pajama top. "Does Philip know?"

Muffy grew calm. "No. Not yet. If we can't find Mimi quickly, Nell, I'll have to tell him."

"What's quickly?" I was getting ready to argue whatever number she put out there.

She was at a loss. "Ten minutes?"

I nodded. We'd give it fifteen. I took the Coleman lantern I save for the evening soirees we've never had yet at the Villa Orlandini and tossed Muffy my second-best flashlight. Stuffing my tootsies into my Blundstone boots, I shoved my phone in the pocket of my sweater, jerked my head toward the door, and we hurried out into the night.

"Has she got a flashlight?" I asked Muffy, tugging my sweater tighter around my middle.

"I think so. I couldn't find it in the room."

We agreed not to shout—it might alarm Mimi—and we'd use Muffy's smaller flashlight until we absolutely had to bring Philip into the search. Not to mention the police. At the very thought, my stomach tightened. Wherever lights were off inside one of the buildings, and the doors and windows fastened, we slunk around the exterior, checking the bushes, and headed for the next place. Muffy and I covered the dormitory, the barn, the cloister, the main building, Pete's cottage, my abbess's room, and the annex Pete was using as an olive oil production space.

"Now what? Has it been ten minutes?" Muffy's voice was tight.

At that moment, we were standing in the moonlight, my lantern and Muffy's flashlight turned off, at the corner of the annex. I knew we were both dreading a whole raft of inevitables—namely, tell Philip, get into a couple of cars, and head out to the roads.

"The olive grove," I answered, "won't take long," I added.

While my eyes scanned in that direction, taking in the ghostly, ghastly dark forms of Pete's trees, it was then I saw it. A flickering light, but not in the grove, more like a hundred yards from the border of the grove. And yet, not exactly in the woods where Stella hunts for truffles.

The flickering light went off.

Muffy saw it, too.

Finger to my lips, I whispered, "Let's go."

Cutting across the gently rolling property, we skirted the fountain, where the statue of seventeenth-century sculptor Francesco Mochi's *Saint Veronica of the Veil* looked lurid in the scattered moonlight, and kept close to the dormitory. A quick glance to the left told me lights were off in Chef's first-floor apartment, in his dreams no doubt cooking up some mischief for the next day. There was a figure moving outside of the moonlight, scuffing at the ground, and I couldn't make out who it was. Or what it was doing.

We closed in just as the moonlight inched past the towering trees where the truffle woods began, and Muffy suddenly pulled up short and flicked on the flashlight. "Philip!" she said, rousing the nightjars in the nearby branches.

At one a.m., Philip Copeland, still in his clothes from our cocktail party at Sottovoce, turned as though coming together out on the villa grounds after midnight in a chilly November was the most natural thing in the world. I had to admit, but only to myself, that I couldn't decide about this man, who had the unusual quality of being at ease everywhere. I suspected money did that for you.

But it was a bad fit for Nell Valenti. Unlike Copeland, I had to study every inch of a place, indoors or out, before I could begin to feel at home. And even then, it was kind of doubtful. "You're a real fish out of water," an early boyfriend had meant kindly. Like telling someone she's a good dancer or spiffy dresser. But I had heard the truth of it. Maybe I kept looking for some natural element for me that just didn't exist.

"Evening, Muffy," said Philip, his smooth cheek catching the moonlight. Tucking a small flashlight into his breast pocket, he added with a crinkly smile at me, "Nell."

"Can't sleep?" I tossed at him.

A beat. Then he raised his hands. "Got me." Then, "What brings you two out?"

When I watched Muffy inhale like it would have to get her through the rest of her natural born days, I said quickly, "We were on a hunt." A Mimi hunt, but for the moment, I kept that part to myself. Maybe we'd get lucky, and Philip Copeland would think we meant moonflowers or scorpions. Any minute now, he'd ask whether we left his mother asleep in the barn room, but I could tell he had a pressing question as he walked a few feet to the left and made a sweeping gesture. "A question?" I gave him my most wide-open look.

"The soil," he began, "looks very different here."

"Really?" I had never noticed, but then, I never felt much of a draw to this back corner area by the woods. "How so?"

He seemed to temporize. "It has kind of a hard, churned look. Like something had been cleared away at some point. Did the woods used to come out this far?"

I told him I didn't know. "You're thinking it was cleared for construction?"

Copeland drew out his pocket flashlight and turned it back on. "I stepped it out." The beam from his light caught me raising my eyebrows, and he gave a little laugh. "Working with numbers keeps me up," and he added, "sadly, but the night air and stepping out a mysterious patch of land, now that will put me out." I watched him count out fifty paces, swinging the light in an arc as he went. Just as Copeland turned and we shone our flashlights at each other, he spread his arms as if to say, *There you have it. Fifty feet.*

Aside from my Coleman lantern, I had no illumination,

and the thought crossed my mind that this was one of the problems of dealing, basically, with the public. The tiresome possibility that they'd go off on tangents that veered away from the tidy confines of tomato sauce classes. Just as I was trying to fashion the kind of response—something midway between excited and bored—that would satisfy our wealthy guest, from up the hill and out of the darkness came shouts. *"Nella! Nella, sei tu?"* Is that you? I recognized Rosa's voice.

"Sì, Rosa." I called to her. *"Che cosa c'è?"* What's the matter?

"Ho bisogno di vederti subito, capisce?" I need to see you right away, capisce? At that, a small flash of light grazed the top of the nimbus of white hair on the tall figure beside her in the dark. Blowing out her great relief, Muffy tilted her head toward me. "I've got them. It's Mimi."

"It's my mother?" called Philip, alert, as the three of us went trotting up the hill.

"Yes, Philip," said Muffy, reasonably, "but I've got her."

He wrapped his mother in a hug. "Are you all right? Mom, are you all right?"

Mimi murmured something incoherent, her eyes still terrified.

I caught Muffy's sleeve. "Can you get her to bed?" I whispered.

"Directly." Then, "Philip, dear, I can take care of things." She patted her old school friend on the shoulder. "Meems, let's go make some tea and see how many school songs we can sing."

At that, Mimi brightened a bit. "Muffaletta?"

"I'll just see you both home," said Philip, who linked arms with his mother and started toward the barn.

Muffy stepped close to me and said quietly, "Come by."

Then she added, "Knock softly." For a second, Muffy caught my eye. "And thank you." She hurried to catch up with them.

I stood shivering at the thought that we were all spared having to search for Mimi Copeland beyond the villa property. Out in the dark on country roads where locals drive much too fast. Would a disoriented eighty-year-old woman alone in the dark on unfamiliar roads be able to jump aside in time? Not even the moonlight could have helped. Sometimes, moonlight isn't enough.

After I heard the barn door close and watched as Copeland's shadow crossed the property, I joined him on the crusty fifty-foot patch of ground. In silence, we busied ourselves clicking pens, patting pockets, and adjusting lanterns. He hummed something unidentifiable. I couldn't decide whether to leave him to his sleepless prowlings or try to help.

His expression was friendly as he narrowed his eyes. "Nell," he said, lifting his gaze to the stars, "I wonder if we're standing on the villa library. Abbeys this old had libraries, and sometimes they were separate buildings." At my raised eyebrows, he added, "Very flammable."

"I can tell you're a man who's dug at crusty ground with ballpoint pens before."

"Oh, not so much," he said with a smile. "I'm just a sap for the research of others." He shrugged, then muttered shyly, "I like architectural drawings."

You'd think he was admitting he liked bobbins.

Or ziti.

*A*fter Philip Copeland and I parted ways in the courtyard—with him heading to Annamaria's old room in the dormitory, although I think he was just being a good egg in telling me he had "all good confidence" he could now sleep—I headed toward the barn room. Recalling the last few minutes in Copeland's company, when it was all I could do to keep a straight face, I'd told him with stiff respect that tomorrow I would ascertain the precise whereabouts of the—bibliographic—nay, bibliophilic holdings of the Orlandini family.

Bumping into Rosa, I hit her with it. "Rosa," I said in Italian, "is there a library at the villa?"

"You want some books?"

"No, Philip Copeland was asking."

"No, no library here." She moved on. "Signora Copeland, very sad."

I wasn't ready to move on. "But this was a convent. Where are the archives?"

"You mean like old missals?"

"Papers, documents, drawings. The history of this place."

"Oh"—Rosa nodded, puckering her lips—"that building is gone."

"What do you mean 'gone'?"

Rosa waved me off. "Very, very old. All the way back to the first Veronicans."

A library from the sixteenth century . . . now gone? "Well, where was it?"

She rolled her bundled shoulders toward me. "I don't know." Rosa switched into English. "Before my time," she offered, then bit her lip in suppressed delight. "I say all right? Before my time?"

"*Perfetto*. Now, what happened to the library building, Rosa?"

She patted my arm as she turned away. "It was bombed."

Bombed.

It certainly made an interesting footnote to the history of the Villa Orlandini. A story of hard use during wartime. How could I work this bombing loss of a library into the website for the cooking school? In some classy, Olympian kind of way that wouldn't appear to prospective American gastrotourists as just some cheesy opportunism? We were selling fantasy celebrity kitchen "experiences," not the kind of existential horror that saps the appetite for osso buco right out of you. This current generation of Orlandinis—including even Chef himself—missed World War II altogether, so it must have been Chef's parents who lived through an Allied bombing raid.

As I knocked softly at the door to the barn room, I decided I'd ask Annamaria.

Muffy opened the door halfway, finger to her lips. In the large, dimly lighted room behind her, I heard wracking sobs coming from Mimi Copeland, who was lying on her bed clutching a pillow to her chest.

I mouthed, "Will she be all right?" When Muffy responded with short, tight nods, I added, "What happened?"

Her eyes filled. "She woke up and thought it was 1961 and Camp Caribou all over again."

"So it was a happy memory."

A short laugh. "She snuck out. We were always sneaking out at the Camp Caribou retreat. Dashing around in the dark, looking for the other girls." Waiting to see, Muffy explained, what they'd got in their flasks. Share some cigs. Top each other with stories about Amherst men and Harvard men . . . and Holyoke women. Getting tight, getting crude, dreaming about breaking out. Muffy jerked her head to the great dark villa grounds behind me. "And then she couldn't find the others. No girls, no familiar cabins or benches. No Muffaletta. She couldn't find her way back to me. And she was terrified. When Rosa happened to find her, Mimi was huddled against the stone wall, shivering." She looked at the threshold. "And moaning."

A beat. I had to ask. "Is she safe here?"

"You mean, do we want to cut and run? Big mistake and all that?"

I nodded. In the background, Mimi turned on her side, her white hair like clouds, her back bony, and the cotton blanket too little. "There's a down comforter on the top shelf in the closet."

"Thanks," said Muffy. "We'll be all right. All of us. I'm here to see to that," she said with an odd emphasis I didn't quite understand. "Ziti Variations is important for her. She's not just here for the ziti." As she told me good night and slowly closed the door, Muffy Onderdonk and I held each other's eyes until—without taking a step—both of us were out of sight.

7

The next morning began inconclusively. Not sunny, not misty. Since Annamaria was cooking for the Veronicans that day, the rest of us went into town on our own. Reminded of the new world order, Chef was gurgling in the kitchen like a mutt confronted by a competitor, hanging on to a marrow bone. "Chef," I told the others brightly, hoping this was indeed the case, "remains behind to prepare the kitchen for this afternoon's hands-on lesson on ziti dough." I drove the T-Bird, Mimi beside me in the front, Philip and Muffy in the rear. For half the ride, I regaled them with anecdotes about Forno di Carlo, even treating them to the dangerous knowledge that Chef was jealous of Carlo Giannini's rustic bread.

"Oh ho ho," cried Mimi, savoring this tidbit. I could tell she was concocting some special way of ribbing Chef, which was fine by me. Chef would never go big and dramatic in front of a guest at the villa. He would have to chew and swallow the tidbit in much the same way as he exaggerates his mouth's experience with Carlo's bread. Having slept through the crisis of the night before and having been informed of it by the splendid Rosa, he was feeling contrite.

As he waved us goodbye with two helpings of Rosa's excellent *sfogliatella* in his mitts, he actually yelled, cupping his pastry-filled hands behind his ears, "I little bit hard of hearing." This irrelevancy, I knew, because I knew how he worked, was meant to explain his unruffled absence when Mimi was missing. Nobody else in the T-Bird understood what he was getting at.

Mimi was paler than usual but doggedly cheerful. Now, as we rode and I came up empty on any more anecdotes, I could tell she was trying to double-whammy her host, Chef, by cooking up something having to do with his jealousy over Carlo's bread and his being hard of hearing. Philip Copeland was silent, his elbow propped on the armrest, his forefinger stroking his lip. Muffy, gazing out her window, looked very alert, for which I was grateful. We parked around the corner from Forno di Carlo's and hoofed it.

Market days in Cortona found shopkeepers setting up tables on level spots in Piazza della Repubblica, shaking out colorful cloths to cover them. Local women with net bags dangling from their forearms ribbed the shopkeepers they knew well. These were old flirtations. A coffee shop rolled out a cart sporting a silver urn. Benedetto Ricci, director of the Cortona Chamber of Commerce, his thin hair levitating in the morning breeze, was angling monster speakers on the street to float recorded Italian music around the piazza.

Carlo Giannini stepped out of his bakery to welcome us.

But from the looks of him, I couldn't imagine a worse time for demonstrating to a few American strangers how to grind grains of whole wheat into flour. He might be keener to demonstrate a leap from the bell tower of the Palazzo

Comunale. His red-rimmed eyes signaled either a whole lot of drinks the night before, a whole lot of tears maybe an hour ago, or possibly both.

As he shook my hand, I stepped close to the man and said in Italian, "Is this a good time, Carlo? We can postpone." Although if he jumped at postponement, I didn't know how to make the revised schedule work. We'd probably have to skip the demo altogether.

"Today, no time is a good time." Then he addressed the Copelands with the practiced grave air of an undertaker escorting the family to the recumbent beloved. "*Per favore*, come inside."

We followed him to the back of the shop, past the chattering stroller moms and white-haired native sons waiting their turn in overcoats that had served for decades. Directly behind the baker, I could see he was wearing a clean white T-shirt and baggy chef pants under a brown waxed canvas apron. Carlo's taste extended beyond the ovens. And if I wasn't mistaken, he had ironed creases in the short sleeves of the clean white T-shirt. I liked the attention to detail, especially on a day when it seemed to me like his first customer must have been the devil himself. Or, for that matter, herself.

On the worktable at the center of Carlo's kitchen was a round bluestone grinder that looked friendly enough at about a foot in diameter but which I knew from my cooking school days weighed about fifty pounds. The grinder held a smaller stone set into a larger one, and as you cranked the handle, turning the smaller stone, the whole grains of wheat, set into the open top of the receptacle, fall between the two stones, where they're ground. Flour is pressed out from the thin interface between the stones. The purest artisan bakers still enjoy the hand-grinding process—some even grow their own wheat—but for large-volume baking, electric commercial grinders are the way to go.

Carlo stacked three large ziplock bags alongside the stone grinder, and I felt touched he had prepared for this demo even beyond ironing his shirt. One bag of whole grains for each of the Copeland Party of Three. As he handed out traditional white bib aprons to Muffy, Mimi, and Philip, Muffy remarked in perfect Italian that he had a beautiful shop here. A nice icebreaking comment. Carlo paused with an apron hanging from each hand. His face was as grave as if he'd just been informed a broken fingernail had been discovered in a loaf of rustic bread. *"Mille grazie,"* he intoned, trying to control his voice, and added in brave *inglese*, "Five *generazioni di* Giannini bake here."

Mimi breathed, "Here?" She turned wide eyes to the rest of us. "Right here?"

"Giusto qui." Right here. His mouth twitched.

"Quasi duecento anni," murmured Muffy. Almost two hundred years.

Bracing his arms on the worktable, Carlo nodded absently, his mind elsewhere. No one spoke. Somehow we all sensed the baker was working up to something. "Whole building," he gestured as though he were snapping a frisbee, *"molto, molto vecchio."* Very old.

"Dicciassettesimo secolo." He sounded funereal.

"Seventeenth century," I translated, my brightness a little subdued.

His jaw worked. "But pretty soon . . ." he said bitterly, lifting his fine dark eyes to all of ours, and snapping his fingers without so much as an abracadabra, "condominiums." He enunciated every syllable with a vacant smile, like a man who had forgotten to down a raft of medications that very morning.

What was he talking about? This venerable block of businesses nearly as antique as the cobblestones underfoot? Soon to be razed and "repurposed" as condos? Where was Carlo getting his information? When the aprons were donned, Carlo bit his lip approvingly. Raising a fist, he whispered, "We grind the wheat. I show." A perfectly common way to begin a cooking demo, only for the life of me, at that moment, Carlo Giannini sounded like he was about to demonstrate how to dismember a corpse with exactitude and verve.

But he had their attention.

And at the rate any of the three Copelands could crank the handle and grind the grains, I could catch the train into Florence for the rest of the day. For my party of three wealthy Americans here at Forno di Carlo—was it Mimi who asked just then if *forno* meant "hell"?—they had a colorful instructor with deep, dark interior spaces no one could reach with a long-handled pizza peel. Their time here would fly like hell-hawks from the underworld.

I slipped out, conveying to one of the bakery ladies that, should anyone need me, I would be next door. Amid many shrugs and eye rolls, they conveyed to me: So what? Did I have more loaves of *pane rustica* to put on the empty shelves? Did I have screaming babies to make them forget everything they had ever learned about making change? Until Carlo's, I had never stepped into a bakery where despair turned out such delectable baked goods.

Next door, I craned my neck to look inside the Chamber of Commerce for Benedetto Ricci. Maybe he'd have something to add to the generalized gloom at Forno di Carlo. But no Benedetto. The red-haired girl who was staffing the coffee cart seemed to sense what I was after and jabbed a manicured thumb toward the end of the block. As I started in that direction, I sidestepped the monster speakers, which roared into life with a whir of music that settled into Bene- detto's usual playlist. Diplomatically, I once told him, "Very eclectic." At which he spat and laughed, "Is mish- mash." The random shuffle landed at "Brindisi," aka "The Drinking Song" from *La Traviata*, which at ten in the morning on a Friday seemed a bit premature.

No Benedetto.

Pressing on, I started to cross the alley between the city blocks, then pulled up short, pretending to be fascinated at the window display in a *tabacchi* shop. Smokes, souvenir postcards, and lotto tickets required a lot of study on my part as I gave the couple just across the alley at a small bistro the side-eye. Renata and her assistant, Jason. I'd know her wild hair and his faux-retro overcoat anywhere. Although their voices were raised, I couldn't hear what they were talking about, so I eased myself around the corner of the tobacco purveyor's place into the pleasantly shadowed alley. In one short dash, I was on the other side and inched my way, like a cartoon character, along the bistro's sand- stone exterior wall. Getting only as close to them as I dared still left me about eight feet away. If one of them suddenly scraped backward in the chair, the jig would most definitely be up.

As an easy blind—in case the bakery ladies had been mistaken and I was now the subject of a manhunt—I stud- ied my phone, but my ears belonged to Renata. "I don't know how in the hell you got that idea, Jason. I never led you on."

"What a liar you are, Renata, and I never saw it." He sounded bitter.

"Oh, stop it. Haven't I paid you well?"

A beat. "I thought we were building something. Working toward something. Together."

I heard a cup pushed violently aside. Hers? "Oh, come off it, for God's sake, Jason. You're not my . . . boyfriend." She said it like a breathless teenager. "You're my lawyer."

His voice dropped. "I thought I was more than that. I thought—"

"And you're not a kid, so quit mooning around. It's disgusting."

A beat. "Renata," he said, with what I can only call admirable firmness, "I gave up a job offer from Rosenberg and Estis to come here with you."

"Oh, so what? There'll be other job offers."

"I'm not so sure. You don't think word gets around? I'm the one who gives up an offer from a top real estate firm to go play personal attorney to a bad player."

She stifled a laugh. "So you've really been doing your homework."

"I'm your lawyer. Whatever you don't tell me, Renata, I find out other ways."

"Boy detective." She added facetiously, "So hot."

Angry. "I was good enough for you two weeks ago."

"Yes, good timing for you in some ways. I don't like sleeping alone, which surprises everyone, considering I don't particularly like people—"

"No, really?"

"—and bad timing for you in others, what with turning down the job offer of a lifetime."

"So you see it." He was incredulous. "I won't get it back. Didn't you care enough?"

"Care enough?" Words strange on her tongue.

"Care at all, then."

She sighed. "Here's how I see it. You've been useful to me. In the boardroom, in the courtroom, in the bedroom. Although"—she let out a sigh—"if you must know, in bed you're a little too young to be so old-school."

He said nothing, probably since breathing was about all he could manage.

"Still, I'll keep you on, Jason—"

"You'll keep me on."

"—even after this little tantrum, because I need those other skills. It's not going to be easy turning this inherited pile of dilapidated shops into luxury housing. You'll have documents to file and, I'm guessing, palms to grease. Same for the pathetic little olive grove." My heart drooped as I took a chance to step closer to their café table. Renata went on in a musing way. For all I could tell, she was doodling on a napkin. "I may even lose some friends."

"Get yourself another lawyer, Renata." Jason pushed back his chair so violently that it toppled. Then, "As for losing some friends, can you really be so stupid not to see you don't have any?"

"You're leaving?" The tone was creepily indifferent.

"I've got fences to mend."

A brittle note crept into her voice. "Actually, Jason, you don't. I needed your help so badly, you see, that I called Rosenberg and Estis after you turned down their offer—"

"You did what?"

"—and told them I was your former employer and thought they should know about the embezzlement."

"The—"

She sounded frustrated with herself. "It was just a form of insurance."

And then I heard a loud slap, a small cry, and the gasps of passing shoppers.

* * *

Back at the villa, Muffy and the Copelands proudly carried their hand-ground wheat flour into the kitchen, where Rosa and Sofia fussed over them. Altogether, Muffy confided to me, they had ground enough flour for the biscotti for this afternoon's tea. The three gallon-sized ziplock bags filled with the whole grains that Carlo had provided them were nowhere to be seen.

Instead, a jubilant Mimi, with a good deal more color in her cheeks, held up a quart-sized bag with the results of their combined efforts. While Rosa and Sofia stood blinking tactfully at the bag, Mimi flexed her thin muscles, and the kitchen became a place of unexpected gaiety.

Muffy leaned into me. "The melancholy Carlo will machine-process the rest that we'll be needing for two days of ziti and bring it by this afternoon."

"Before lunch, I hope. Chef will be teaching you the dough, and then you'll be extruding."

Muffy nodded serenely. "Carlo knows." She touched my shoulder. "Lovely man."

I eyed her. "Are you matchmaking?"

"Well," she temporized, "you'd have to like an atmosphere of torment, of course."

I crinkled my nose. "Could be a little tough to have around the house."

She said airily, "I suppose so."

"Besides," I added, "I have a boyfriend." I remembered Renata's mockery.

"Ah."

"The Orlandini you haven't met yet."

"Oh," said Muffy brightly, "the cover boy?"

"You read *Bellissimo!*?"

"I like to keep up on my 'life arts.'" She rolled her eyes. "Actually, no, I couldn't possibly care less, but Philip does. He brings Mimi his magazines and journals when he's done with them." She went on, "That *Bellissimo!* piece is where he heard about the cooking school. He passed that issue on to Mimi to whet her appetite for a ziti extravaganza."

Rosa and Sofia set aside the bag with the ground wheat flour and motioned to the Copelands to help themselves. What they made sound negligible, like maybe the guests could expect a turnip or half a cabbage, turned out, when they swept off the napkins that covered the platters, to be a spread for a wedding feast. Impressed, Philip inclined his head, and his mother squealed.

"Remember," I raised my voice, "after lunch, Rosa will escort you to Arezzo to the farm of our cousin, Oswaldo Orlandini, where you will pick fresh what we need for the next two days. Chef will provide the list."

What I was secretly hoping was that the quirky Oswaldo wouldn't see them as heaven-sent farmhands and overwork them. That was where Rosa Bari came in. For some reason we could never quite sort out, Oswaldo feared Rosa, a goofy state of affairs we were happy to cash in on occasionally.

In my room, I sat on my rug in a sunny corner, nibbled on the rolled slices of carpaccio I had wrapped and pocketed from the "little lunch," and thought about what I had learned. Apparently, the icy Renata had inherited that *"molto, molto vecchio"* block of shops and came to town now with big American plans to raze them and develop the property. But inherited from whom? Did she have ties to Cortona? It sure sounded like it. She was what a stricken Carlo had called *un fantasma*. A ghost. How did he know her?

But what interested me even more was her throwaway crack about the pathetic little olive grove. How could Pete's olive grove—right there on Orlandini property—be part of this mysterious inheritance? Renata had made it sound like Jason, had he stayed on as her personal attorney, would have plenty of documents to file on that score, too. And palms to grease? What did this unpleasant woman mean? Who was her dead benefactor? And how long has she known about this inheritance?

And where could I uncover more information?

*W*aving *arrivederci* to the Phantom as it pulled noiselessly out of its parking spot and headed toward the gate, Chef and I argued through our smiles. He can slap down as many different opinions as cured meats on a platter. He dealt "Why you no making *Hot Chef* video?" "How you expect me do *Hot Chef* video if Annamaria home watching TV?" and "You *sous chef* today—no argue—no time off" before the Rolls even turned left out of the gate. I gave him a long look, the kind of look that left no doubt what I thought about the chocolate brown jumpsuit he was wearing. Defensively, Chef eased the material around his waist. Shoehorning a word into the one-sided conversation, I agreed to help him set up for the afternoon in the kitchen to make pasta dough, and as we headed toward the main building, I brought up what was really on my mind.

I gave it my best shot in Italian. "The building that was bombed, Chef."

"Eh?"

I knew Chef himself wasn't even born when the villa was hit, but he had to know something. When he was child, it was the sort of story that gets aired at birthdays, saints' days, holy days of obligation, and pub crawls as part of the local lore, filed under "There but for the Grace of God . . ." or "Had I Not Felt Called to Have a Few at the Pub . . ." depending on where the narrator turned for salvation. "The building"—here I pointed repeatedly toward the woods at the back of the property—"that was"—since I didn't know the word for bombed, I mimed an explosion. With sound effects.

"Ah, *sì*."

We struggled over who was going to hold open the door. I let him win.

"Was your family here?" I added, following him inside. "During the war?"

I had to listen to a thin stream of disbelieving comments that ended with the biggest *Just how crazy did La Bella Nella think the Orlandinis were?* I decided to sidestep it as a rhetorical question and see what he answered as we strode down the hall to the kitchen. Apparently, the Orlandini family—Chef's parents and grandparents—decamped to Bellinzona, Switzerland, in 1938, where they stayed with other Orlandinis, and I could tell by his expelling air out of the side of his mouth, which made a sound like a whale's blow hole, that he didn't have a clue about their names. And in all of his seventy years, it struck me, he had never even wondered about them.

"Come back here"—he stamped his feet just to be sure I got the concept of "here"—*"dieci anni dopo."* Ten years later.

In the kitchen, where the afternoon sunlight was skimming over the windowsills, I placated Chef by donning an apron, and together we rolled the wheeled cart holding the industrial-sized pasta extruder into the center of the beautiful new kitchen, next to a large stainless steel utility table.

"Which building was destroyed?"

His large features seemed to draw in by his nose. An effort of memory. *"L'infermeria."* So he heard, he was quick to bluster, but it was before his own time. The shrug and smirk implied it was of no consequence. Or interest. Suddenly, he lifted a hand like a traffic cop. "No." Again, "No." He titled his head back, trying hard to recall what must have felt like conversations from back in the day when these folks were building aqueducts. "Was bathhouse."

"Okay, Chef, what's next?" I brought over the bag of flour the Copelands and Muffy had ground by hand.

"No. No." Chef's head swung left and right. Staring at his right foot, he finally offered, "Was *infermeria. Sono sicuro*"—I'm sure. Leaving history behind like unpaid bills, he said imperiously, as if he were marshaling an army, "Bring out eggs."

"Did anybody die?"

Deflated. *"Non lo so. Chiedi ad Annamaria."* Ask Annamaria.

I must have looked forlorn, so Chef turned slowly away from me and headed to the Liebherr side-by-side fridge. While he extracted six eggs, he mused in Italian that while the Orlandinis were in Bellinzona, they had permitted the Veronicans—housed in their new convent home about fifteen minutes away for the last one hundred years—to use the villa in any way they saw fit in exchange for keeping an eye on things. With that piece of information, I adjusted my thinking. The building bombed into rubble might have been an infirmary, but surely not during the tenure of the Orlandini family.

Would it have been repurposed? If the villa had ceased to be a monastic community, where the sick were tended right on the site, what would the secular new owners, generations of Orlandinis, have used it for? That building must have dated from the sixteenth century, like all the others, but even if the nuns throughout those three hundred years had used it as an infirmary, in modern times, it would have served some other purpose.

In front of me, Chef was arranging a clean dish towel in the shape of a wreath on the utility table and gently setting the eggs inside. He smiled. He was enjoying the visitation of an idea. "You find plans of old villa. Better"—he shot me a dark look—"than Annamaria, that bad—" Like a school-boy caught badmouthing his gym teacher, he clamped his lips shut and banged around among the measuring cups hanging on a rack for a one-cup measure.

He had a point.

Plans of old villa.

And there I was again, back with Philip Copeland, who wondered about a villa library.

No books, Rosa had said.

As Chef and I finished the setup for the ziti dough–making afternoon, I found a complete lack of library hard to believe. Even if this generation of Orlandinis—well, Chef—preferred scanning the papers for the bocce scores, it couldn't account for 150 years of other Orlandinis, possibly readers. It was just too many years of residence at this villa not to have acquired classics, first editions, prints, local histories, blueprints, drawings, deeds, leases, purchase orders—and a lot of those, I'd think, from the tenure of the Orlandinis. I watched Chef position his black toque on his gleaming head and then sync his phone to the sound system.

But what about the Veronicans of the Veil who had in-habited the villa for those three hundred years beforehand? What about missals, illustrated manuscripts, maps, Bibles, records of births and deaths? Into the swelling strains of the studio orchestra came Vic Damone asserting, "You don't have to say you love me, just be close at hand." For some mysterious reason, this song was one of Chef's favorites. *"Questa canzone, sono io"*—he'd say with a manly thump at his chest. And I couldn't figure out just why, considering Chef Claudio Orlandini wanted everybody to tell him they love him all the time. He owned practically every recorded cover of it. Dusty Springfield, Elvis Presley, Connie Francis, Robert Goulet, Tom Jones. But it was the Damone version that stirred up some tender heroics in Chef he thought needed airing every so often.

As I set out three mixing bowls, my mind turned back to the mystery of the villa library. I couldn't banish the image of an indistinct, shadowy pile of reading material that was—rather like any tender heroics in Chef—missing.

No missing," said Annamaria matter-of-factly when I tracked her down by phone in the convent kitchen on the southern outskirts of Cortona. She put me on speaker. Quickly we covered the health and whereabouts of Chef (well enough, cooking, grumbling, wearing an ugly jumpsuit), Pete (also well, except for head swelled to the size of a beach ball, still in Rome), Rosa (so very happy, what with shooting Chef with the evil eye), Sofia (most definitely a dark horse), the guests (sleepless in Cortona, exceedingly good sports), and myself. Myself. To my great surprise, I dodged that one.

Instead, while she described how, for the sisters' dinner, she was making omelets with garlic, Gruyère, cremini mushrooms, and fresh parsley, demonstrated on YouTube by Jacques Pépin, I found myself wondering if I should describe the schemes of a dangerous newcomer to town named Renata. Undecided, I took a few seconds to envision the reaction of Chef to the news that Pépin had buttered and béchameled his French way into a Tuscan sous chef's kitchen life. No use warning Annamaria. From Chef, she's known better and she's known worse. So when she told me without any hesitation that the library of the villa wasn't missing or destroyed in the rubble of what had been the infirmary or the bathhouse, or was nonexistent in the very first place, I felt a thrill.

In the background, I heard the neat little chops I had come to associate with Annamaria at work on an onion, a bunch of parsley, eight ounces of cremini mushrooms. Of course, she made a disclaimer, she had no firsthand experience with the events. "No, no"—I smoothed over it—"of course not." But when the Orlandini family fled to Switzerland, the Veronicans packed up all the books, documents, manuscripts, ledgers, drawings, plans, and so forth, all of which they thought were too precious to risk in the run-up to a world war. Considering the Allied bombing of October 22, 1944, that documentary rescue effort showed foresight.

"Where had it all been housed at the villa?" I asked.

Still in Italian, Annamaria chirped, "In the old infirmary."

I breathed. "So that building *was* the old infirmary."

"Until the Veronicans sold to the Orlandini family."

"And then?"

"A library. And storage."

"And now, *niente*."

"*Sì, é vero.*"

"Did all those books and documents"—how to put it?—"survive the war?"

"As far as I know."

And now we had arrived. "Where?"

"You will have to ask *Suor* Ippolita Cordovana, Nell." I heard her sauté the mushrooms.

I sagged. "So you don't know?"

"Oh, no," said Annamaria in a lively way. "This is the last I know. The sisters, they get those books and papers *nel Museo dell'Accademia Etrusca*."

"The Etruscan Museum." I marveled. "Right in town. On Piazza Luca Signorelli."

"Nell," said Annamaria, and I could tell she needed to get off the phone, "you come talk to Sister Ippolita. She know more."

"Is she the convent historian?"

Annamaria let out a laugh. "Sister Ippolita Cordovana is ninety-six years old." She added, "Nell, *lei era qui*."

She was there.

When Muffy and the Copelands got back from Arezzo, hauling net shopping bags filled with Montoro onions, eggplants, fresh parsley, bay leaves, carrots, celery, and plenty of San Marzano tomatoes, there was a scene of near wailing when Rosa realized they had forgotten to swing by the butcher's and get two pounds of braising steak. I saw my opportunity, either to grill Sister Ippolita or to scour the holdings at the Etruscan Museum to uncover the villa's history.

"I'll go," I said valiantly.

Sofia offered to take my place in the kitchen—done.

Rosa offered to wash the vegetables and prep them for the next day—done.

Chef used Vic Damone's "April in Portugal" for some lip-synch.

Mimi, measuring out the oil for her flour, bit her lip, delighted with Chef.

Eyeing the hefty extruder, Philip rolled up his sleeves.

Muffy, shooting me a quizzical look, cracked eggs into her mixing bowl.

I hung my apron on a hook. With a quick *"Ciao!"* I hurried out of the kitchen, down the corridor to the school office, where I grabbed my cranberry fleece coat and jailer's key ring. Before leaving, I remembered what Philip had suggested about the architectural plans exhibition—"Go to the Met website and check it out"—and I booted up the laptop.

On the Metropolitan Museum's classy and colorful site, I clicked on Upcoming Exhibitions and found three—two coming up within the year, the third well into next year.

CHANGING THE IMAGE, IMAGING THE CHANGE

The Art and Revelation of Architectural Plans. In a Eurocentric survey of the advancements in architectural drawing, this fascinating exhibition presents a documentary record of cultural change as seen through the lens of architectural developments. From the palladios and palazzos of Italy to the estates and monasteries of Great Britain, advancements in draftsmanship respond to the accumulation of wealth. Particularly intriguing are the edifices that inspire renovation over several centuries, made apparent in the pairings of drawings and plans for a single structure.

At the bottom of the second paragraph was one line: The exhibition is made possible by the Philip B. Copeland Foundation.

How nice to have that kind of money. The Copeland Foundation was single-handedly bankrolling a major exhibition at a world-class museum of art. And Philip Copeland himself had been so . . . casual about it. For my part, at that moment, I felt a tingle of excitement at the thought that I could provide something of interest.

Heading outside, I had a mission.

Philip had done a tidy job of parking the Rolls out of the way of the villa vehicles, and in a flash, I was heading into Cortona in the T-Bird on a midafternoon in November. I knew I couldn't just drop into the Veronican convent to call on Sister Ippolita, who—despite what Annamaria told me—might not be quite such a good resource at ninety-six as she had been, say, even ten years ago. But even if she shared as many diamond-sharp memories of 1944 as we had San Marzano tomatoes getting a nice bath from Rosa, I felt better about making an appointment with her. I only hoped I had time to pull it off tomorrow, when the kitchen would be awash in ziti shells, tomato sauce, and Copelands.

Clouds strayed in front of the sun as I entered the downtown section of Cortona, and I flicked on the windshield wipers as a windless drizzle began. Prowling side streets near Piazza Luca Signorelli for a parking spot, I had to widen my search. At least, I figured if I got closer to Piazza della Repubblica, I could find my way walking to the museum. Motorcycles zipped by me, tourists with selfie sticks strolled, and I made my way down Via Ghibellina, just a block off the piazza.

As I braked near the corner while a group of uniformed schoolkids did a cluster run across the street, I happened to catch sight of the Hotel Italia. It happens sometimes in life, it seems to me, when circumstances grab you by the neck and shake you silly, long enough to let the old way you saw things die not with a bang, not even with a whimper. Just die. Your hands look different, your cry is one you've never heard, and blindness would have been a blessing. For in that moment, up the lopsided step to the arched entrance of the Hotel Italia, sprang Renata, Carlo's wild-haired *fantasma*.

Right behind her, with his hand on her back, was Pete.

8

I never made it to the Etruscan Museum.

I barely made it to the butcher's.

Having to choose between the two, at the museum I could only gaze from a distance at iron knives in acrylic cases. But at the butcher's, ah, at the butcher's I could get supremely lucky and watch some trusty Wüsthof blades go snicker-snack. Collapsed against the back of the T-Bird's seat, I allowed myself five minutes of hot tears—I actually set the timer on my phone—because I made a point of never spending more than those five minutes on any heartbreak that comes out of a he-done-her-wrong scenario. Season one, episode seven of *The Dr. Val Show*.

That piece of advice—or what the brand calls ReVALation—occurred lots of times in the nine years my father's been on cable TV, the studio audience shrinkabees being what they are. But season one, episode seven, when I was twenty, I heard it, and needed to hear it. Dad, incredulous, to blubbering woman: "Martine, Martine, why would you cry more than"—big expressive stage shrug—"five minutes over this husband who's cheated on you with five different women?" Camera close-up on Dr. Val, who did his trademark clown horn sound effect everyone loved and added, "This year alone!" Rimshot from the drummer of the in-house trio.

But it made a convenient kind of sense to me.

I drove past the Hotel Italia and made my way to the butcher's shop on the other side of town. There I sat, parked, putting off getting out of the car only to find out my appendages weren't working. Quite simply, I couldn't make sense of what I had seen. No matter how I turned it over in my hands. First of all, Pete had lied. He wasn't in Rome; he was in Cortona. To be fair to him, I couldn't say whether he had just arrived. Second, did he actually even know this Renata? Is it possible he just happened to be entering the Hotel Italia at the very same time she was? To be fair to me, I could hear my father on the clown horn four thousand miles away.

Say, though, Pete did not know this Renata. Say their entering the hotel at the same time was coincidental. All that dispelled was whatever I thought was going on with Renata. It doesn't, let the record reflect, dispel (a) that he lied to me, and (b) he was jolly well going into the Hotel Italia for something or someone . . . else, having lied to his girlfriend, Nell. Still not good.

There were sufficient imponderables that I decided to suspend judgment.

It never fails to make me happy when I can suspend judgment.

A few rounds of alternate nostril breathing, and I was good to go. I would buy two pounds of braising steak for the next day's ziti alla Genovese. I would make an appointment for tomorrow, perhaps around lunchtime, to visit Suor

Ippolita. I would tell an ecstatic Chef that we would film his audition video for *Hot Chef: Italian Style* tomorrow at 8 a.m.—yes, that early, no arguments. My quarrel wasn't with Chef; it was with Pete. And I wanted to put as much behind me as possible between now and when the Copelands climb for the last time into the Phantom and ease on up the road toward Aeroporto di Firenze, Peretola. I wanted to meet my responsibilities.

And be done with them.

Which meant, I realized as I got out of the T-Bird, I hadn't suspended judgment one iota.

And very, very far away, I swear I could hear a rimshot.

I turned over the braising steak to Rosa, who in turn promised to hand it off to Annamaria the next day. I had dug around in Chef's closet with him to pick out a flattering and filmable outfit, not an easy task. When the time came, the Copeland Party of Three were in high spirits, taking turns at the extruder. And Chef had miraculously produced dinner all on his own, which turned out to be a sensational Cacciucco, a fish stew, served over toasted hunks of home-made *pane campagnolo*, a garlic-rich bread. For wine, he offered either Prosecco or Moscato—and I knew the Moscato was really for me since he knows it's just about the only white wine I'll drink.

I bestowed a quick kiss, which only made him heave into a loud chorus of "You Don't Have to Say You Love Me" to the delighted cries of Muffy and Mimi. Philip hung on to a wry look. After dinner, Muffy and Mimi strolled to the common room, where Mimi played what she could re-member of "Für Elise" on the villa baby grand, and Muffy told me in a whisper that tonight she'd lock them both in.

Philip said that farmer fellow—clearly, the odd cousin Oswaldo—told him there's a cool quartet playing tonight at the Globe in the Piazza Luca Signorelli. Off he went in the Phantom. These Copelands were very self-reliant. An excellent student class. Alone, alone, alone in my room, I downed the last of my Moscato, refused to think about Pete, and turned out the light at 10:03. It was the kind of falling asleep that happens sometimes, when your body feels like it just plain disperses, every part easing off from every other part. Like a spreading puddle thinning out all around the exquisite edges. Until finally, even the edges go.

The morning of the day we filmed our audition video for the show *Hot Chef: Italian Style* started out promising. I was directing, Rosa was filming, Chef was starring, and the sprightly Sofia was providing wine and sandwiches. All the really key jobs were covered. I had an appointment for around noon with Sister Ippolita, just after midday prayers. Hers, not mine.

I discovered Pete had left me a late voicemail, saying he couldn't wait to see me and he was looking forward to being home. I have to admit, I liked hearing his light baritone. His soft laugh, his sexy pause over the word "see," his way of packing a lot of good freight into the term "being home." Pure Pete. But maybe I didn't know him.

Could I really be quite that big a chump?

I just couldn't believe it.

When I stood still, breathed, and smiled for no good reason at all, I actually felt a little better. So I dashed around the grounds of the Villa Orlandini to decide on a location for our establishing shots meant to entice the *Hot Chef* producers. For this task, I had allowed an hour. It took about ten minutes to eliminate the broken fountain, where the skull-smashing murder of my ex-boyfriend occurred; the beautiful old villa barn, where just a month ago, a guest succumbed to mushroom poisoning; and the courtyard, where I confronted the private detective my father had hired to keep tabs on me, Nell Valenti, designer of the Villa Orlandini Cooking School here in Tuscany.

What was left? The dead garden with its bent, dried-out stalks? The woods along the back of the property, which would really only establish just how unkempt the grounds were? The compost heap? Lucky thing I was pretty sure the Moraiolo olive trees owned by Pete would meet the requirements: interesting vegetation, a good panorama of hillsides and fields, and a sense of the exotic flavor of the villa's setting. Otherwise, I'd be smack out of options. But the crew seemed game, so off we went. I tried not to think about whatever Renata had in mind for what she called "the pathetic little olive grove."

What I hadn't counted on was world-famous Chef Claudio Orlandini's interpretation of "establishing shots" for *Hot Chef*. At the sight of him prancing and leering through the olive grove like a satyr in a chef's jacket, I figured out what he was going for. He thought he was establishing that he was a hot chef. This sequence we could definitely save for *Local Maniacs Italian Style*, but not for a top-rated culinary competition program aired in twelve countries. When I loped toward him, calling to our cinematographer, Rosa, to pause the filming, Chef's eyes widened and he changed the game. Suddenly, he was chasing me through the olive trees. *"La Bella Nella,"* he said with a whoop straight out of a spaghetti western.

"No, Chef!" I yelled, *"No. Tu non capisci."* You don't understand. *"Smettila!"* Quit it.

He leaped out at me from behind a tree, turned to Rosa, who apparently was still filming, and now cackling, took a stance fake-beating his chest.

"Smettila!" I cried, for all the good it did, or all the good it ever did with this overgrown toddler who was in the pantheon of top five culinary celebrity chefs globally.

When I started a long-winded explanation as I ran backward about why he mustn't run around, and why he must look dignified at all times, I tripped over a tree root, fell, and rolled down a small incline at the back of the last row of Pete's trees. That time, the whoop was entirely mine.

I came to a stop against something soft that gave under the sudden slam.

Clutching at the stumpy grass, I steadied myself, caught my breath, and turned on my side. My roadblock was a heap of flesh draped in a Hermès beaded shawl in vermilion and white. She was back, this time sleeping it off, and without the trusty assistant. "Renata"—I elbowed her—"wake up."

The shouts from above told me the illustrious film crew was heading our way, and I was pretty sure the fluent Italian-American opportunist Renata, who had arrived just two days ago, would not like to be filmed sprawled in the Tuscan winter furze.

"Renata," I hissed through gritted teeth as I gave her a mighty shove, "are you drunk? Wake up!" My final shove, which included one of my feet for good measure, succeeded only in flipping her over. Not a quick flip, mind you, but a flip of agonizing slowness, the kind that seems barely responsive to things like gravity. At the final flop, one of her arms fell gracelessly to her side.

Which was pretty much when I noticed the swollen purple face and bloodred eyeballs that were way past seeing anything at all. With a gasp, I crab-walked two feet away from the body, taking in only her long mop of curly hair dyed raven, wondering just how long it would take before Chef pitched the murder as a selling point for offering him a spot on season three of *Hot Chef: Italian Style*.

I t was Rosa who came up with the old Crime Scene tape she had been keeping in her room in the dormitory for reasons that weren't quite clear to me. When I eyed her, where Sofia, Chef, and I blocked the Copeland Party of Three from approaching the disaster that was now Renata, she gave me an arch look. Then she hotfooted it past me in her black soft-soled oxfords to where she began stringing the tape from tree trunk to tree trunk, stepping back to give it marks for artistry.

Chef got busy with the guests, offering up the very best Orlandini flimflam, something about *"un'asino morto"*— dead donkey, who could argue?—down below, in a vague gesture meant to take in everything from Tuscany to the Rock of Gibraltar. When it became clear the Copelands and Muffy wanted to peer at the dead donkey, Chef tapped his foot impatiently, and landed on his most persuasive argument against it. He pinched his nostrils together as his other hand waved away the smell. Had that argument not worked, I knew he was quite capable of describing busy maggots and exposed innards.

Fortunately, unpleasant smell achieved consensus among our guests: better to beat it. At that, Mimi and Muffy gamely chugged up the small hill at the back of the villa property, wrangled by Philip. When they were out of earshot, I deputized Chef to find Pete, Sofia to phone the carabinieri, and Rosa to tell Annamaria to please avoid preparing any red meat dish for dinner. That left me to guard the body until the carabinieri arrived, most likely in the person of Commissario Joe Batta.

Chef, Rosa, and Sofia disappeared up the hill.

With just the dead Renata for company, I turned slowly toward her in the cool midmorning light. When a breeze fluttered her hair and raised the edge of the beaded shawl, it almost looked like life, and I felt a wash of sadness toward this woman I really didn't even know. I drew closer but stopped just short of touching her curled fingers.

There are usually those predictable scenes in TV murder mystery shows when—upon the discovery of the body shot precisely through the heart in broad daylight in fine weather in an open field—some chump stammers, "There must be some mistake." These are the scenes where I laugh heartily on my way to the kitchen to refill the Cheetos bowl.

But at the exact moment I recognized the dead woman, I had but a single thought: *There must be some mistake.* As if someone had mistaken this poor woman who had strewn business cards and bossed assistants and didn't make a complete jackass of herself in high heels for someone else. In broad daylight, in reasonably fine weather, and in an open field just past the olive grove. You can see how that might happen.

But what was she doing here? Again?

I started to shake uncontrollably.

I admit it, I was bitter. While I waited for someone to turn up and relieve me of my guard duty, I found a gnarly exposed root of an olive tree around twelve feet away from the corpse. There I sat, averting my eyes, and immediately felt myself sink into a demifunk, the kind I get when I think about what my life would have been like if I hadn't been an only child and my parents had someone else under the roof to gnaw on in their free moments. But my lack of distracting siblings, a topic that was always on the Nell Valenti infinity loop, didn't stand a chance in light of my recent history, which now included a fresh murder.

Granted, it hadn't technically occurred on villa grounds. Technically, the Silver Wind Olive Grove was Pete Orlandini's property. Adjacent, yes. But indistinguishable from the acres owned by Chef Claudio Orlandini, also yes. To an outsider, the murder of Renata was just another in what was becoming a long bloody line in the recent history of Orlandini-associated murders. How could I possibly save the cooking school from what was rapidly shaping up to be a bad reputation in Cortona, Italy? In fact, we should be so lucky just to have a bad reputation. That would indeed be trading up, the way things were going. I had every self-pitying right to be bitter.

Turning up first, no surprise, was Annamaria. Here she came, tall and stately, alerted by Sofia, with salt-and-pepper hair, bearing a silver tray with an espresso pot and demi-tasse cups. She was back on the job as sous chef, but only half-time, and she was immovable. It was a job. It no longer seemed to be her life.

She handed me the tray with a thin smile. *"Aspetti,"* she said in a quiet voice. Wait. Then she circled the tree, edged down to where the remains of Renata lay, and considered the scene. I had hoped for something kind of a cross between wacky and upbeat—"What, her? This one? Say, this isn't so bad, never saw her before in my life!"—but I knew that for that kind of response, I should have asked for Chef. Instead, Annamaria sighed one of those bottomless, expressive Italian sighs that covered everything bleak from the bad thing that happened in the Bari family four hundred years ago all the way up through the ages to the substandard Roma tomato crop this year.

"So." This had to be Annamaria's favorite English word. "So."

I nodded my complete understanding.

"Ecco la strega." Turning away from the sight, she made a single gesture, the kind my mother used when she wanted me to move my muddy boots elsewhere. *Ecco la strega.* Behold the witch. Her voice was flat and laden with doom—the kind of one-note clang I associate with the end of days.

She pulled up a tree root or, at any rate, shared mine, and took charge of the tray, which, in my hands, was shaking. Oddly, I was consoled by the tinkling of the demitasse spoons. Tilting her beautiful, imperturbable head, Annamaria poured out our espresso.

"Grazie," I managed to choke out at her for her kindness.

With raised eyebrows, she slipped a biscotto into my demitasse cup. We regarded it in silence, considering how the proportions between cup and biscotto seemed all wrong. Behind us, the poor dead woman had no opinion. After a moment, Annamaria shrugged and sipped her own. We stared companionably at nothing while the espresso lasted.

Finally, she murmured some little string of Italian nothings and stretched musingly. "Finally, *la strega è venuta a casa.*" She dabbed at her lips, shaped like the ocean's best swells.

I turned to her. "The witch has come home?" What could she possibly mean?

"Oh, *sì*, Nella." Her gaze fixed on distant figures hurrying into the olive grove. "Signorina Renata. I recognize *al momento. Molti anni fa, capisci?*" It was many years ago.

I set my cup down on the tray. "Renata lived here?"

"In Cortona, *sì*."

"She grew up in Cortona?"

Annamaria leaned away. "No, no, no, not so long. A few years. *Come un adolescente.*"

A teenager. I felt unprepared for this revelation that the dead woman had Cortona ties.

"Her father"—Annamaria swelled dramatically—"famous singer. Lodovico Vitale."

Of course I knew the name, but never put it together with *la strega* sprawled strangled to death behind us.

"Did you know her?" Now I was just keeping the conversation alive, not expecting much more information.

"Ovviamente!" She lifted her shoulders.

But why *"of course"*? "And Chef?"

"Chef, Caterina—Pierfranco's mother—" She was waving off days gone by like a pesky mosquito.

I got the idea. "And Pete?"

A beat. At that, Annamaria Bari turned to face me. Her hands got very still, there between us in midair. "Pierfranco?" First she gave me an incredulous look. Then she jerked her fine head toward the motionless shape not twelve feet away. *"Quella strega,"* she told me, "is how you say his"—her eyes narrowed as she found the exact words—"ex-wife."

C hef, who was wearing a full-zip knit jacket in the popsicle colors of his bocce team, had somehow figured out the photo shoot might have to wait a day. Annamaria organized our expresso things and started up the hill, letting me know she would take charge of the school's guests. But it was the incomparable Rosa Bari who had news I could only liken to a last-minute reprieve by the governor: Commissario Giovanni Battista Onetto is attending a videoconferencing workshop in Rome and won't be back until tomorrow. That alone would hold me in the good news department, but I couldn't imagine what the homicide unit might want to do in terms of the corpse, the crime scene, and lunch.

Without my saying a word, Rosa stood nodding that tight little nod of hers that seems less like an agreement than an affliction. *"Chè?"* I tossed out. And then I heard the unmistakable sound of a motorcycle roar into the courtyard, where it blurted to a stop. I knew. The Polizia Municipale had arrived in the person of a helmeted blonde on a motorcycle. The first time I met her, Pete called her Serafina, and Serafina called him Pierfranco. I was given to understand either those two shared a common ancestor, mixed drink at the local watering hole, or set of silk sheets. She wore blue twill pants, a thick zip-up jacket, a white bandolero with a holstered gun, and no makeup.

As the cop Serafina headed toward me, escorted by Rosa, who was practically skipping she was so happy for something to relieve the domestic boredom of this private party of Philip Copeland and his vague and lovely mother and her bestie. Once again, her eyes sweeping the scene, Serafina came striding, taking in the lay of the land, not to mention the corpse. Serafina was all business, a nice contrast to Rosa, who was gamboling like a spaniel with its tongue lolling. When the two of them came to a stop in front of me, Serafina shot me a smile and Rosa widened her eyes in a way that said, *Finally, someone who can take charge.*

We exchanged very small talk. How have you been? Fine, and you? I can't complain, now where's the body? I had forgotten how good Serafina's English was. I showed her. As I gave the cop room to take in the crime scene, studying the dead woman from a crouch, her gloved hands dangling between her knees, I saw that she still wore blue twill pants, a thick zip-up jacket, and a white bandolero with a holstered gun, but this time, her flawless skin glistened with product, topped by volumizing mascara, swaths of blush, and strokes of rose-tinted lip gloss. I thought if I could somehow work the crime-solving biker Serafina into the *Hot Chef* audition video, Chef Claudio Orlandini would land a spot in the lineup.

"Her name?"

"Renata Vitale."

"And you are—?"

"Nell Valenti. Designer of the villa cooking school." I was rather cheered she didn't remember me. It meant the local law might not have quite come to think of me yet as queen of the house of death. "I found the body."

"Time?"

"Half an hour ago."

"Did you touch the body?"

Not my first crime scene, missy, I wanted to say. Instead, I covered my fall, my roll, my soft landing. As I spoke, I felt like an onlooker to my own report, hearing myself slip into one of those false precision points of view. Officer Serafina's pen poised midair as she listened to me declare something about how although technically rolling into the corpse may constitute "touching," it may not strictly fall within the definition of said action established in the criminal codes wherein "touching" signifies willful intention as per an act of the hands. Finally spent, I had the good grace to sag.

And Serafina had the good grace to move on. "Was the dead woman a guest here?"

"A guest?" To keep from getting giddy at the thought, I bit down on the inside of my cheek. "No."

"Yet you know her. How?"

"I met her in town. Just yesterday." True and verifiable. What I didn't want to pass on to the lovely blond cop was that, apparently, the dead woman used to be married to my boyfriend. If I could stick to answering the questions precisely, I would be okay, and connecting the dots to Pete Orlandini would fall to somebody else. I only knew it couldn't be me. My heart was already hurting enough on that score. But I started to feel light-headed, and she showed no inclination to stash her notebook. All I could see ahead of me right then was a vast wasteland of questioning, and no hopes of keeping off the subject of Pete and the dead Renata. The very little I knew was so damning.

Was it Annamaria's biscotti? Too much sugar? Not enough? The espresso, then? Too early? I took a step or two backward as Serafina eyed me narrowly. "Scusi—" was all I managed as I turned away from her with dreamlike slowness, and threw up.

I lay alone and unbothered on my bed in the abbess's room behind the closed door and drawn shades. Not dark, not light, just something in between. Which described me perfectly. It was Sofia who got me to the room and Annamaria who hovered close enough to tell me she'd handle everything and Chef who yelled we'd finish the video later.

Even from where I was lying, squinting at a little black blot on the ceiling, wondering if it was a bug or a hole, I heard the commotion in the courtyard as more of the local law arrived. Lifting my phone, I checked. Just after nine a.m. For now, I let the consequences of murder swirl around me, directed by other hands. In time, when my stomach settled, I took a slow, cool shower, where I stood unthinking in the stream of water and cried for home.

Who had she threatened? Even if she didn't know it?

What information did I have that could possibly be any help?

How would we ever be able to establish some normalcy for the Copelands, who were paying an exorbitant amount of money to have the Villa Orlandini to themselves? Between Mimi's nighttime wandering and now a murder, just how much danger were they willing to face?

As I dried off, I believed I had never felt a softer towel. I slipped into an indigo blue knit dress over black tights and boots. Then I phoned Annamaria, who picked up before the second ring.

"Pronto?" Her voice was clipped.

I switched into Italian. "How far has Serafina gotten?"

"She's talking now to Rosa. Staff first. How are you feeling?"

"Good enough. Is Chef there?"

"Yes."

"We have to make plans about the Copelands."

"Agreed."

"Have you heard from Pete?"

"Not yet."

Depending, I thought, on what he's been doing for the last eighteen hours or so, he may already have the news. "Annamaria, we need to come to some decisions."

"About Ziti Variations."

She was always one step ahead. "Yes"—I went on— "when I get back. I've got an appointment—"

"Sister Ippolita?"

Make that two steps ahead.

9

*Sister Ippolita Cordovana met me in the refectory, where she was sweeping after the noontime meal. She was a little woman in a gray twill contemporary habit that buttoned up the front, was belted with a narrow cummerbund, and came nearly to her ankles. Covering her head was a Veronican white veil that directed her hair down her back. White, thin, barely touching her shoulders, brushed back after a lifetime, her hair didn't need any help to know where to fall. The habit seemed almost too heavy for the tiny Ippolita, who looked like she was the last in line to raid the community clothes closet. Her sweeping was done with quick, short strokes, some of which missed the floor, but they matched the quick, short steps of the hunched and smiling nun.

We shook hands—hers were large—and I took in her face, with its long nose and eyes dark like BBs and thin smiling lips. Her skin, tucked with laugh lines that had long ago deepened into folds, was marked with popped capillaries and age spots. When it became clear she didn't have a word of English, I switched to Italian and walked by the old nun's side. At ninety-six, she had a brittle quality to her voice and not a lot of range. But her mind was quicker than her broom.

When I explained how Annamaria sent me to her for information about the old library at the Villa Orlandini, she nodded with a lot of chin bobbing as though I had raised a weighty question. As she whirled her memory back more than eighty years, she slipped the broom across her shoulders like a milkmaid's carrying pole.

"Cosa vuoi sapere?" What do you want to know?

She and I stared at each other while I tried to figure out how to answer that in a way that would get me the most information. Philip Copeland had set me, unknowingly, on this little investigation, and I couldn't even say why I felt intrigued. But I wanted the story.

I told her I wanted to know about 1938, when the books were packed up.

I told her I wanted to know about 1944, when the old library was bombed.

She grunted in understanding, rocked the broom across her sloping shoulders and told me. She was a twelve-year-old local Cortona girl who helped in the kitchen in 1938. When Hitler and Mussolini palled around in Rome, *la famiglia* Orlandini decided to sit out *la puzza*, the stink, with relatives up in Switzerland. Before going, they made a deal with the Veronicans: you can make use of the villa, your historic old convent, in whatever way you need, in exchange for caretaking.

"Così abbiamo fatto." So, said Sister Ippolita with a casual shrug, *we did.*

What with the fall of Austria—she tsk-tsked with a mighty sigh—and all the book burnings, Mother Superior thought it wise to pack up all the books and papers in the library at the villa and store them elsewhere. Ippolita went along to help for those two days of work.

Interrupting her, I touched her arm. "And these books and papers included what belonged to the Orlandinis?" I asked in Italian.

Oh, yes, a hundred years of Orlandini, three hundred years of the Order of St. Veronica of the Veil. They packed it all, except for everyday holy books. A few Bibles, a few missals, a current log of holdings, just to keep things straight. Sister Alfonsa thought it best. When I asked Sister Ippolita if Sister Alfonsa was Mother Superior, I got a vigorous "no, no, no," with a gentle gesture. Sister Alfonsa, she corrected me, was *il custode*. The caretaker.

"At the villa?" I wanted to be sure.

"Alla villa." Sister Ippolita folded her hands and pressed them against her thin smiling lips. I caught the broom as it slid off her shoulders. Sister Alfonsa Cambi was a very good woman, a clever woman. She came late to the religious life. At twenty-eight, said the little nun solemnly. But by then, when she was caretaker at the villa during the war, she was nearly forty. "Sister Alfonsa," breathed Ippolita, *"era un'artista."* It was if she had uttered the words for angel or magician or visitation by the Holy Mother.

An artist. What could be better for a woman like Alfonsa Cambi? The run of the Orlandini villa, solo, setting up her easel wherever she pleased in exchange for some light duties. "The books and papers you packed, Sister Ippolita . . ." I said in Italian, "how did Mother Superior decide on the Etruscan Museum in town?"

And she told me she overhead Mother Superior and Sister Alfonsa deciding it was because the Veronicans could "lose" them there, stipulating to the museum personnel that the villa material would go into the archives—which meant deep, deep in the basements of this great palazzo from the thirteenth century. And, Ippolita added, wrapping her fingers around the broom handle and bringing it down from her gray-clad shoulders with a flourish, *"una buona decisione,"* a good decision, considering the night of—her eyes closed as she tried either to remember the date or forget the events—October 22, 1944.

"The bombing." I said softly.

"Sì," said Ippolita, since "bombing" is a word that seems to cross language barriers. Parting her short legs, she took a stance and leaned her wrinkled chin on the tip of the broom handle. They heard the planes—how wonderful, the Allies. Off to bomb the locomotive yards near Bologna. A spree. And then in the night sky, they heard the whistle of falling bombs, very close, and thought it must be an accident. So very close. Sister Ippolita was just a postulant then, but there was no way she wouldn't go along with the search party. They climbed, eight Veronicans, into the convent truck and raced to the villa. There were fires and rubble, and in the yard, the bodies of Sister Alfonsa and . . . *un uomo.*

"A man?"

The brave Sister Elena checked at the time. She said the dead man looked like Leon Eckhardt.

"Leon Eckhardt," I repeated, wondering if Sister Alfonsa—the artist, angel, magician—had a relationship outside the scrutiny of the other Veronicans. "A special friend?" I asked tactfully.

At which Sister Ippolita chuckled. *"Quanti anni pensi che io abbia?"* How old do you think I am? And then she informed me merrily that she was neither sixteen nor dead.

No, she went on, not—with air quotes—a special friend. He was a Swiss German who worked in Berlin and came through and stopped in Cortona on his way to the Vatican. And then, like a child asking if I'd like to see her Victorian dollhouse, Sister Ippolita Cordovana asked, her voice high, if I would like to see Alfonsa Cambi's art supplies.

After that terrible night—she gave me a sorrowful look—the Veronicans packed up her things from the villa and brought them back here. "You still have them, after all these years?" I felt amazed.

Alfonsa Cambi was their only loss during the war. *"Sembrava giusto."*

It only seemed right.

B ut taking a look at Alfonsa Cambi's art supplies would have to wait. When my phone trilled at me, I learned from Annamaria, whose voice was high and tense, that the police chaos was upsetting our guests, that we had many things to decide, and that Pierfranco has just returned from Roma. All of these items on her list were her way of telling me to kindly put everything aside and hurry back from the convent. With many *grazies* to Sister Ippolita, I made a plan to return that evening for the tour of the long-dead Alfonsa's things. The interest I felt was small and respectful, aimed more at Ippolita than at anything I could possibly learn from the tour. Somehow my asking about those dates in Cortona's war history lifted the heart of the ninety-six-year-old, who only rarely got a chance to talk about them.

I made good time getting back to the villa, but I couldn't pull into the courtyard and had to leave the T-Bird as close to the outer villa walls as possible. Apparently, members of the local crime-fighting authority didn't put much stock in carpooling. The scene of the crime techs' small van, Serafina's motorcycle, the coroner's SUV, the coroner's van, and a nondescript rental car, which had to be Pete's ride from Rome, crowded the Rolls Phantom, which looked like it had just wandered into the wrong party on New Year's Eve.

And then my eye caught the dark sedan I had come to associate with the Grim Reaper, or the homicide detective with the *carabinieri*, Giovanni Battista Onetto. Wasn't he supposed to be out of town at a cop convention? Did he ditch all the PowerPoint presentations and Prosecco just to see what bloody-minded things were going on at the Villa Orlandini again?

And then there was Pete. I stared, unable to get out of the car, my gaze fixed on a little green-and-black garter snake whose head was peeking out between the stones of the villa's wall. The serpents had entered the garden. Was Pete just another one of them, one I had somehow missed just because I cared for him? I didn't know. And I hated it that I didn't know. I could choose just to have faith that I didn't have all the facts—or, for that matter, any facts at all—and maybe this was one of those stand-by-your-man moments you hear about in song and that only ever seemed likely to rocket the rag-headed stander up well into the chump zone.

But I was in a new position. I cared. And for the life of me, I couldn't tell the high road from the low road. But I couldn't erase the image of Pete following Renata into the Hotel Italia. He was in Cortona on the sly, on the lie, a day ahead of time, before anyone at the villa knew about it. Already, I pushed the heels of my hands against my eyes, I had too much information. Trembling, I stood up out of the

T-Bird, shut the door firmly behind me, and headed toward the entrance. Whatever Pete had going on in the last few days, it left me out, and maybe that was a good thing. Especially if it included murder. I would just have to face it all.

As I made my way through the maze of vehicles, it was Sofia who ran up to me, shooing me along with limp fingers. *"In ufficio,"* she managed. In the office.

With a quick look in the direction of the olive grove, I saw a small swarm of crime scene techs processing the site. When I realized Sofia was right behind me, I said to her over my shoulder, *"Dove sono* the Copelands?"

Annamaria had arranged for Vincenzo's housekeeper to bring Stella the dog and take the Copelands to the woods to hunt truffles. A solid idea, I thought. Annamaria at work.

Then Sofia brightened. *"Com'è sta* Sister Ippolita?"

We entered the main building, where the warm air seemed to hang in an indeterminate way, and the smells included more than just a sauté of onions and garlic. There was unfamiliar soap. There was unfamiliar cologne. When I reached the office, Sofia scurried away. That bad? I wanted to ask. I stepped over the threshold, where Annamaria gave my upper arm a quick rub. By the long window stood Chef, who looked like he was trying to rub his lips clear off his face. Behind the desk sat one of the two men I only ever see when the world crashes.

Dr. Val Valenti turns up a moment before the crash. The man at the desk that I had personally chosen for my command center, back one month ago when my role at the villa was more extensive, was Giovanni Battista Onetto, or Joe Batta, who turns up a moment after the crash. This was the man whose skull was a good likeness of a death's head and whose noisy addiction to hard candies could unsettle even the steeliest of suspects at murder interviews. Instead of the usual translator, it was Serafina who took notes and navigated the language shoals.

But I didn't care about any of them.

Even seated, Pete dominated the room. He twisted around when I entered, and we looked at each other. In his dark, lovely face, all I saw was pain, and it had nothing to do with the murder on his doorstep of his ex-wife. It had to do with me. I raised my eyebrows a millimeter in a question I knew he'd understand. He shook his head in a millisecond, and I had my answer.

Did you do it?

No.

It was like trying to have a conversation about a book you were both reading, but the other person was much further along in the tale and couldn't give anything away. Tentatively, he started to stand, and with a sob I hardly recognized, I covered the space between us in two bounds and threw my arms around him. His heart was pounding, or maybe it was mine, and we patted each other in a buck-up sort of way, and Joe Batta cleared his throat. Behind me, a chair pushed up against my legs, urging me to take a seat. Annamaria had moved one to the perfect spot, not on the same plane as Pete's, but not as far back from the desk as Annamaria's. I sat.

Joe Batta folded his hands. He was wearing a wine-colored turtleneck under a black collarless sport coat. With a thin, cadaverous smile, he gestured at the spread of confetti-colored Gummi Bears laid out in a clump on a napkin before him. He rumbled in my direction about no hard candies because tough cases made two fillings fall out and he does not have great dental coverage on his plan. Then he motioned for me to free a few toppled gummies from the pile. Citing the fact that I lost my appetite, I demurred with thanks.

Content he had played host, Joe Batta resumed his interview. "Did you know the victim Renata Vitale was in town?" He rattled off in Italian.

Pete drew a breath. "Yes," he said quietly. "She called me."

"Were you accustomed to hearing from her?"

"No. Not at all. We weren't in touch. I haven't seen or spoken to Renata Vitale, my ex-wife"—his eyes moved toward me apologetically—"in almost twenty years."

"Ah!" Joe Batta held up two fingers. Between them was a pinned gummy bear. "You are wrong."

Pete looked confused. "More than twenty years? I don't think so, Signor Commissario. We got married at eighteen, went off to Cornell for college"—I could tell as he noted each life event he was doing the math—"and split up at twenty-one." He spread his hands. "I'm forty."

Impassively, Joe Batta reached for a file folder. "And that is where you make your mistake."

Pete tried to figure it out. "Was she not eighteen?" Before the homicide detective could reply, Pete scratched his chin. "No," he declared, so very sure, "she was eighteen. My ex-wife and I"—he shot a steely look at Joe Batta—"were both eighteen when we got married. You can check the records."

"We did check records, Signor. And yes, you were both eighteen." With the edge of his palm, he made a neat little square of Gummy candies, where everything slid neatly into a pattern. Then he lifted his eyes and said softly, "Only she was not your ex-wife."

Pete was silent.

"The murdered woman, Renata Vitale"—Joe Batta inhaled—"was your wife."

* * *

*A*t that, Chef exploded, only I could tell he didn't know where to direct his anger. For a brief moment, he even considered me. Some vestigial good sense made him cross Joe Batta off the list, too. On general principle, he glowered at Annamaria, who sat unperturbed, and then Pete got the full force of it. The gist, in effusive Italian, seemed to be a time-honored parental gripe: *What were you thinking?* What were you thinking, marrying *quella strega* back then? What were you thinking keeping it a big secret, you're such a big shot? What were you thinking leaving it to her to get the divorce she just happened to forget about? What were you thinking not plugging the cooking school to that *Bellissimo!* reporter? What were you thinking leaving me alone with these ziti-loving Americans so you can swagger around Rome—you, a married man!

"Pop," said Pete, standing with an effort, then pushing Chef in the direction of the closed door. "Go braise something." Chef huffed and swelled and scowled, first at the rug and then at nothing at all. Pete and Annamaria exchanged a look, and in one sleek motion, she was out of her chair and shepherding Chef out of the room. Then Pete came over to me, ran his hands down my shoulders, and spoke very quietly. "We'll talk later, Nell. Right now I have to stay and—"

"Just text me," I murmured.

"Signor," said Joe Batta, straightening up in the chair, and signaling Officer Serafina with a snap of his fingers. His voice, when he spoke, had a curling quality. "Do you have something to tell me?"

With practiced ease, Serafina set down her notebook,

pulled out her phone, and clicked on an app. They were recording the rest of the interview.

"Yes, Signor," said Pete, who turned away from me, "I believe I do."

It struck me hard as I moved leadenly toward the door. No, it wasn't an interview. In that moment, Joe Batta and Serafina believed what they were about to get from Pete Orlandini was a confession.

I n the common room, Philip Copeland had started a fire. During the time I was in the office with the homicide cops, Rosa and Sofia had moved the furniture closer to the fire—its pops sounding like gunshots—and were plotting in a corner about refreshments. I sank into the love seat and, with no feelings at all, took in the others. And the wall bearing the brand, hand-painted in sprawling gold leaf, of the Villa Orlandini Cooking School: *Tutto Fa il Brodo*. Everything Makes Broth. I looked away.

There was too much everything, too much broth. All I wanted in that moment as I let the warmth from the fire surround me was to grab a sketchy falafel from the vendor at Columbus Circle who's held that prime spot in Manhattan forever. In fact, I wanted to go to work for him, where the biggest decision on any single order was whether to slather the tahini sauce from left to right or from right to left.

But even that might be beyond me.

Muffy Onderdonk had swiped off her floppy purple hat and wrangled her white hair into a short ponytail. Her bright eyes were on me. Mimi Copeland was smiling as though there was no better place than this small group of fire lovers who let the fire do all the talking. Philip was inscrutable, his hands in the pockets of his YSL micro check pants, probably chapters ahead of the rest of us in weighing all the possibilities. In swept Annamaria with the tea cart arrayed with what I recognized as her pickled egg salad crostini topped with prosciutto. Carafes of sparkling water and dark-roasted coffee also made the trip, followed by Chef, who was wearing his chic black chef jacket. At the sight of food, everyone perked up.

Wordlessly, companionably, Chef and Annamaria plated crostini and poured coffee.

"Un pranzo leggiero," said Annamaria at length. A light lunch.

Before I could dig in, I needed to have the conversation with the Copeland Party of Three. I had planned on spitballing all the possibilities, all the plan Bs and detours that having a murder on the premises entails, answering their questions, fielding their proposals . . . but what I blared was, "So what do you want to do?"

Chef and Annamaria looked a bit surprised at how we materialized so quickly at what should have been the very end of the conversation, but I could tell I had the approval of Rosa and Sofia (two thumbs up).

It was Mimi who spoke. In those delicious minutes before a popping fire, where lovely touches like draped prosciutto and heavy linen napkins remind us that murder doesn't cancel every last bit of civilization, I could see the strengths of the Mimi Atwill who made her society debut over fifty years ago. With slow deliberation, she set down her plate and rested her hands in her lap.

"Although"—she sent around a wide smile that netted all of us villa staff—"Philip and Muffy and I are deeply sorry for your trouble, we sincerely hope you lovely, fun, and talented people are game to continue with Ziti Variations. It is"—she lifted her left hand, where rings glittered—"we believe, a good distraction for you. And for us, well . . ." She lifted her thin shoulders. "This is a dream of Tuscany you are providing us, and tomorrow is my eightieth birthday." She stole a glance at Muffy, who confirmed it. "And speaking for myself, I'm hoping for"—Mimi Copeland rose and twirled once—"a ziti cake," she proclaimed with a laugh and a raised fist.

Just then I had a glimpse back across the years of a wealthy twenty-year-old Wellesley girl romping at Camp Caribou, sneaking out for forbidden wine and smokes before all the heartache and responsibilities would descend that even money couldn't help.

T he afternoon brought the clamor and joys of kitchen life. At least for a while. Chef rolled out two unusual— but classic—ziti recipes: ziti alla Genovese and ziti lardiati. In a clatter of pots and laughter and whatever best of Vic Damone that Chef had not yet played for us, aprons flew into place, even over Philip Copeland's YSL duds, and the smell of simmering tomato sauce was soon filling the space. Muffy supervised Mimi while she sliced up the braising steak with an alarming eight-inch chef's knife, and now with steak and not the veal of offending Bologna, Chef was more in his natural element of pure showmanship.

Sofia stood by Philip Copeland, who won her wordless smiles and nods as he showed surprising talent for mincing pig back fat, otherwise known as *lardo*.

"My son," Mimi announced, gesturing grandly with her hand, "lover of all things porcine."

"Hear, hear," cried Rosa most unexpectedly.

With a bow, Philip brandished his knife. "Purveyor of arcane fats."

"Slicer of—of bacon!" cried Sofia.

By then, we were all laughing.

Mimi clasped her son's face between her two hands, then gave him a noisy smooch.

Not to be outdone, Chef was pulling out all the stops as he regaled them with the fact that, to win the coveted Protected Designation of Origin certification, the back fat must come only, only, only from pigs in one of four Northern Italian regions.

I could tell the Copelands thought he was kidding.

When Pete stopped in unexpectedly, looking somewhat paler than usual, I made the introductions. I could even find it in me to joke that Pete was dean of the Villa Orlandini Cooking School.

Muffy, whose sleeves bore tomato stains, quipped, "I hope you don't put me on academic probation."

What a good laugh we all had, then Chef thunderclapped his hands and announced with a playful grin that if we want to eat, we cook.

Pete and I stood on the threshold of the kitchen, and he brushed my temple with a familiar kiss. "I'll be back later. I'm meeting Joe Batta in town."

"For a drink?"

I could tell he was withholding something. "To sign my statement. To answer more questions. *Sta bene*," he lapsed into Italian. "I'll be back." Resting his palm on my cheek, he started to turn away.

"Pete!" It came out a bit louder than I had hoped. "How long have you known you were still married to her?"

He stood very still. "Not quite a day."

"She told you in person?"

He looked away. "Yes."

And my next four words held a universe of sadness and confusion. "At the Hotel Italia."

He didn't look away from me. "Yes" was all he said. And was gone.

10

I figured I had two hours. The Copelands were up to their designer necks in pasta, tomato sauce, and Chef's booming personality. They didn't need me. In fact, as I got to know these three, I didn't believe for a second I was what anyone would call indispensable. But I persisted in thinking that I represented the Villa Orlandini Cooking School, so I needed me. I needed me to show up. Be present. Available. Participatory. But factor in the likes of Annamaria, Sofia, and Rosa in the kitchen—no matter how much larger and more commodious we had just finished making it—and Nell Valenti was just one more five-foot-eight pillar of flesh taking up cooking space, which always bore a strong resemblance to a Tilt-A-Whirl. So I split.

But not before calling ahead to the library of MAEC, the Etruscan Academy Museum in Cortona, and giving someone named Fabrizia—daughter, I established, of Benedetto Ricci, director of the Chamber of Commerce—a heads-up that I was on my way. In Italian, I told her I was interested in what I'm pretty sure I termed "the documentary holdings" in the Villa Orlandini archives.

With a youthful and charming lilt, she disclosed that she didn't know precisely and exactly how much of that "sort of thing"—she made it sound like naughty postcards—they actually had in the museum's archives, but she would check. "But if we have them," she informed me, "they do not circulate. You are welcome to peruse them in the reading room. With gloves." Here we agreed she would provide gloves, we bid each other an energetic *arrivederci*, and disconnected.

I had considered bringing Philip Copeland himself so he could take a gander at whatever the villa archives had to offer, leaving me free to daydream, but rejected it. I never like going in blind to a situation if I can help it. Half blind, fine, that's probably my baseline here in Italy, anyway. But Copeland's offer to include Villa Orlandini architectural drawings in a major exhibition at the Metropolitan Museum in New York meant little Nell had just been plunked down in yet another unfamiliar element—that of world-class arts organizations and the money that loved them—and at least I could do some legwork.

If there were drawings, and if they were at all presentable, I could either take photos with my phone or make a separate trip with Philip Copeland in tow. I could come through for the Orlandinis, all right, but I wouldn't go in blind. If it came to nothing, nothing was a circumstance I knew, and the billionaire philanthropist presently mincing back fat in our kitchen would sensibly move on to something else. All I had to do was be seen as having come through for the team.

If the drawings weren't good enough for the Met, maybe we could frame them and hang them in the common room.

But if they were good enough for the Met, the promotional possibilities for the cooking school were astronomical. First, don't fret about Pete. Not just yet. Second, MAEC (which helps with First, see above). Third, check out the Met's website. As I parked the T-Bird a block and a half away from the Museo dell'Accademia Etrusca, I legged it around the corner to Piazza Luca Signorelli. As I stared at the tall square facade—another unblinking and inscrutable medieval fortification—I thought we must have made a mistake. I was expecting the kind of branch library we have at home that houses toddler story times and tax forms. This building was a Cortona landmark. A Tuscan landmark. An Italian landmark, for all I knew. It was, to be fair, an actual *palazzo* in its earlier days. Three vaulted Roman archways, four tall stories, the soft colors of sandstone, a peek into an interior courtyard. Inside, I made my way up to the fourth floor, where I found the library.

Presiding alone over ten stacked rows that ran the length, the width, and very nearly the height of what felt like a secret room was a young woman who I assumed was Fabrizia Ricci. Slim navy blue pants topped by a cashmere sweater in lighter blue. Her soft waves of light brown hair were clipped together at the back of her head, she wore no makeup—at no loss to her good looks—and her glasses looked like drugstore cheaters. At first, she didn't hear me come in, so I caught her sitting in one of the twelve old red leather armchairs with what looked like art books spread out on one end of the polished wood of the single great reading table that filled the space.

When she turned a page in an oversized, very old book, I noticed she wore membrane-thin silicone gloves, just like anyone cooking in Annamaria's kitchen. Inside the doorway was a stand with a couple of open boxes of gloves in front of a sign that started with ATTENZIONE! and included enough exclamation points that I knew a rule when I saw one. I grabbed a pair.

"Ah!" she breathed when she caught sight of me in the doorway. Her smile spread evenly across her face, her teeth nearly translucent.

"*Ciao,* Fabrizia."

"*Benvenuto*"—she spread her hands fondly—"*nel mio piccolo regno.*" My little kingdom.

While we made some small talk, I looked around the Etruscan Academy's library, practically hidden away on this top floor of a palazzo built hundreds of years ago. A rarefied atmosphere for the life of the mind. There wasn't a public computer anywhere in the room. The first four stacks of these wall-to-wall leather-bound books were locked behind wood doors, but perfectly carved ovals kept them visible behind crosshatched wires.

You could smell the books, and maybe a pinkie could reach through and tickle their spines, but they were off-limits in the most tantalizing ways. The higher stacks were open, packed tightly, looking no less valuable than the locked volumes below. A brass chandelier hung over the table—not close enough to help readers, I thought—and framed portraits appeared over the highest stack, too far away to identify.

I quietly pulled the door shut behind me.

Set out on the reading table, awaiting my groping, were three large metal boxes with hinged lids. On one, the smallest of the three, a precise hand had written *La Famiglia Orlandini* in ink on what was now a yellowed rectangle of paper and was held in place with curling adhesive tape in a state of exhaustion. The other two metal boxes were labeled *Santa Veronica del Velo,* embellished with a hand-drawn crucifix. Same yellowed paper rectangle, same exhausted tape.

Naturally, I wanted to take my time through the Orlandini box, looking for what, I couldn't say. Birth certificates of unknown *bambini*. Loose photos of Orlandini ancestors in military uniforms. Eviction notices. Expired *passaporti*. Official divorce decrees. Letters never sent. Letters received and never answered. The good, tantalizing stuff. Orlandinis had inhabited the villa for a hundred years before World War II, when they decamped for eight years and returned at war's end. Since then, I figured Chef and his family had new places to keep family and business records. But this. This metal box held many older narratives, but probably not the historic architectural drawings that might interest Philip Copeland and the Met.

So I pushed aside the box marked *La Famiglia Orlandini*.

With a slow pull, I used both hands to angle one of the St. Veronica of the Veil boxes closer to me. This one alone was a lot heavier than the Orlandini box. I couldn't help groaning. Did Fabrizia lug these up four flights from the palazzo dungeon? Shooting her a look of disbelief, I found her grinning at me. "Elevator," was all she said. In English. With a certain amount of trepidation, I pushed open the lid, preparing myself for a slapdash stash of stuff, totally disorganized, considering how quickly Sister Ippolita had mentioned that they packed. But my heart lifted when I eyeballed the contents. File folders! Better yet, labeled file folders! I held one up and shook it happily at Fabrizia. We shared a moment of keen appreciation for organization.

These cardboard envelope-style folders were uniformly the khaki green color of the World War II era. Into a calling card–sized clear plastic front pocket, this file was labeled

"1800–1850 *Purchase Orders*." The next one was labeled "1800–1850 *Official Correspondence: Vatican*." The third file was labeled "1800–1850 *Official Correspondence: Other*." Fingering my way quickly through the stack, I realized the nineteenth century had brought with it—in addition to the Kingdom of Italy itself—a penchant for record-keeping. This box got me back as far in the Veronicans' history as the mid-1700s.

A quick peek in the other box, which was lighter, went back to their beginnings in Cortona on the grounds of what was now the Villa Orlandini. But Sister Ippolita made it sound like the packing up of holdings from the convent's library in 1938 had resulted in many boxes. Here were three.

I turned to Fabrizia. *"Niente libri?"* I asked.

I could tell she was hoping I wouldn't ask. *"Molti libri, certamente."* She gave me an apologetic look but went on to describe that, from what she was able to track, it had been easier for the museum to integrate them all into the general holdings of the library. She shrugged. *"Era tempo di guerra"*—It was wartime. In the interest of accuracy, she muttered, *"Quasi"*—Almost. In short, who had time to do anything else? To make a special collection? No.

Brightly, she added, in Italian, "But you can find them now in the digital catalog."

What I didn't point out to Fabrizia is that before doing that, I would have to know exactly what title or author I was hunting for. She held out a small hope that somewhere in these files—she gestured to the metal boxes in front of me—I might come across the original handwritten catalog of the Veronicans' books.

As I nodded, I realized that in the interest of time, I wouldn't need the books.

Thumbing through the labels on the file folders themselves, I worked my way back to the mid-1700s, where I discovered the first useful image I had seen. Too large for a file folder, it had been backed with cardboard and slipped into a clear plastic sleeve. I peered closely at it. In the style of Antonio Visentini, this plan of what I knew as the Villa Orlandini had been drawn in 1747 in pen and brown ink. Excited, I took out my phone and ran my measuring app the length and width of the sheet, and noted it measured 22 $\frac{9}{16}$ inches by 16 $\frac{3}{4}$ inches. At the top, my eye caught the words *"La Ristrutturazioni"*—a renovation, a restructuring. With less than an hour until the museum closed for the day, I had no time to study the plan. All I could do was take its picture.

In the remaining metal box of documentary archives Sister Ippolita and several other Veronicans had stored and brought home to the new convent in 1938, until they found a permanent home in the Etruscan Museum, I located one more architectural plan of the convent on the villa grounds. And this one was the original, like the later one, backed with cardboard and preserved as best they could in a clear plastic sleeve. Slightly smaller than the *ristrutturazioni* plan of two centuries later, this original plan for a convent for the Order of St. Veronica of the Veil was drawn and signed by Vincentio Rossi in 1571 in pen and brown ink. I took its picture.

Baby steps. No point in bringing Copeland until he checked out the photos and decided whether to include them in the Met exhibit. But it occurred to me I could hedge my bets and asked Fabrizia if she could set aside these two historic architectural plans for me. "I have to consult an interested party." When she asked, I told her a day or two at most. When I heard my phone vibrate against the reading table, I shot it a quick glance.

A text from Pete.

Suddenly, all I wanted was some fresh air.

And a seat at a lone table at a café. For, say, half an hour.

Where I could enjoy a San Pellegrino Chinotto—a fizzy citrus drink—and inventory what wits I had left. Philip Copeland had to feel pleased with what I've done on his project in such a short time. From here, his ball. About the murder of Renata Vitale, I felt the stirrings of questions and actions, but I refused to give them any room to breathe. Instead, I thanked the capable Fabrizia and dashed down four flights, pulling up short when I hit the street.

At the nearest café, I sank into a wrought iron chair, just about ten feet away from a table of tourists, and ordered my Chinotto. It was that time of day in late fall when light shrinks. Like some great, invisible shutter is closing over the daylight. For me, it always seems peaceful.

When the Chinotto arrived, I tapped the text from Pete: **Need to see you ASAP.**

Somehow, this didn't sound like putting his signature on a line. I texted, **Where are you?**

They've arrested me for Renata's murder.

Just then, I had nothing more to ask.

*S*erafina seemed apologetic about the whole thing. Since I didn't trust myself with reparking the T-Bird in the failing light and with encroaching horror, I flung two bills on the café table, made a mess trying to pour my Chinotto back into the bottle so I could take it with me, gave it up, and half ran the five blocks to the *comando* of the local carabinieri on the narrow Via Dardano. The station's stone-and-mortar exterior with an attractive fanlight over the entrance and just a modest sign to identify the cops within, looked more like a boutique *pensione* than the local HQ for Italy's gendarmerie. Rushing up the two steps, I stepped inside, still barreling ahead before my eyes could adjust, which was when I ran into Officer Serafina. Not even her own branch of law enforcement, but it looked like she had stuck around to ease everyone's way—Pete's, mine, any other misbegotten Orlandini who might turn up sobbing.

She cast a quick eye around the joint, where Joe Batta was nowhere in sight, and motioned for me to follow her. We slipped through a steel door she had left slightly ajar, and we hotfooted it down a corridor that Hera Neri must have painted the same insane asylum green that Philip Copeland's room was now sporting.

"Cinque minuti, tutto qui, capisce?" Five minutes. She made a gesture with her arm toward Pete, but I had already spotted him, and then Serafina strode back up the corridor, discreetly out of earshot, where she got busy with her phone.

Aside from the man standing at the bars inside a cell, I found myself looking at a scene so terribly unfamiliar to me that I might have been mysteriously set down on the moon. A cot, a barred window, a toilet. We interlaced our fingers through the bars. He'd have to open up the conversation because I knew I wouldn't get through a single sentence without breaking down, and then where would we be? There was such a stricken look in his dark eyes I couldn't imagine what he had to say. With just five minutes to hear his story, I couldn't help myself. I prompted him. "The Hotel Italia." Oddly, it felt like a place to start.

He nodded, grateful for a focus. "I hadn't seen Renata for twenty years, Nell—"

"More or less," I smiled weakly.

"You heard that, right, and it was true. I hadn't talked with her, written to her, or even"—he exhaled—"thought about her. You have to believe that. She said she'd get a no-fault divorce, and I was so happy to be done with her that I went off to live my life. Once, a few years in, I tried her old phone number, and it worked, and I asked her if everything had gone all right. Yes, yes, she said, all done. She's got the papers if I ever needed them, so goodbye already. End of a harebrained chapter, a cautionary tale about youthful stupidity."

"There are plenty of those. Go on."

He did. He was actually in Rome still when he phoned me. Not ten minutes later, Renata Vitale called. She was coming to Cortona and she wanted a meeting. As his wife, half of Silver Wind Olive Grove was hers, and she thought they should talk it over. So he rented a car and tore up the highway between Rome and Cortona, and made the trip in under two hours. Following her into the lobby of the Hotel Italia, he realized he had forgotten everything about her.

If anyone had asked him before that day what Renata Vitale looked like or talked like or smelled like, he couldn't say for sure. He had so totally forgotten her. And then there she was in all the same old discrepancies that came washing back over him. Her wild dyed hair and her designer heels. Her hippie cloaks and serious pantsuit. The little things hadn't changed. But as they sat in the lobby for their meeting, he realized the big things hadn't changed, either. She was scheming and self-absorbed.

And he hated her.

It surprised him, as she spoke. As she laid out her plan with an indifference that was chilling. As for him, he was in five kinds of shock. Shock that she turned up after all those years, shock that they were still married, shock that she was claiming half of the olive grove he had loved and tended for years, but it was all just beginning. Because then Renata Vitale went on about her plans for her half of the property . . .

"What were they?"

She was going to bulldoze the trees and build luxury condominiums. All very nice. Think of the view! Straight into the Val di Chiana! As Pete went on, I remembered seeing Renata and Jason in the olive grove, when Renata was regaling him with the plans, the vision, the view. She confessed to Pete she had absolutely no idea he owned property back in the land that time forgot, not until she saw the new issue of *Bellissimo!*

And there was Pierfranco Orlandini, right there on the cover, flanked by those gnarly olive trees. Inside the magazine, of course, she learned more about the little olive business, and she saw this fabulous opportunity to take her career in property development international. Straight into Tuscany, still a tourist hot spot, however overrated.

Her grandmother Pia Vitale, drying up down in Key Biscayne, had popped off recently at the tender age of ninety-three, and the old bat had willed her only grandchild, Renata, the one investment she had managed to hang on to in the old country—namely, that block of buildings right on the Piazza della Repubblica. Well, Renata fancied herself a landlord, and she could just pull down those monthly rents from little shops like, oh, Forno di Carlo.

But then came *Bellissimo!* and she knew for a fact that she, Renata Vitale, had been thinking too small. Raze the entire moldy, decrepit block, erect more luxury condos in the same style as she'd have going on her half of Pete's property, and she would be flaunting what she was coming to think of as the Vitale brand.

"So," I said slowly, sensing our time was nearly up, "to Joe Batta, that's your motive."

"Well," Pete frowned, "there's more. She had a right to half the property. But"—he looked past me to some murky future—"she would only consider a divorce if I turned over the entire property to her."

I felt hot. "That's extortion, Pete."

"Depending on how you look at it. There are plenty of divorce settlements that look a whole lot like that."

"But she was making a divorce contingent on your giving her the property."

"Nell"—he sighed, studying his feet—"it's not so clear," he said. "I don't own the olive grove outright."

"What do you mean? I thought you did."

He nodded. His beautiful face lost some expression. "Recently, I took out a mortgage on it."

Motives for murder just kept stacking up. "Why?" My voice was soft.

His voice was even softer than mine. "I needed the money." He could barely get the words out, and in the way he raised a palm and looked away, I could tell that was all he was going to tell me. He flung up his hands. "A story for another time, Nell," he said with energy. And that was the first time Pete Orlandini really reminded me of his father. When a book was closed, the pages were glued together, it was tied up with string, then locked. If any questions persisted, then the book was incinerated.

For a long moment, we said nothing. Suddenly he looked troubled.

"What is it?"

"You should probably know I have no alibi."

At that piece of information, I nodded for a while at my shoes. "That's not good." Like it or not, I realized I was in the lousy position of having to solve the murder of my boy-friend's ex-wife, who wasn't really his ex, and the afore-mentioned boyfriend had no alibi and plenty of motive. To top it off, he trusted me enough to investigate the crime but not enough to tell me why he needed money. In that moment, seeing Pete Orlandini locked in a cell wasn't enough to keep me from feeling ill-used.

I was steamed. "You need to convince me," I said coolly, "that your need for money has nothing to do with this murder."

"It doesn't, Nell," he said, pressing his eyes shut and wincing. Then he waved off the matter as inconsequential. "I owe a silent partner, that's all. Nothing to do with Renata."

I actually hated hearing him call her Renata, as though we were all on friendly terms. But I let it go. "How did the meeting with her end, Pete?"

Managing a laugh, he said, "She handed me a business card and told me she was sure we could agree on terms." Pete sank onto the cot. "And then I left in a daze." He drove halfway back to Rome until he was so worn out he just pulled off at a scenic overlook and slept in the car.

I stood there silently, watching him wring his hands. Then, "Anything else I can use, Pete? Anything at all?"

He looked up at me. "She got a couple of calls as we were putting on our coats." One was from someone named Jason, who she put on speaker and reamed out because when he got to the airport, he found he still had her day planner in his briefcase. They argued over whether he was willing in this godforsaken lifetime to turn all the way around and bring it back to her in person, or whether she'd just have to suck it up and get it by courier and he'd send her the bill. They argued over whether he could still catch the express train to hell, or let's see, whether he had damn well already arrived there when he had gone to work for her a year ago.

When Renata got the second call, she immediately took it off speaker. Oh, yes, she had said into the phone, stepping away from Pete, *I'm happy to hear from you . . . Later tonight's fine. My day never ends . . . Hotel Italia, right in town . . . See what? . . . Romantic.* Pete shot me a twisted smile. "Apparently my beloved wife was making a date."

With, very possibly, her killer.

*S*erafina saw me out. *"Grazie,"* I murmured, and she gave me a sympathetic smile. Plus a little squeeze on my upper arm. It began to look to me like a day when words were hard to come by. Then she found a few. With her eyes half-closed, she dipped her head. "We let him keep his phone."

"Oh." Good to know we could stay in touch.

"Special circumstances," she added.

"What are the special circumstances?"

"We like him." Serafina gave me a slow wink. "And bring a change of clothes."

I wondered if Serafina would insist on being present when he changed.

"In *Italia*," she purred, "we are not barbarians. In jail we wear our own clothes."

As she started to head back into the station, I had a thought. "Serafina," I said, "Renata Vitale had an assistant, a man named Jason Zale."

Serafina let go of the door handle and crossed her arms. "Go on."

"He was her lawyer. I overheard them fighting at the corner bistro, and he quit."

"Is that all?"

I spread my hands wide. "Pete heard him on a call that last afternoon with Renata. He was at the airport. I don't know which one." It sounded so lame, but it was an interesting lead.

"It was the Firenze-Peretola Airport. Zale was booked on Alitalia Flight 103 to JFK. We called ahead to the gate." She lifted her wrist, pushed up her coat sleeve, and glanced at the time. "Signor Zale should be arriving in Cortona any time now." Flashing me a smile, Serafina disappeared back into the station.

I walked thoughtfully back to the T-Bird, two blocks out of the action at the heart of downtown Cortona. I was yearning for my mind to wander over the possibility of Jason Zale being either a source of information about Renata's movements over the past few days or . . . a suspect. But my chances of getting my hands on Renata's day planner before Joe Batta did were slim.

Still, I'd try to get a conversation with the man, at the very least. I could unsettle him with knowledge I'd gleaned glued to the bistro wall, around the corner and out of sight. Snatches from his argument with Renata floated back to me. Lovers, Rosenberg & Estis, embezzlement. I could push a thumb into any of those and see what the angry, heartbroken Jason Zale did with it.

"Pronto?" said Annamaria in the low, rustling voice she uses on the phone when she's caught in the kitchen at a sensitive moment in the stirring of a risotto. But risotto would not be sharing the menu with two very grand ziti dishes, so she must be paging through her cookbook collec-

tion for a fresh idea. I asked her for a quick rundown on
Copeland Party of Three and an ETA for the evening's dinner. Eight p.m. for the dinner, since the Copeland party expressed interest in truffle-hunting with Stella again, and then
Signora Copeland might need to lie down for a little rest.

"Send Rosa with them, Annamaria," I reminded her.
"We always need a school representative to be present."

She agreed, then mentioned her workday ended at six
today. Rosa and Sofia would serve the meal and take care
of the cleanup. If Pierfranco returns in time from whatever
he's off to, then she was sure he would help.

All of a sudden, it occurred to me Chef and Annamaria
were missing the news.

And Rosa and Sofia were on their own.

As I inhaled longer than I had any right to expect my
lungs to play along, I found myself longing for the Chinotto
I had to ditch to get to Pete. "Annamaria," I managed to
enlist my voice of deadly calm, which I try to whip into
action when discussing future plans with my parents. I
didn't know which Annamaria would respond: the explo-
sive one, like the fireworks finale that rattles your teeth, or
the low-key one that trundles right off to the *malocchio*
workshop in her head. "Annamaria, Annamaria—" Unfortunately, the more I repeated her name by way of opening,
the more alarmed she'd become. "They've arrested Pete for
the murder."

A beat. Then she said something extraordinary. "Yes,"
she said musingly, as though weighing whether the clams
in the bowl deserved a white sauce or a red sauce, "I
thought they would."

"You did?" There went the voice of deadly calm.

"Pierfranco is the obvious choice to kill *la strega*. She
would do him much harm."

She made it sound like a holy obligation. Like a few knights had drawn lots.

"Could you please tell Chef and the girls?" We always spoke of Rosa and Sofia, who are twenty years older than I am, as "the girls."

"Yes. What more?"

"He needs a change of clothes. When you get off work, would you be able to drop them off?"

"Via Dardano?"

"Yes."

"Sono onorato," she intoned. I am honored. It was Annamaria Bari's way of saying, *Now you're talking.* Before we hung up, she added simply, "I will stay, Nell. I will take Pierfranco's things to the *comando*, but I will come back to the villa. My place is here." And, with that, she was gone.

As I turned the key in the ignition and the trusty T-Bird sprang to life, I decided I could stay away from Ziti Fest for another couple of hours. As long as the Copelands and Muffy were traipsing around in the truffle woods while the excellent (strictly from a truffle-snuffling point of view) Stella showed off, they didn't need me. In the Copeland file I kept on my phone, I spotted Philip's cell phone number, then texted him the photos I took at the Etruscan Museum. I felt a little fizz of excitement, wondering whether he'd snap up the historic architectural plans from the convent days of the Villa Orlandini.

I thought they were in really fine condition for drawings anywhere from three to five hundred years old. The sheets themselves were intact, no folds, no discolorations, and the pen and brown ink the draftsman had used was faded but still legible. The plans by Rossi and Visentini were two hundred years apart, and the value now seemed to lie in comparing them. What changed? What disappeared? What was added?

11

If I was going to be digging through more archives, putting a brave face on a double dose of ziti dinner, and providing the evening's entertainment for the high-rolling Copelands, I would need a bracing triple shot espresso at Caffè Vittoria, just up the street from the Etruscan Museum. Chilled, I think more from Pete's arrest than anything in the air temperature, I slipped over the threshold and into the warm, high-ceilinged, yellow-walled interior and took a table near the wall of sparkling windows, where I clutched at my sweater while I warmed up.

I turn to espresso whenever I need a nerve tonic. If it's late in the afternoon, I find the salutary effects last well into the wee hours. At three a.m. I could be counted on to take every quiz ("What Tattoo Are You? Take the Quiz!") posted on Facebook. Or I will linger longer over all gall bladder posts or play games, wherein I'm pronounced a genius if I can find the only M in a grid of Ws. So it's not terribly often that I down a triple-shot espresso.

While I waited for the nerve tonic to take effect, which

I compare to the moment Stella the truffle-hunting pooch is paralyzed into attention at a nondescript patch of turf in the woods, I found myself wondering why Jason Zale took off quite that fast for home after quitting his job with the odious Renata. Or had he? That had happened yesterday.

Did he leave Renata at the bistro, pack his bags at the hotel, and get a shuttle to the airport? Or not? Or . . . and I had a lot of respect for this kind of subterfuge . . . had he made a great show of doing all those things (packing, checking out, yelling *"Ciao, tutti!"* to a dozen strangers) and then, after nightfall, doubled back and lured Renata to her death?

But there were a few unknowns to that scenario.

Where had he spent the intervening time? If he didn't have a car, how could he get around so easily? And why the olive grove? To throw suspicion on Renata's husband, Pete? Ah, but did Jason Zale know Renata Vitale was still married? A key point. And as the triple shot sank in, I knew the answer. He *had* to know. Her plans for the vision of development in the central piazza—and, by that logic, the olive grove—she had to have told him as her lawyer.

She herself even mentioned he'd have documents to file and, if necessary, palms to grease. As her lawyer, he had to be privy to her plans if only to know which wheels to set in motion to further those plans, and Jason himself—in that wretched argument—had whined to his merciless boss that he thought they were in it together.

I found myself hoping I could pump Serafina for information on Joe Batta's upcoming interview with Jason Zale. How good was the guy's alibi? Anything interesting or incriminating in Renata's day planner he had forgotten (had he?) to toss on her bed before he took off in a snit? Could I manage to snag him myself for a sleuthing tête-à-tête? I'd have to stay alert for an opportunity.

Then my mind slid off to considering the other phone call Renata had received when she and Pete sat in the hotel lobby and she was systematically dynamiting his world. What was Renata's part of the brief conversation? Happy to hear from the caller, a late—romantic—date to go somewhere and "see" something. Could it possibly have been Jason Zale on the other end?

I liked the idea.

But from the way he recounted the story, Pete hadn't picked up on any tone on Renata's part that could help identify the caller. Could Renata have been guarding her tone just because she and the mysterious caller had an audience—namely Pete? I'd have to shelve this line of thought for a while and just hope for a tidbit that would enlighten me on that phone call. For now, in the hour and a half's reprieve from villa duties that I had left, I had an opportunity to learn more about Sister Alfonsa and Leon Eckhardt, who died in what the nuns believed was an accidental Allied bombing raid while en route to a strategic Nazi rail yard farther north.

Depending on what I found about the clever Alfonsa Cambi, I felt the simmer of a great, fresh idea. We could mount a permanent display of her brief caretaking years at the villa during the Nazi occupation of Tuscany. Framed examples of her art, photos (if I could find some), ledger pages, journal entries. Highlight any passages pertaining to cooking at the villa or donating food to hungry Cortonans. Hang even grainy photos of Alfonsa in an herb garden. We could provide an historical immersion experience for the American foodies descending on the villa for our work-

shops. What a perk! A century of cooking at the Villa Orlandini! I understood why the Veronicans had gathered up
Alfonsa's belongings and stored them.

If I could pull off this permanent display, I'd be making
a contribution to memorializing this nun who died in the
chaos of those times. The villa was more than the Orlandini
family home, with the exception of the war years, over two
hundred years. And it was more than the original site of a
religious order. For nearly all of its five hundred years, the
property had been private—Orlandinis or nuns—and a
sanctuary.

Then came the war. When nothing was private or off-
limits.

With that realization, I looked up from my espresso.
Was that why I felt so drawn to Sister Alfonsa and Leon
Eckhardt? Why I could relate to them? In a sad way, I suddenly saw my whole childhood had occurred in a kind of
war zone. An only child of high-profile parents. I was just
another dark corner that required stadium lighting in Dr.
Val and Ardis Valenti's pursuit of a TV audience, a brand,
and wealth. I was the kid. And I was fair game. And not just
to an insatiable media beast. To them. When I was finally
old enough not to be their fashion accessory, I became
trouble. What I couldn't earn for myself, there stood the Dr.
Val empire to make it happen anyway. Team spots, class
play casts, single rooms at camp and at college.

When nothing is off-limits, things feel cheap.

But there was nothing cheap about Sister Alfonsa and
Leon Eckhardt.

There was, instead, mystery. Two people dead in a
bombing blunder. So little about what happened—and
about them—was on display for public consumption that I
wondered how they managed to keep their history tucked

away. Out of sight. Off-limits. Right away, with no more knowledge than I had at that moment, I admired those two. And I believed if I kept at the research, I would learn more about each of them. Maybe they had something to teach me. And, with so many years in between the end of their lives and my sleuthing, I couldn't hurt them. I savored the last few drops of my espresso.

With my eyes on the foot traffic outside the Caffè Vittoria, I called the convent and got Sister Ippolita on the line. I apologized for wanting to change the plan, but I was hoping to come now to see Sister Alfonsa's belongings because I had work duties back at the villa for the rest of the evening.

"Va bene," she yelled, *"vieni adesso."* That's okay, come now.

I paid my bill and went out into the failing November light, walking fast because of the chill, disappointed the nerve tonic hadn't warmed me up. But I'd settle for the bug-eyed sharpness I felt. The T-Bird and I made good time to the Veronicans' convent on the outskirts of town, and it was Sister Ippolita herself who opened the oak six-paneled door with a brass letter slot. She had to use both hands and tug, with some fancy footwork thrown in.

With nods and smiles, I fell in behind this energetic ninety-six-year-old as she headed down the wide hall, past sizeable wall niches containing statues of the Virgin Mary, Jesus, and Saints Anne, Joseph, Veronica, Peter, and Francis. Twosomes and threesomes of talkative sisters crisscrossed our path, bobbing *buona seras* to me, and Sister Ippolita was single-minded in her tour to the basement.

Pushing open a metal door with her shoulders and hips, she led us down a stairwell that must have been remodeled in the fifties, what with its hefty railing, wide even stairs, and yellow brick walls. The soundproofing was top-notch, as the lively chatter overhead was lost to us. Ahead, there was one option, a heavy metal door bearing a small bronze plaque embossed with the word STORAGE.

The room proved to be large, and at some point, a freight elevator had been added for moving furniture into storage. I was struck by the warehouse feel of it, with floor-to-ceiling stacks of open metal shelving along the lines of Costco back home. We strolled along the boulevard of storage, passing boxes of books, retired paintings and sculptures, bins of devotional objects, racks of used habits, row after row of footlockers, chairs in need of reupholstering, racks of new habits sheathed in plastic, a pew missing an arm, a table missing a leg, plumbing pipes, keyboards, old monitors, two bicycles, boxes of floor tiles, and a few sinks.

Labels proliferated, especially on the footlockers, which appeared to contain the belongings of the current residents of the Veronican order. I passed some smell of mildew, mothballs, cedar, and rust. At the end of the boulevard in this tour of historic storage in the life of a religious order, Sister Ippolita rounded a corner, and set apart from all the rest of the not-quite-discarded stuff was a smaller unit of open shelving that bore the label ALFONSA CAMBI, 1904–1944. Nothing had been set on the lowest shelf, which was just a couple of inches off the ground, and I wondered if it was a precaution in the event of seepage. One shelf up were large, colorful, hand-woven grass baskets holding the finery of the dead Sister Alfonsa, stylish dresses before she replaced them with a habit, and smocks and loose drawstring pants that bore blotches of paint. For all time.

Stockings with seams, bras, slips, briefs—the lingerie of the dead. Bandanas, sun hats, half-used lipsticks and face creams. A silver bangle bracelet. A natural bristle hair-brush. My fingers sifted through it all. Sister Ippolita stood happily two feet away, her hands crossed in front of her. She knew everything in this collection well. Nothing here was new to her.

On the shelf above Alfonsa's clothing was one item: a beautifully hand-carved wood box with a lid and broken latch, which measured maybe eleven by seventeen inches. When I reached for the box, I turned with a questioning look to my guide, whose smile dimpled her cheeks. One hand gestured in the direction of Alfonsa's keepsake box.

Only, when I carried it over to a small, bruised table that had all its legs, what I discovered inside was more than mere keepsakes. If Alfonsa had used a desk in the villa, this was the accessory that kept it organized. In the six years she served—by agreement with the Orlandinis—as villa caretaker, two identical soft-covered ledgers kept the villa accounts for all six years.

Alfonsa had recorded monthly checks to cover basic expenses from the Orlandinis hunkering down in Switzerland, and when the boiler finally blew in the main building, the Veronicans had helped cover the cost. In turn, Alfonsa had written checks on the villa bank account to cover bills from plumbers, electricians, and an assortment of handymen.

A log, ironically dubbed "My Travels" by the manufacturer, kept frequent brief notes about interesting thoughts and occurrences that would shed light, down the road, on the villa's experience during the war years. Some entries were located in the wrong record, it seemed to me. Occasionally, Alfonsa recorded *Rec'd, 4 Aprile 1939, eight pane toscano, Shipped 6 Aprile 1943*.

It was unclear to me why this record of bread income

and outgo, on the average of two times a week, wasn't recorded in the ledger book along with visits from plumbers and handymen. And the absence of costs mystified me. She was being supplied with Tuscan bread, which she, in turn, shipped out. My best guess was that these were charitable transactions. Was she feeding partisans?

Rec'd, 24 Gennaio 1940, thirteen pane di Altamura,
Shipped 27 Gennaio 1940

Rec'd, 10 Settembre 1943, nineteen Brioche, Shipped 12
Settembre 1943

After that date, shipments dropped off significantly in the year leading up to the bombing deaths of Sister Alfonsa and Leon Eckhardt. A couple of loaves here and there. And nothing recorded for the week of October 22, 1944, when they died. Alone on villa property. In fact, the more I scrutinized her entries, I made an interesting discovery.

From what I could tell, there was no overlap between "the bread business" and Leon Eckhardt's presence at the villa. I'd have to check more closely, but it also looked to me like there were no handymen or tradespeople on-site during the couple of days Eckhardt was around, en route from Berlin to the Vatican. His visits—unlike the bread shipments—Alfonsa recorded in a rather hurried hand in the bookkeeping ledger.

Pensione, L. Eckhardt, no. 211 Spreestrasse, Berlin,
venditore di cornici, 4–6 Dicembre, 1943. £10,000.

So Alfonsa recorded the stays of the Swiss German Leon Eckhardt, frame salesman who lived in Berlin, as a guest of what she called the *pensione*, or guesthouse, where he had stayed a total of six times in that final year. On that particular visit, which was the first she recorded, he stayed two nights and paid ten thousand lire for the room—approximately six bucks. Although she accounted for his visits in the blue bookkeeping ledger, she lumped them all together on a separate page instead of where, chronologically, they actually occurred.

And because all seven entries were listed in black ink, it made me wonder if she had copied over the information from some other source—if any at all—at one time. Interesting. As if it somehow had occurred to Sister Alfonsa that she needed to have a formal record of those guesthouse visits—that *pensione* source of income—somewhere, in case she was ever asked about him.

Aside from the log and the ledgers, Alfonsa kept some newspaper clippings, mainly about the deportation of Jews and the arrests of *partigiani*, partisans. And there were just a few personal letters, tied together with discolored, fraying string. Three from Berlin, two from Siena. The ones from Siena were written by Alfonsa's mother and contained family news. The three from Berlin sported envelopes with the identical handwriting.

A quick peek inside the envelope on top told me they were written by Leon Eckhardt. To be studied later. "Sister Ippolita," I said in Italian, turning to where she sat on a settee with a spring that had sprung through, "may I borrow these letters? I promise to return them. But, for now," I winced when I glanced at my watch, "I have to get back for dinner."

She nodded genially, but then the dimples disappeared right off her wizened face, and she held up both palms. *"Per prima cosa, guarda qui,"* she intoned. First, look here.

She moved over to what looked to me like a poster bin on wheels, the kind you find in art museum gift shops that invite you to paw through the stock. Between the two bars, front and back angled apart by forty-five degrees, was a collection of the clever, artistic Alfonsa Cambi's artwork. Oils, watercolors, studies, sketches, some on canvas, some on paper, some on hardboard. In a footed brass umbrella stand were rolls of canvas, stretcher bars, braces, and tools.

Holding my breath, and with two hands, I pulled each painting and drawing toward me. From one piece to the next, what I saw was a riot of bold and colorful abstraction, portraits in broad brushstrokes that captured pain and rendered it beautiful, that captured brinks of mood and showed them to be timeless. Some were early pen-and-ink studies of old masters, with plates snipped neatly from a book and clipped to them.

How would I ever decide? I wondered. What gets displayed, and what does not?

A second set of eyes. That's what I needed.

Maybe a third, maybe a fourth.

Maybe Alfonsa Cambi deserved better than a section of wall in the Villa Orlandini common room.

Crouching, glancing nervously at my watch—I had fifteen minutes to stop playing hooky and get back to the villa for dinner—I slid a box out from a bottom shelf of the rolling bin. I gave Sister Ippolita the side-eye.

She shrugged indulgently. *"Le sue pitture,"* she sighed, *"tutto prosciugato."* Her paints. All dried up.

A quick check inside told me she hadn't exaggerated. Still, there was the unmistakable smell of oil paints. Faint, down through the forgotten years. Tubes squeezed from use, cracked from disuse.

The palette was poignant, an exhibit of its own, really,

showing us almost eighty years later the very last colors Alfonsa was using before her death. As I tilted the box to the side to see if any light in this dim, gentle space would bring more life to the palette and paints, something shifted, and I realized a very thin piece of wood had been trimmed and set beneath the content, creating a kind of false bottom. From beneath it peeked the edge of a paper. In that moment, I had to make a quick decision.

In a friendly way, I asked Sister Ippolita if the nuns have used Sister Alfonsa's paints.

She frowned and waved off the very idea. "They are not ours," was all she said.

Remarkable.

"Sister, may I borrow this paint box for a couple of days?"

A ripple of alarm crossed her face.

"I promise I won't use the paints. I just want to study Sister Alfonsa's paint box." And I said what I knew was true. "The villa wants to honor her life and her work."

In her enthusiasm then, Sister Ippolita hit three octaves of permission and delight.

She insisted on carrying the tied, stacked letters, I carried the paint box, and we headed chattering in boisterous Italian together back up the stairs.

I consider myself a reasonably self-disciplined person, but when I left the paint box unopened, stashed under my bed, to get to dinner on time, I decided what I was asking of myself was unduly harsh. Painful even. As I sat, now nibbling on capicola and black olives, I was reminded of the time I had filled in for my mother on the Dr. Val set for a week when she came down with the flu. When some people immerse themselves in cross-cultural experiences, it usually means they host an exchange student from Gambia or take a small birding cruise down the Amazon, where they really never have to get off the boat. Or . . . they take on a cooking school start-up in Italy.

But I—I took on producing (i.e., playing border collie with a clipboard) five days of my father and his followers, who looked, to me, like it was a coin toss for them between getting tickets for the *Dr. Val Valenti Shrink You Very Much* television show or *Live with Kelly and Ryan*. There is just such a thing as too much self-sacrifice.

Somehow I got through the big Ziti Fest meal. Without, that is, hotfooting it to the abbess's room, locking myself in, drawing the blinds, pulling the curtains, and slowly, slowly opening the paint box. As I sat, instead, enjoying antipasti in the common room with Philip; Mimi; Muffy; Chef; Annamaria; our elderly neighbor Vincenzo and his imperious truffle-hunting ace canine, Stella; his housekeeper, Jenna; and our cousin and farmer, Oswaldo, all I could see was the perfect setting for an exhibition of Sister Alfonsa's life and work during the Second World War.

"Any progress?" Muffy turned to me.

Suddenly, the room went quiet.

"Oh, yes," put in Mimi, her shoulders hunched excitedly, "any progress?"

Philip scrutinized a mushroom canapé like a pathologist. "Rosa," he announced, "keeps us posted on any"—I watched him stop himself before becoming the third person to use the word "progress"—"developments in the case."

Chef puffed out his cheeks. "Murder is no putting, how you say, wet blanket on things." He shot up, and opened his arms wide, taking in the company. "What do you say, eh?"

I eyed Chef. I guess one dead body does not a bummer make.

But they all knew a cue when they heard one.

"So very sad, dears," said Mimi, "but we hope our presence offers some—some—" She was at a loss.

"Distraction?" put in Muffy, who clapped an arm around her friend.

"Normalcy?" offered Philip.

Oswaldo lifted his hands skyward. "The truth will . . . show up."

"Pete is no killer," said Annamaria, as though she had insider knowledge. I studied her.

"Maybe lady killer."

"Sofia!" That was me.

She was quick to explain. "Cover of *Bellissimo!* Practically a movie star."

Since I didn't want to get cornered, I changed the subject. "Did Stella come across?" I asked Jenna, a young strawberry blond American who had moped her way through one of our workshops a month ago until she found a housekeeping gig with Vincenzo. And Stella. And—here I shook my head—apparently Oswaldo. Jenna kept patting all three of them.

"Oh, yes," she fluted, "one black beauty of a *tartuffo.*" She plucked the costly fungus out of a pocket and held it up for view.

Eyeballing it, I thought it came in at about two ounces, a quarter of a cup. Stella, for her part, sat smug and serene, tucked in against Jenna's legs, and fixed me with one of those neutral expressions I have come to expect. It masks her continual low-pitched growl that she can make sound like a faucet's been left running somewhere in another room. Aside from her talent with truffles, Stella is a dog ventriloquist. She and I honor an uneasy peace.

Oswaldo, I have to give him credit, was crouched in goddess pose alongside Chef, who sat forward in a chair, his hands clasped between his knees. This farming cousin, whose hairline began not far from his crown, whose fingers ran arpeggios on invisible instruments, was commiserating with his uncle, Chef, over the arrest of Pete. The little tableau had a kind of confessional feel, with Chef murmuring a stream of inaudible comments to his listener, whose head was shaking in auditory pain. Yes, the world is just that bad, he seemed to communicate to his uncle.

The Copelands were regaling Annamaria—who sat with a frozen smile and faraway look in her passionate dark eyes—with woodland tales of this good "doggo." Philip made a nice offer to buy the truffle for a sporting hundred bucks—Vincenzo straightened up with interest—but Jenna declined. "It's getting to the end of the season, and we'd like to keep this lovely truffle for our own use."

"Then," announced Philip, folding a hundred-dollar bill and handing it to Vincenzo, who disappeared it as swiftly as an ATM machine, "thank you for a wonderful experience." It was a tip. Classy.

Mimi and Muffy exchanged stories with each other about every little bit of the tramp through the truffle woods, which for Mimi seemed like an enchanted forest. Everyone savored the 2015 Excelsus, the super Tuscan from Castello Banfi, and in the large absence of Pete, it was Rosa who built the fire.

We all dug into the two types of crostini Annamaria had spread across the antipasto platter, one a dried fava bean pâté, the other a black olive pâté. When it was time to head for the chapel dining room to enjoy the results of Ziti Fest,

I worried that Annamaria's frozen smile went on a little long, so in my own imitation of Oswaldo, I crouched next to her, ignoring Stella, whose head was busy butting my thigh.

"Is terrible," she said simply. I didn't have to ask. She meant Pete. "Seeing him, how you say, *in carcere*,"—in jail—"broke my heart." She slid me a look. For the sake of the guests, the smile was in place, but she was suffering. "Worse than Chef," she whispered.

"A different love."

"A different hurt."

I leaned my head against her arm, just for a moment. It would have to do for both of us. If anyone can come to her feet regally, it was Annamaria Bari. Pressing her lips together, she rose, and addressed the others. *"Andiamo,"* she said, gesturing toward the doorway.

The wine came along with us, carted by Sofia, and we flowed reverently into the former chapel of the Veronicans. Chef escorted Mimi, on the eve of her eightieth birthday, to the head of the table, and aside from that guest of honor, it was open seating. Stella's toenails clicked on the plank flooring as she made her way under the table and close to Vincenzo's feet.

Just as I was about to insinuate myself between Philip and Annamaria—the two I figured most likely to enjoy their meals in silence—my phone trilled, and I excused myself, stepping out into the corridor that was heady with the aroma of the meaty ziti alla Genovese ragù. In the low light, I could barely make out the caller ID—Carlo Giannini, my new baker pal. *"Ciao, Carlo, com'è stai?"* We continued in Italian.

"I am always the last to know." A statement of fact. "I like knowing bad things as soon as possible."

"The murder, yes. How did you hear?"

"No," his voiced soared, "not the murder. The murder is a good thing." I could hear him brush it aside. "I mean Pierfranco. I didn't know he was married to *quella strega*. And now she's—" Here he made an up-the-spout whistling noise. Since that pretty much covered it, I didn't know what to say. Carlo's voice dropped. "You should come talk to Ricci and me."

"Benedetto?"

"Of course. We may have information."

I said the dutiful thing. "You should tell the cops."

"No, no, no," he said in a fatigued way that let me know I would need remedial help in Italian intrigue. "We're not sure the information is right, and we want to try it out on you first." Then, "The cops already questioned all of us on this block, but I could tell none of the rest of us tenants had a clue what the witch was planning. So." This he spoke declaratively. "This seemed to Ricci and me like the kind of very special knowledge you only get after working almost thirty years with yeast." I heard him inhale. "Delicate knowledge."

"Okay." I gave in. "When?"

"When can you come?"

Would I ever get to bed that night? First I had to figure out what the Copelands would enjoy in terms of the evening's entertainment, and then I would scamper back to my room and discover what the Sister Alfonsa's paint box held beneath the false bottom she had installed. And now I had to buddy up with Carlo and Benedetto, no doubt to receive information that would be of no earthly use whatsoever in the murder investigation.

"How about ten thirty?" I didn't want to rush my way through the culinary culmination of Ziti Variations. In a day and a half, the Copeland Party of Three would be heading back in the Rolls Phantom to Florence and, from there, home. I wanted Mimi Copeland to have something to remember—and who knew how long she'd remember it, really?—but I could help shape the present wonderful mix of voices, colors, snippets of conversation, and feeling of joy, whether she liked it quiet or rowdy. "Ten thirty, Carlo. The bakery?"

"We'll let you in."

I couldn't resist. "Why me, Carlo? Why not Chef?"

He made a sound between a snort and a *fft*. "He doesn't like my *pane rustica*." He went on, "Claudio Orlandini is not *simpatico*." This may be his only sentence in English. It seemed fitting.

We ended the call, and I hurried back to the table, where I found the only empty seat was between Chef and Oswaldo. Just as I started to tell myself that it was not my day for catching a break, I remembered Renata Vitale, squelched the voice in my head, and took my seat.

12

❧

Annamaria—because it could only be Annamaria—had outdone the table settings, and I had never before seen these gleaming, round acacia wood dinner plates. I fingered the tablecloth, deciding it was handwoven natural linen in a subdued salmon color with a muted gold design of botanical prints. The wineglasses were mahogany. At the center of the table were half a dozen square glass candleholders, each a different height, dabbed in gold leaf, burning salmon-colored candles. It took my breath away. Rosa and Sofia served the two dishes made from scratch by Philip, Mimi, and Muffy.

There's nothing quite like homemade pasta, and I couldn't stop smiling as the Copelands swore up and down that the fact that they ground the flour themselves shot the ziti right into the stratosphere. Everyone agreed. To offset the heaviness of these ziti dishes featuring *lardo* and braised steak, Chef had made his grilled fennel and blood orange salad, topped with sliced red onion, fresh mozzarella, and a heavenly combination of fresh hand-torn basil and mint leaves. Wine was poured as Chef cued up a loop of *The Best of the Ink Spots*, and the perfect harmonies and easy sway of "I Don't Want to Set the World on Fire" made Philip Copeland quip something about too many red pepper flakes in the Genovese ragù.

Holding her wine aloft, Mimi, on the last night of her seventy-ninth year, toasted us, all her new friends, and added, "'Three be the things I shall have till I die: laughter and hope and a sock in the eye.' Dorothy Parker, darlings." She raised her glass a little higher, then sipped, smacked her lips, and declared, *"Mangiamo!"* Immediately, she bent to Muffy and whispered, "Did I say that right?"

"If you meant to say, 'Let's eat,' then yes."

Beaming at everyone, Mimi set down her glass and raised her fork. "I was never very good at languages."

And with that, we dug in. When her wineglass ran dry, I could tell Annamaria lapsed into thought about the beloved Pierfranco. She caught my eye, her expression pained. Her widespread hands gestured at the glorious spread of food at the table, as if to say, this is not what Pierfranco is having for his supper. And then her lower lip quivered. For once, Chef caught what was happening, that something subtle was being expressed. And for once he rose, moved behind Annamaria, and planted a kiss on the side of her neck. Her hand came to rest on his cheek.

Nothing was spoken.

Chef took his seat.

Sometimes moments are just that small and quick.

For those two, maybe it was a start.

I just hoped it wasn't a tumble back into old habits.

At that moment, it was the trusty Rosa who floated a question in broken English. "What we do *stasera*?" What's on for the evening?

First of all, I thought it might be a mood lightener, and second of all, it was clear Rosa was joining the party. Mimi, Muffy, and Philip signed on for whatever we proposed. I was in, although I'd have to make my excuses around ten o'clock to get back to the Piazza della Repubblica in time to conspire in the bakery with Carlo and Benedetto.

Suddenly, Sofia cleared her throat and set down the water pitcher. "Arlecchino Dancing is much fun." It was like a Tripadvisor review. She picked up her pitcher and continued to make the rounds. Not far from Cortona, Sofia elucidated, and I translated, this very fun place was a dance club with live music, separate ballrooms for young and old—"Do we get to choose?" Mimi laughed—crazy lighting and boring crowds.

The level of glee sank. I jumped in to revive it. "I believe Sofia means it isn't a wild place."

The level of glee shot back up, if not quite to the ziti-infested stratosphere, then at least a respectable height from the ground. Arlecchino Dancing, then, was the choice. I had an idea, something about two birds, one stone, and left them alone sitting back with the last of the wine and talking unintelligibly about proper attire for a dance club.

I checked my phone, then made the call. "Carlo? You and Benedetto, meet me at Arlecchino." Surely we could be coconspirators in a quiet corner, discussing secrets as subtle as yeast to the background bounce of an accordion.

*S*idesteps, low claps, high claps, spins. Sidesteps, low claps, high claps, spins. I sat with a Chinotto in a red fake-leather banquette and watched a crowded dance floor do a line dance Rosa informed me was called the Manitosa, which was reminding me of a step aerobics class I took a couple of years ago at the Ninety-Second Street Y in Manhattan. Our whole villa gang, which I was increasingly beginning to think of as Copeland Party of Eight, was out on the dance floor at Arlecchino.

The place, I had to admit, got the job done. A bar, tables, stage, live band, dance floor, columns with strobing white lights, klieg lights, spotlights, pulses of colored lights, even a disco ball hanging in retro readiness should the need arise. As I sipped my Chinotto, I realized the dance club reminded me of Friday midnight disco soirées at a bowling alley not far from the Lincoln Tunnel on the Jersey side.

For the locals at Arlecchino, the dress code appeared to be what I think of as trip-to-Costco casual. T-shirts with glitter butterflies. Last year's jeans. The occasional brave white shirt. Do some errands, have some pasta, head for Arlecchino. Nothing for show. Nothing for showing off. Everyone here came to dance.

Without Pete, I felt benched. But when the brunette chanteuse in off-the-shoulder white stepped in front of the other performers grooving to the live band up on the stage, Annamaria became a hot property. The accordion wheezed into *"Quelli Eran Giorni,"* which turned out to be "Those Were the Days" Italian style, but coming from this brunette's pipes, every bit as dark and hopeful and hopeless and nostalgic as the original. In the dancing Arlecchino crowd, this number was an opportunity for a foxtrot.

Chef, guarding his expression, held out a hand for Annamaria, who, guarding her expression, took it. Out to the dance floor they went, and, like the rest of the crowd, danced nearly at arm's length apart. He looked off in one direction, like he was following a bocce blunder, and she looked off in the other, as though she were waiting for the train to pull into the station. Still, they moved together in a way that was old and familiar, and I was pretty sure the lovely man in Siena wouldn't get anywhere, after all, with the imperious and sensitive Annamaria.

Suddenly, a hand was held out in front of me, black sleeve rolled up partway over the forearm, part of a tattoo visible. It wasn't Philip Copeland, for me the only other potential dance partner in Copeland Party of Eight. It was Carlo the brooding baker, who murmured in Italian, "It's better to talk on the dance floor." He shot a quick look around.

I shot a quick look around. Sofia was foxtrotting with Philip Copeland, Rosa with a server I had seen at Tempero, and Muffy and Mimi with each other.

"I left Benedetto at home," Carlo explained, although the way he said it made it sound as though he was talking about the family dog.

Before I knew it, he twirled me into his arms, and we both took a step back. We smiled at each other, those wan smiles that express something about following the rules, whether they're rules or not. Sternly, coming more out of what he'd like to think about himself than anything he'd have to straighten me out about, he went on. "I do not hustle Pierfranco Orlandini's . . . girlfriend." Lucky for him he didn't say "Pierfranco's woman," which would have left him looking silly standing all alone on the dance floor. Into the five-second conversation gap, he lobbed "Although he hustled mine."

Step, step, slide to the left, just as the off-the-shoulder brunette crescendoed, "Those were the days, oh yes, those were the days."

"What are you talking about?"

"Twenty-three years ago." This was uttered in what I call Italian doomspeak.

"Could you be more specific?"

To effect a modest spin, he clamped a hand on my rib cage and urged me to continue around. "Renata Vitale."

"The *fantasma*."

"The dead."

"Go on."

"In high school," he said, "we were in love." This he spoke with the kind of expression I've seen on my father trying to get a fix on something he sought to dredge up out of the swamps of memory. *I'm pretty sure I always liked the Stones better than the Beatles, yes, I'm pretty sure.*

"All right." For want of anything better, either on the dance floor or in high school.

"At last, she broke it off. I couldn't understand. I had a good future as a baker." There was something in his voice just then, a little self-mockery, maybe. "A couple of months later, she turned eighteen and disappeared."

"Ah. Enter Pierfranco."

Carlo nodded once, slowly. Over the years, understanding it from every other point of view. "Only I didn't know it then. I was a grade ahead and was already rolling barrels of flour into the storeroom at Forno and trying my clumsy hands at *semelle* rolls." He lifted his eyebrows and gazed straight into my eyes. "We were done. She was gone. Her parents, too, who were just slumming here, to tell you the truth, what with her papa's celebrity."

I recalled what Annamaria had told me. "He was a singer. Lodovico."

"One of those. Too big for two names."

I laughed. "Well, where I'm from, Lodovico would have needed both his names."

Carlo smiled and moved on. I could tell there was more. "There's more."

I murmured.

The crooning brunette had just finished the third reprise of *"Quelli Eran Giorni"* and was launching into the "la-la-la-la-la-la-las," when Carlo went on, "You should know"—he lingered over the "know," even in Italian, and pulled me a little closer, not wanting to blare what he was about to say—"I moved the body."

The way he said it was kind of offhand, like he was telling me he had put the broken chair out on the tree lawn for special pickup. "You did what?"

He squeezed his eyes shut and gave me a series of tight little nods. *Someone had to do it. It was the right thing to do. In a pinch, I would do it again.* Those tightly shut peepers spoke to me in all those ways. "Ssh, ssh, ssh," he cautioned. "I moved the body. Less"—here he held up an index finger in front of my appalled face—"because of the wounded heart stuff twenty-three years ago, although surely the cops will look at that—less for that than for the meeting she had held with our little tenant group just two hours earlier."

I wanted clarification. "Tenants of the building block she just inherited."

"Of course. She called a meeting."

"Where?"

"At Benedetto's." I supposed the Cortona Chamber of Commerce was the logical, if ironic, place for that meeting, considering Renata Vitale was about to reduce that block full of commerce to rubble.

"And?" It was all I could manage. I sounded stern.

The music had flowed rather seamlessly into one of those self-important soaring tenor ballads that really don't say very much but take a lot of time doing it. I must have looked puzzled, because Carlo Giannini slipped in, *"Ti sposerò perché,"* he said, "which means I'll marry you because you know and understand me.'"

"Aha." I breathed. "What happened at the meeting, Carlo?" It was a slow number, and we didn't lose a beat, in either the dance or the suspense.

"Renata Vitale told the nine of us shopkeepers that we were *finito* in this location." His lips thinned out. "She actually said 'this location,' as though this four-hundred-year-old building for the ages was just another place for food trucks to do business outside a football stadium." He stood against the window inside the Chamber of Commerce and watched her evict everybody, out by the end of the month, in time for the wrecking ball.

Of Renata Vitale, in that hour of lavishly flung pain, all he saw was how cruel she was, and he had never seen it, not in the seventeen-year-old sweetheart. Although probably—probably—it had been there even then. It just didn't have enough money or power to find its voice. At that meeting, nothing was negotiated because nothing was open to negotiation. Nothing was, when it was all said and done, even really discussed. Benedetto and the others, well, they didn't know what to say or do. "Lita, you know Lita, who owns the tobacco shop—"

"By sight."

"She cried, 'But, but, you're a daughter of Cortona. Cortona is your home.' The others shouted their agreement." His mouth was wry. "Renata said, 'Only as long as it had to be, then I got the hell out.'" There was no reason for a meeting, Carlo concluded. Everything she had to communicate to the nine shopkeepers could have been handled in a form letter either from her or that boy-toy groupie attorney she lugs around. "So," declared Carlo, "I realized she just wanted to deliver the anguish. She wanted to see it. In person."

We had come to a place in the music for a spin, so we did. "So, when I discovered her much later, dead on my back doorstep, well, down a couple of doors, all in the condemned block, I called Benedetto, and we moved the body. If," he shrugged, "one of us had strangled her, I was buying us some time for remorse or flight or—I don't know what. I wasn't thinking straight. It was awful. Awful makes awful. That's how it is."

Suddenly Carlo Giannini remembered he had brought me a treat, two bakery-paper-wrapped *pizzicati*, butter cookies filled with Nutella, and slipped them out of his breast pocket. I gave him back one, with thanks, my mind reeling, and we nibbled our way off the dance floor, avoiding the rest of the crowd. "Dead, she was awful. But alive, more awful still."

"So you moved her to"—I ran out of breath before I could utter "the olive grove."

"Across the piazza. In the parking lot behind the hotel."

I was stunned. "Just"—here I made an impatient gesture—"on the pavement?"

"No, next to a couple of parked cars." He considered. "Well, yes, on the pavement."

I inhaled deeply, and some cookie got sucked down my windpipe. When I stopped coughing, I managed, "Carlo, this is bad."

"Nell," he said reasonably, "I know it's bad. It's worse. I was rattled." He pulled me around to face him. "What she was doing to all of us shopkeepers in that block was cruel. If we're all innocent of her murder I don't want suspicion and arrest and trial to be Renata Vitale's parting gift, reaching up from the grave to do any more harm."

"You know she wasn't found in the parking lot, right?"

It was Carlo's turn. "What?"

"I found her, Carlo, I found the body in Pete's olive grove."

He looked at me with great compassion. "I should have brought you more *pizzicati*, Nell."

"When did you find out about Pete?"

"That they were married? She told me. That last night. Which doesn't look good for him."

"Or for you."

"Yes, of course," he readily agreed. "This is why I brought this sensitive information to you, Nell."

"Save the best baker in Cortona."

"Save your boyfriend . . . and the best baker in Cortona. You've got to investigate."

It made all the difference to me, then, that I didn't have to make this next statement myself. "I will—come clean—to the cops, Nell. You just give me the word, okay?"

Mimi and Muffy pulled us over to the dance floor for the cha-cha slide—to about seventy sets of clapped hands came the instructions, "To the left, take it back now, y'all"—and I slipped in between Rosa and Sofia. Rosa likes any activity where she gets to hop, and Sofia likes any activity where she gets to stomp, so I was in a lively section of the line. Carlo set himself up next to Annamaria, who was still playing it cool with Chef but was at least keeping the *malocchios* holstered.

While I took it back now, y'all, I couldn't help wondering who had relayed the strangled Renata to her next final resting place in Silver Wind Olive Grove. Although I wouldn't admit it to anyone I happened to know who was at present cha-chaing real smooth, I felt a pang for *quella strega*. In just that moment, Renata Vitale felt to me like a pathetic woman, a hometown girl who grew up resentful and vindictive, who had plans to develop luxury condos where olive trees used to grow, with a fabulous view . . . to die for. She got the death but not the view.

Who found her body between two parked cars behind the Hotel Italia . . . and moved her again?

I left Arlecchino ahead of the others, but not before giving a quick hug to Annamaria. And not before Carlo promised to see that everyone had a ride home. On my way back to the villa alone in the T-Bird, I found myself turning over what was beginning to feel like a key question in this murder: Why was Renata Vitale's body moved to the olive grove? It was such an unusual spot to dump a body. Tomorrow I'd call to see what the coroner had to say about how and when Renata had died.

But, no matter, if she was strangled behind the imperiled block of shops, Carlo was correct, any one of the nine shopkeepers—alone or in a group—had a motive. Had the killer counted on that somehow? Had Renata's place of death been chosen for precisely that reason? Or had it been coincidental? For me, the really interesting question was why the killer had dumped her among the olive trees. *Why there?* Considering there were plenty of other, oh, impartial spots—fields en route to the train station in Camucia, forests on the way to Florence, even Lake Trasimeno, if you've got a chain and a cinder block along for the ride.

Why the olive grove?

Or, maybe more to the point, anywhere at all on the grounds of the Villa Orlandini?

I parked the T-Bird in its traditional spot, nose almost to the wall of the dormitory, shut her down, tapped my phone flash on, and locked up. As I crossed the cloister walk and made my way down the path to the abbess's room, I heard a scops owl somewhere close, its one-note call like a friendly little snore in the dark. My room felt warm, a place I could trust—but not before turning the lock. Very methodically, I hung up my jacket, with my eye on Sister Alfonsa's paint box, a mere corner of it peeking out from under my bed, and kicked off my shoes, my eye still finding that alluring corner.

Finally settling in, I checked my phone. Three calls from Pete. One voicemail. "Nell, where are you? Why haven't I heard from you? Call me, okay? I don't care what time it is."

It was late, I was tired, but I felt bad I hadn't talked to him since my visit to the jail.

The call woke him up. "Nell?" He was groggy. I knew how he looked when he was groggy. Not *Bellissimo!* cover worthy. "Where have you been?"

"Out dancing." I'm sure there must have been a better way to put it, but his attitude got my goat.

"Dancing?" For that second he was a tenor. "I'm rotting here in jail and you're out—"

"First off," I felt my jaw tighten, "You haven't been in jail long enough to rot, so please spare me the dramatics." I heard him suck in some breath. "I've been entertaining the fancy guests of the cooking school in what has turned out to be my nearly 24/7 job."

There was silence.

"I'm sorry," he piped up. Then, weary, "My life's out of control."

I temporized. "Not really, Pete. You've just had to hand off some control to me." I left myself open to some smart late-night retort and waited. When none came—wise man—I continued. "I've got some news on the case."

"The name of the killer?" he murmured.

"No, sorry. I know that's all you want to hear." I heard him snort. I decided to go for bright. "Renata wasn't killed in the olive grove."

"Okay."

I thought somehow that fact would cleanse the olive grove in his mind. Somehow his life's dream was a pristine thing apart from the murder of his wife. I offered my other discovery. "The night of the murder, she held a meeting of the merchants in the block she owns downtown."

"Uh-huh."

"Renata announced she was throwing them all out and developing the real estate." At more silence, I thought perhaps I had to make the point more clearly. "Motives for murder, Pete." Then I couldn't help adding, "Other than yours."

"Well, that's good." Then, "Is that it?"

I bit the inside of my lip. "Yes, that's it."

His voice was soft. "I thought there'd be more."

At that moment, I realized he was scared. Just plain scared. And too scared even to admit it. I stumbled across the high road. "There will be, Pete. Just be patient."

When we said good night, it sounded nearly normal.

With a sigh, I drew the shades, pulled shut the curtains, cranked up the heat, and turned on my desk lamp and electric tea kettle. Still feeling the effects of that triple shot espresso late that afternoon, I rummaged in my canister of tea bags and chose something with enough chamomile to give me a chance at sleep. While I waited for the steam whistle of the kettle, I pulled the paint box out from under the bed and set it carefully on the table.

I told myself, as I lazily circled my spoon in the darkening water, not to fan too much advance excitement into discovering the secret paper under the false bottom of Alfonsa's paint box. She probably kept a running shopping list for paint supplies. What better place to secure it until she could get to Florence to buy them?

It was wartime, and by 1944 German troops had overrun the countryside, securing the land after Italy left the fight, and Allied troops had invaded Italy and were heading north. How safe would even a former convent be in the push to secure ground? To common Italians, did nothing seem important anymore, or did everything?

Carefully, I lifted out contents of the paint box and set them aside, the tubes, the smaller brushes that had been jammed in, the makeshift palette. I sat staring for half a minute at what I now knew was a false bottom. For some reason—maybe leaping ahead to the imagery in our future display of Alfonsa Cambi's life and work—I grabbed my phone and snapped a picture. And then snapped another one, closer, where the hidden paper was just visible beneath the side of the false bottom. And that was when I realized I loved documenting moments. In fact, I wished I had snapped a picture of the estranged Chef and Annamaria dancing their foxtrot truce.

I positioned my fingernails under the false bottom, gave it a soft jostle, and lifted straight up. Beneath it lay a carbon copy of what looked like an ordinary bit of correspondence. Paper clipped to that was a scrap torn from a book, quickly inked with a crude hand-drawn map and few lines of description.

2/

place, I favor beneath the statue of Veronica, but it is
likely to undergo repairs in the next few years, and so we
take a risk. This place is only my temporary home, Leon,

and whatever spot we choose has to be quickly accessible
if I must flee. Once the family returns, after the war, I
will no longer have access to the interiors. So I favor a
temporary outdoor cache for these valuables of MMC
and VVG until you feel it is safe to go the rest of the way
to the Vatican. For now, partisans, fascist gangs,
American soldiers—all Italy is battleground, and this
place could be quickly overrun and the fate of the
valuables grim. I must act quickly. I have a new idea for a
cache that might work in the short run. All will be
decided before you arrive on the 19th with the VVG.
Give me the name of my next effort so I may make a
good start before I see you. Be very, very careful in
everything, Leon, especially with your work in K-F.
Remember me to your kind sister, Gerda.

Regards,
A.

Well, it wasn't a shopping list for paint supplies.

Sister Alfonsa, what—in addition to bread handouts—
were you up to?

What I held in my hand was page two of a letter to the
Leon Eckhardt who had later died with Alfonsa in the bombing. A carbon of page two. Presumably, Leon had the original of both pages one and two. Maybe the carbon of page one
had simply been lost. Or maybe Sister Alfonsa hadn't needed
a copy of the first page of her letter to Leon—especially if
she hadn't addressed anything important or relevant to their
common interests. *How's the weather in Berlin, Leon?* I re-
read page two—the only page she had kept, hidden, beneath
the false bottom of her paint box—and believed she wanted
some kind of record for herself.

Without a date, which would have been included at the beginning of the letter, whatever she was documenting didn't need to be date specific. Although . . . I studied it more closely . . . it was clearly after the Allied invasion of Italy, which a quick Google search told me was the summer of 1943, and the villa took an accidental bomb just over a year later, in October of 1944.

If this half of a letter was somehow a record for Alfonsa, I could narrow it down ever better. This letter came after she already had the valuables of MMC but before Leon brought the valuables of VVC. Was his arrival that she mentions on the nineteenth actually October 19, three days before their deaths? Or months before? I could ask Sister Ippolita if she would check Leon's stays recorded in the guest log.

I asked myself for my first impressions of this carbon copy of a half letter.

Holding it in two hands, I straightened my arms for an overview. First, I thought I could eliminate Leon as a love interest for Sister Alfonsa Cambi. It was the wrong tone. What, rather, it did suggest was a warm working relationship. What interested me ever more was the careful nonspecificity of Alfonsa's communication. No date, no language that gives away the exact location, either in Italy in general or a villa-former-nunnery outside Cortona in particular. Along those lines, she avoids putting down on paper that she is a member of the St. Veronica of the Veil religious order, which, if the paper fell into the wrong hands, would narrow a search.

The only hint—inadvertent, I'd say—to Alfonsa's location is that it's somewhere in Italy north of Vatican City, since we know from Ippolita that Leon Eckhardt was a Swiss German working in Berlin. Alfonsa is looking for a cache for valuables before Leon feels it's safe to go "the rest of the way to the Vatican." Wherever Alfonsa lives, however Alfonsa lives, and whatever Alfonsa is up to, it is somewhere between Berlin and the Vatican.

How carefully this clever nun and caretaker of the Villa Orlandini during World War II uses language. To Leon Eckhardt, nothing she says would be mystifying. He knew the abbreviations and vague references: MMC, VVG, K-F. The statue of Veronica, the unnamed, absent family, the valuables. But to anyone else, like me, really, Alfonsa's letter was a masterpiece of ambiguity.

Tomorrow was going to be a long day, what with checking in on the class in dessert ziti (Would Mimi get a ziti cake on her eightieth birthday?), visiting Pete in jail, tracking down Jason Zale, and the morning outing to Lake Trasimeno that I'd arranged for the Copeland Party of Three through Manny Manfredi's Cucinavan, once they had expressed strong interest and I had checked their signed liability waivers. Since Annamaria had, in her good soldier way, volunteered to be the school representative on the lake excursion, she deputized Rosa as sous chef for the day, and I had bought some sleuthing time.

I eased into bed and had every intention of turning off the last lamp standing, but sometimes even a triple shot espresso gives up in the daily struggle to buy more waking hours. I slept, for no reason of night fears, with the light on.

13

🌿

The morning dawned crisp but promising, and even the November mists were biding their time. As we stood in the courtyard, Annamaria turned to me. "Call me," she said with some anxiety, "if something go wrong with Pierfranco." I wondered exactly what else, aside from a murder rap, could possibly go wrong with Pierfranco. Still, I promised her I would, and that Chef expected them back and ready for the dessert ziti class at two p.m. As the Copelands ambled toward their ride, I wrapped the still-beautiful Mimi in a birthday hug.

Philip, cool and warm all at the same time in a Burberry black quilted jacket, quipped, "I'm pretty sure it's my birthday, too."

"Oh, ho, ho, Mr. Naughty," said Mimi, swiping her son with her fleece scarf. Their voices faded. "My William was always after the girls."

"This is Philip, Meems," corrected Muffy quietly.

Mimi peered at her son. "Ah, so it is." She looked disappointed.

"Mom, really!" said her son with a halfhearted little laugh.

Must be terrible, I thought, watching them. Always the second-best child.

And then it struck me. I was always my parents' second-best child, too. And the only one they had.

I didn't know which was worse.

"William," Mimi said with spirit. "So full of life and joy."

"Time to board Cucinavan," boomed Manny. "Best tour company in the length and breadth of *la bella Italia*! Step right up."

I reassured Annamaria, who wore a stylish purple wool coat I thought might want to sit next to Muffy's hat, which seemed particularly low around her ears this morning. With one smooth wave, I yelled in English for everyone to have fun, and as the Copelands hollered back at me, Annamaria ascended the two steps into Manny's twelve-passenger gleaming white Cucinavan. Over the microphone, the irrepressible Manny Manfredi was telling a joke about Italian wedding nights. Followed by weak laughter. Followed by Mimi Copeland announcing to no one in particular that she didn't get it. The front door slid shut, and Manny pointed the van down the driveway, swerving for just a second as he turned up the volume on Rosemary Clooney singing "Mambo Italiano."

Fifteen minutes later, I found myself prowling around Cortona in the T-Bird. It was an ill-formed plan, to say the very least. Find Jason Zale. Finally, I gave up the let's-see-what-happens approach and called Officer Serafina.

"Pronto," she said in a breezy way, and from the traffic noises on her end, I figured she was stopped at a light on her motorcycle.

"Serafina, Nell Valenti."

A couple of revs, then she continued in English. "No news. Pierfranco slept well."

"You stayed at the jail?" Which was more than I could say. I felt outplayed.

"No. I check with Commissario Batta."

A difficult thing, when the nongirlfriend shows more consideration. "About how Pete slept?"

A merry laugh. "You think I have nothing else? No, I check on interview with the victim's assistant. Joe Batta happen to mention."

A sudden thought. "Serafina, Pete overheard Renata Vitale get a call from somebody late that afternoon, and she made a date for later. Did you get her phone?"

"*Sì, sì,* already done."

My heart pounded. "You got the number of the caller?"

"Routine."

"And?"

"No good. It was a burner."

I was slow on the uptake. "A—?"

"Prepaid phone. Loved by dealers. One call, then *pht*, trash."

So, she was telling me, not traceable.

The light changed and Serafina roared into life. "Serafina," I shouted to be heard over the traffic, "do you know where Jason Zale is staying?" Just then a truck blew past the cop, the driver's hand riding the horn. Serafina launched into a string of Italian invective that sounded like curses tumbling just inside the benefit-of-a-doubt zone before a *malocchio* got flung. I pressed her. "Zale, Serafina. Where's he staying?"

"Hotel Italia."

"One more thing. Did the coroner come back on the time of death?"

"No, but call me later, *bébé*," she said flippantly. In my head I heard Lauren Bacall say, *Just whistle.*

"Grazie," I said, and ended the call. Driving slowly through the parking lot behind the hotel, I snagged a spot away from the other cars, locked up, and headed toward the piazza.

*F*or this conversation, I wanted a very public place. So it couldn't have suited me better that I found Jason Zale sitting on the steps of the Cortona City Hall. In his hands was a take-out cup of what I supposed was coffee. On his lap was a white bakery bag—one of Carlo's?—with a flaky *sfogliatella* and a couple of chocolate biscotti lying on top. He definitely looked the worse for wear. Hair uncombed, shoes scuffed, and eyes staring at some image of his own rotten luck. Maybe he was mourning the death of Renata, maybe he was replaying her cruel argument with him, maybe he was wondering how he'd ever get out of Italy if the cops looked more closely at him. Or maybe he was devising some pretty attractive way of getting Rosenberg & Estis to consider him again. That it was just a matter of time.

"Jason Zale?" I tried to sound friendly. He sat six steps up from the broad, flat stones of the piazza, which put him a head below my eye level, but I didn't feel comfortable sitting just yet.

His eyes looked dully at me. "Who are you?"

"Nell Valenti. We met the other day at Forno di Carlo, the bakery." Not technically, but given the way he looked, he might not care.

I had to give him credit. He was squinting at me in an effort of memory. "You're friends with the baker."

"New friends."

"Oh, wait, now I remember. You chewed us out about the olive grove."

"The trespassing on private property. Correct."

Unfortunately, Jason Zale revived a bit before my very eyes, words like "trespassing" and "private property" providing him a shot of lawyer tonic. "Under the laws of community property, Ms. Vitale owned half of the grove."

I managed a tight-lipped smile. "Her claim has not been established."

He was shaking his head almost happily. "The marriage record was quite clear."

I couldn't take it anymore. Still, all I did was sit. "Did you peruse it before or after you started sleeping with her?"

When he flushed, Jason Zale lost even his faux retro look. "Before. She said it was over."

"Which? The marriage? Or the affair with you?"

His mouth twisted into a smile. "Both." He turned to look at me. "At different times."

"And you turned down the job of a lifetime at Rosenberg and Estis to tag along with Renata Vitale, lend her some credibility, and turn down her sheets."

Now he was just plain agog. "Who did you say you are again?"

"I work at the villa. Which is how"—it was a brainstorm—"I happened to find the body."

"Rotten luck," said Jason Zale, but it sounded insincere. What was he hiding? "How do you know about Rosenberg?"

"You of all people," I said genially, "should understand that I have my sources."

He grunted. Twice. When grunting was done, he heaved a sigh.

In an effort to change the mood, I got chatty. "Terrible

thing, this corpse on villa property. You know what I mean?"

"Very upsetting, I can imagine." He gave the kind of nod I give when I want someone to think I know what they mean.

"Our little cooking school is brand new. A start-up. And"—here I puffed out my cheeks—"picture the publicity." I fanned myself. I rolled my eyes.

"Stinks," said Jason empathetically.

"That woman," I said in what I hoped was a foxtrot side slide worthy of Arlecchino's dance floor, "was real trouble."

"Huh." He agreed.

"Dead or alive."

"To tell you the truth"—Zale found some spirit—"I prefer her dead."

"Less trouble in the long run?"

"You can say that again."

I leaned away from him. "That may be something you don't want to mention to Commissario Joe Batta."

He looked away. I noticed his hands kept bunching into fists. "He got enough out of me. Not everything," he muttered so quietly I could hardly hear him.

"Including Renata's day planner?"

"Oh. Right. I forked that over first thing."

I eyed him, unabashed. "Anything interesting?"

"Since we got here? No. She figured she'd swan around, upset the equilibrium, deal some business cards, and wait to see who sought her out for a meeting." *Or for a murder,* I thought. He went on to tell me that Renata had what she called "pure biz" appointments in town, just to verify her standing— real estate agent, banker, public records. Those she kept on her phone. The day planner was more like a climbing-to-heaven-on-the-broken-backs-of-other-people study guide.

Ruthless moneymaking self-help books. How far she'd read in a day, a week. A fashion consultation at Bloomingdale's. A day/time for her eyelids. A note about which office parties to crash, with Tishman Speyer always at the top of the heap. Which boards to finagle a seat on. Which openings, premieres, and seminars to crash. A day/time for her butt. Which wives to drop hints to about their wandering husbands. Which wandering husbands to offer a chance to head her off. Which Nietzsche quotes—"I kid you not," said Jason—to work into her correspondence and conversation. In the margins of the day planner, though, were inspirational quotes by people you've never heard of.

"No therapist?"

He brayed. "Renata actually told the last one how he should get into another line of work."

"Her life seems a study in alienation." I felt thoughtful.

Jason Zale was thoughtful, too. "She'd tell you something different, but"—Jason brushed pastry flakes off his pants—"she was stupid about people. And she couldn't sense danger. Her path was strewn with potential killers." He actually shivered.

"So," I said, "someone beat you to it?"

He sniffed. "I never even got to that point. I mooned around. Thought she'd fall for me sooner or later. I guess I was at a point in the abuse where walking out was my big rebellion."

I didn't mention to Zale that I had overheard his big moment.

He went on, "They arrested her husband, so Batta must have a case, but he wants me to stick around as *'una persona di interesse.'*" He swung around to face me, then took a sip from his coffee cup. "Sounds the same as it does in English!"

I changed course. "When you left here after the argument—"

He looked petulant. "Who said I left?"

"The cops."

He settled down. "One of your sources."

I wore my enigmatic smile.

"Oh, all right. We argued, I quit, walked it off for about an hour, came back, and had dinner alone."

"Where?"

"Bottega Baracchi, over on Via Nazionale."

"I know it. Then what?"

"Then I went back to my room at the hotel and packed up."

"Did you see Renata?"

"No. I threw my stuff in the car and headed out of town."

"Leaving her high and dry for transportation."

I was his star pupil. "Oh, yes," he smiled beatifically. "The rental was in my name."

"Where'd you go?"

"Straight out Highway 35 toward Florence."

"And the airport."

"After driving around the city for a while. I'd never seen it. I parked in the lot at Piazzale Michelangelo, a great scenic overlook of the city. Beautiful at night."

All very nice, but as alibis went, uncheckable.

I eyed him. "How were you feeling about everything?"

He sighed. "Mixed," was all he said, then pressed his lips tight.

"Jason," I leaned back, hugging my knees, "what can you tell me about why Renata Vitale came here in person?" I was recalling Carlo's point, that she could spread all this misery about ripping out olive trees and tearing down historic buildings to sling some luxury housing around town all via Zoom or email.

He chuckled. "She wanted to be felt. Far away, no personal effect. From stuff she said, some of these relationships went way back, and she had scores to settle."

"Like what?" I said, interested.

Jason Zale flung up his hands. "Nothing, that's my guess. She was someone who thought a lot about settling scores"—he clamped a hand on his chest—"but I thought she wasn't old enough to have scores to settle yet. I think she just wanted an old boyfriend to see how beautiful she was, or an old nanny to see she had no more power over Renata, or an old husband to see how much money she had." He pulled at a flake of *sfogliatella*, then held the pastry out to me in case I wanted a flake, too.

I declined. "Did she?"

"Have money?"

"Any of those things."

He considered. "Beauty, well, I guess it depends on what you like."

"You liked." I reminded him gently.

"Yeah, if she didn't say a word, because most of them were poisonous. I could hardly believe my luck. Renata Vitale and me."

"What else?"

"Power?" I could tell he was undecided. Finally, "She didn't have the kind of power she thought she had. The kind that makes people fall in line behind you, gaga over your charm and savvy and taste and"—he took a breath—"people didn't like her, even when she was doing her best to exert her . . ." He groped for the right idea.

"Personality." I offered.

He nodded. "Her personality." I remembered what I overheard that day, eavesdropping on Renata and Jason's fight at the bistro. When, on the subject of friends, Jason had said to her, *Can you really be so stupid not to see you don't have any?* "But the power she did have was real and dangerous. She . . . knew things about people. She collected—really, almost without trying—facts and tidbits about other people."

"Was she a blackmailer?"

He snorted. "Believe it or not, as money hungry as Renata was, she would think something like blackmail was beneath her. No," he said reflectively, as out of the corner of my eye I saw Carlo emerging from the bakery. "What she knew provided her with a bit of leverage."

"Like bringing up embezzlement." I waited to see what he'd do.

His mouth twisted. "Will you ever tell me how you know these things?"

"No, I'm not Renata."

He gave me a smile. "Like bringing up embezzlement. She knew I've got nothing like that to hide. But the threat runs deep. And the damage runs deep." Jason Zale looked me straight in the eye. "Because my father did. He embezzled. I've seen what it can do. Renata knew I wanted to put a lifetime between me and any hint of that sort of thing."

"So, aside from her threat to you, how did she usually work things?"

"I've seen her say 'Don't I know you?' or 'I hear that was quite a party,' or 'Did your son get out of that scrape?' That sort of thing. She wasn't out for payoffs. She just wanted to be included in exciting new deals and parties out on the island."

"What about money, Jason?" I asked. "Beauty, power, and money."

He nodded. "Right." Opening his eyes wide, he gave me a frank look. "Well, she didn't have any."

"What! She was building condos all over town!"

"Sure," he went on to explain, happy to be in his element, "she had property. That"—he pointed diagonally across the piazza—"block of shops she inherited from her nonna. And of course, either half the olive grove or, if she could dangle a divorce in front of her husband's nose, all of it." Suddenly, I knew where he was going. "She had the properties, but"—he opened his hands wide—"without capital, she wouldn't be able to develop them."

"So, either she would have to sell out to a developer—"

He held up a cautionary finger. "And maintain an interest," he put in.

"Or put together some investors who'd be chumps enough to bankroll her."

Jason's phone blared the first few bars of the "William Tell Overture." He gave it a quick glance. "Huh. It's the *commissario*. I'd better take it . . ." I watched Jason Zale spring up, fly down the steps, and move out of earshot. He and Carlo checked each other out as they passed.

Carlo, his thick dark hair in an endearing disarray, came to a stop in front of me. We smiled, then he jerked his head in the direction of the departing Jason. "Where do I know that guy?" he asked in Italian.

"Renata's assistant. And lawyer. And latest but former squeeze."

Still looking in Jason's direction, Carlo wondered, "What does he drive?"

"A red Jeep Renegade."

"No . . ."

"Yes."

He gave it up and handed me a small brochure. "From Benedetto, in case he misses you."

At a distance, Jason held up his phone, tapped his wristwatch, and briefly waved. I nodded a goodbye and turned over Benedetto's brochure to face me. *Celebrità di Cortona* was splashed across the top in bold white script. Celebrities of Cortona. One of the brochures that Benedetto makes available to tourists who come into the Chamber of Commerce searching for maps and hotel recommendations.

I looked up at Carlo. "Just for fun?"

He shook his head, his hair settling into a new arrangement. "Take a close look at page three, he says. Something he noticed." Then, "I'm off. When I take the next loaves of *pane rustica* out of my oven, I'm bringing two to Chef." Seeing the look on my face, Carlo lifted a hand. "No, no, he has not placed an order. This will be complimentary, just for neighbors."

I knew an olive branch when I saw one. Over the last two months, I'd noticed there can be bad blood that springs up suddenly between people, and if asked, neither of them could tell you why. But it had an air of agelessness. Crazy old battles still fought. Maybe it had something to do with a dead cow, a stolen sweetheart, a ruined crop—from like two hundred years ago. Imagined grievances even a well-placed *malocchio* wouldn't touch. If, for instance, I asked Chef why the bad blood between him and Carlo Giannini, he would say emphatically in no-nonsense Italian, "It just is." A kind of hereditary grudge.

We said a quick *arrivederci*, and Carlo loped back to the bakery, where he disappeared inside.

Pressed onto the top of page three was a pink Post-it note. Written in block letters was a single line: *Lei era al'incontro*—She was at the property meeting. Peeling off the note, I found a splashy montage of colorful photos and captions and skimpy text. Across it all was the name LODOVICO! followed by a barrage of exclamation points.

And there was the bare-chested man himself, with hair as thick as a fantasy wig, scruff, an overbite, a gold necklace, and a thin shiny silver suit with tight pants and a jacket never meant to button, zip, or otherwise obscure a meadow of chest hair. Legs spread, arms raised, mic gripped, head back. All the shot needed was audio. Floating around the page were the titles of Lodovico's hits.

The skimpy paragraph covered the Cortona years, from where his mother's family lived, and he expressed a belief that the seclusion in this unglamorous backwater would enable him to compose the score for the movie he was not at liberty to talk about. And it might be okay for his beloved wife, Bianca, and his beloved daughter, Renata. There were other photos, Lodovico stampeded by fans, Lodovico giving it his all in a recording studio, and one family shot . . . Lodovico in a stagey hug, wide open so everyone could still glimpse his chest hair, with his wife, Bianca, thirteen-year-old daughter, Renata, and the Unnamed Au Pair they brought with them from Rome—because she had been with the baby from the beginning—when they made the move to the hillside backwater.

The au pair stood off to the side, excluded from the expansive group hug, and although she faced the camera, her look was hard to read. But a bit like Mary Poppins being tempted to tell the employer just where he could stick the spoon full of sugar.

It was Hera Neri.

The list of suspects had just opened up. Excited, I dialed her number.

"Pronto?" came her voice, finally.

"Hera?" Suddenly I felt guarded. Not only has my painter pal Hera been on the villa grounds, working, for the last week and a half—I peered at the photo—she and Re-

nata Vitale go back further than anyone else on the scene
that I could name. It was Hera Neri who had more time to
know the dead woman. More time to hate. "This is Nell. I
have to talk to you."

"Is there a problem, Nell?"

A beat. "I don't know."

She was apologetic. "I'm in Milan. My old uncle, Arturo, fell off a curb. But when I get back, *sta bene?*"

"Sure." I deflated.

"I'll text you."

14

 ❧

I was definitely at loose ends. I wasn't quite at the point of
cursing old Uncle Arturo for not watching where he was
going, but I was feeling stymied to find Hera unreachable.
To get in touch with some better information, when I got
back to the villa, I shut myself in the office and googled
"Leon Eckhardt Berlin 1944." I could at least make more
headway on the mysterious history of the Villa Orlandini
during World War II. Two hits, one a piece in *Das Reich* on
the wartime damage to museums, which featured a grainy
photo of two conservationists in a workshop bent over the
damaged frame of a painting by Reich preferred artist Ar-
thur Kampf. From the left, Leon Eckhardt and Hans Weber.
Although the piece did not go on to disclose the location of
the workshop, the image of Eckhardt was clear, what
looked like a man of average height and build; fair hair,
lank and side-parted; eyes so deep-set behind their rimless
eyeglasses that they looked more like slashes of shadow
than anything else.

Eckhardt, forty-seven, a master of frame restoration,

traveled widely throughout the Third Reich, repairing and exchanging frames among the world's most famous museums' holdings. He is also a modest collector of poster art and expressionist painting. "Often," he told this reporter, "at the Kaiser-Friedrich Museum, we conservationists put in long days and longer nights, often alone in our workshop, to keep up with demand. But we try not to denude the galleries!"

Two key bits of information settled on my shoulders like the Tuscan mists of November: Eckhardt traveled widely as part of his job, and often worked solitary nights at the Kaiser-Friedrich Museum in Berlin. What Sister Alfonsa had to be referring to in her cryptic letter as "K-F." But then I let my mind play with the life Eckhardt was describing in the article, and mainly, it seemed to me the man had a lot of what we call "flex time" to do as he pleased. Alone, let's say, in a conservation workshop on the museum's lower level, repairing and restoring frames, but also . . . what? What would also involve Sister Alfonsa, the clever nun with her paints, waiting for the name of her "next effort," also alone, "caretaking" a villa that might be eight hundred miles away?

Was she a forger?

Her wait for Eckhardt to tell her the name of her next effort made me think he determined what she undertook to paint, but how? What made the cut? Clearly they worked in secret, and it was Eckhardt who was the more at risk of the two, as a staff member of the Kaiser-Friedrich Museum in the heart of Berlin at a time when Nazis themselves had a bold mission afoot to plunder the art treasures from museums, galleries, and private collections across Europe.

What would have happened to him if he had been caught? Eckhardt had to have figured a way of reducing the risk. Even if he could play the odds and somehow pull off a switch of a valuable painting hanging in one of the galleries, how long would it take for the forgery to be discovered, scrutinized daily by experts and museumgoers?

I went back to the grainy photo, pondering Leon Eckhardt bent over a worktable in the Kaiser-Friedrich's workshop, so busy keeping up with demand, still attempting not to remove too many works from any one gallery at a time. For those that couldn't wait, that were taken downstairs for repair or restoration, a card was positioned on the temporary space: "Not on View." So, not on view for the public. Not on view for the staff, either, really, placed temporarily in a storeroom.

I saw it then. Nearly the whole thing.

That was when the two of them pulled it off. When a painting went for repair. Off the floor, out of the gallery, and literally out of sight for what, during the chaos of wartime Berlin, could turn out to be months. Closing my eyes, I set my feet on the top of the desk and worked it out. It was Eckhardt who made the choices, the painstaking discriminations of cultural value and taste.

To Alfonsa Cambi, he provided the names of the artist and specific painting, and she got to work. No doubt he took into account where her greatest abilities lay and what size painting he could most easily transport from her studio at the villa in Tuscany to Berlin and the storeroom at the museum. How often could they pull it off? Better yet, how often did they pull it off? At the very beginning, did they have an end in sight? Ten paintings? The end of the war? All of the work by Rubens?

And what did they do with the originals?

It was on a trip to the Villa Orlandini that Eckhardt could take the spanking, fresh copy Alfonsa handed off to him, replace the original in the museum's storeroom, and once he removed it, do what with the original masterpiece? Sell it on the black market to rich collectors? I was unhappy. Theirs was a two-person job. She was a nun. He was an art conservator. I just couldn't picture those two as crooks in a game of high stakes. In a way, the success of their operation depended on the very smallness of it. Far less likely to attract attention.

The second hit in my Google search of Leon Eckhardt turned out to be a piece in the *Sunday Times Magazine* dated almost three years ago. And it turned out to be more than a footnote in the World War II activities of the Swiss German Eckhardt, who figured as just one of several collectors of Nazi graphic art and what was labeled by the authorities as *"Entarte Kunst,"* or degenerate art.

The point of the piece was to consider the heating up of the art market for these collectibles. Eckhardt's great-niece, Sylvette Meyer, points out that her uncle's interest in collecting poster art—propaganda not limited to the Nazis—and a few examples of the work of degenerate artists, which referred to those who produce work deemed incompatible with Aryan ideals and ideology, was in the interest of historic preservation. "Great-uncle Leon attached notes to everything. 'This is crap, and so we must save it,' he wrote on the note for the propaganda posters."

Other notes were attached to the carefully unframed and rolled-up examples of degenerate paintings. "Brave and beautiful, saved from a mass burning." "Altogether original, full of strident colors and power, pulled from the dustbin." According to Ms. Meyer, her uncle was a conservator in every sense of the word. "These treasures," he noted, "which will comprise Lot 37 in the modernist auction at Christie's New York on April 17, will be a good measure of renewed interest in this period."

I wanted to find out whether the lot had sold.
And, if so, who had bought it.

*A*fter tracking down Sylvette Meyer, who worked as a buyer in the Fine Watches Department at Harrod's in London, I called her. She answered on the third ring, and in the background, I heard children screeching, which meant we weren't in the hushed zone of fine watches. Meyer seemed to welcome the diversion of a phone call from a stranger, so I gave it my all.

Actually, I sounded pretty good: Nell Valenti, designer for Chef Claudio Orlandini's Cooking School in Tuscany. When Leon Eckhardt's great-niece gushed that she loved his recipe for ziti alla Genovese, and to please call her Sylvette, I knew I was in. And then it struck me. Trying to keep it light I asked, "May I ask where you found Chef's recipe for ziti alla Genovese?

"Oh, let's see. He posted it maybe a month ago. On one of those Facebook food video pages."

I felt queasy. Now, naturally, I would have to kill the Italian chucklehead. To be fair, right after I got off the phone I would check out the post on Facebook and see just how bad the damage was. For now, I was just easing on down the high road of valuable art. "Sylvette, we here at Chef's villa"—at that she did a whole major scale of "oohs"—"want to mount an exhibition"—no need to mention on what amounts to a living room wall six feet wide—"of the work of Alfonsa Cambi, an Italian nun who collaborated with your great-uncle, Leon Eckhardt"—please don't ask me on what—"during World War II."

"On what?"

I rubbed my forehead. I scratched my cheek. "I'm still

trying to determine exactly what, but we believe it had something to do with his work at the Kaiser-Friedrich Museum."

"Ah, yes."

I let out a breath. "I saw in a *Times Magazine* piece from about three years ago that your great-uncle's collection was coming up for auction shortly."

"Yes, that's right."

I needed to take the long way around. "Were you personally acquainted with the collection, Sylvette?"

"Oh, yes," she said in a way that lingered. "I inherited it, if you want to call it that, from my mother, whose mother was Gerda Eckhardt, Leon's sister." *Remember me to your sister Gerda,* went Alfonsa's page two of a letter hidden for nearly eighty years in a paint box. "The way I hear it, Nell, when he died in Italy, my grandmother cleaned out his Berlin apartment and packed up anything art related. She held on to it all because she didn't have the heart to get rid of it." Like the Veronicans, I thought, who couldn't just trash or give away whatever was left of Sister Alfonsa.

Sylvette Meyer laughed, then hushed her children in the background, who kicked up again. "Leon's art stuff, which is what we called it, became like a hereditary obligation, passing down through the generations. When I got pregnant with my second, I thought I'd spare my children from the hereditary obligation, opened it all up, and got an auction assistant at Christie's interested in the whole kit. Off it went."

"Did it sell?"

"Oh, yes," she warbled at what was a gross understatement on my part. "Let's put it this way," she explained, "I could buy several of the very watches I sell."

I fell silent. Then, "Aside from the posters and the examples of degenerate art, was there anything else?"

"Plenty, really. Things related to Uncle Leon's business, logs, ledgers, letters—you know the sort of thing."

How I'd love to get my mitts on any of it. So I asked Sylvette Meyer my key question. "Who bought the lot, Sylvette?" I could swear my heart was pushing at my rib cage.

"A private collector," she said airily, and I knew where she was going. "I don't remember the name. Actually, Nell, I'm not sure I ever knew it. I can put you in touch with the specialist I dealt with in modern art . . . ?"

Maybe that was the best I could do, but I doubted whether the fact that I was world-renowned Chef Claudio Orlandini's cooking school designer was enough to make this specialist hand over the name of the collector who won the auction. And, really, even if I did get the name, what was I proposing to do? My sense of defeat lifted off me so quickly I didn't even recognize it. Maybe this collector would be willing to lend us some representative piece from Leon's loot to display on our Alfonsa wall.

Or . . . maybe I could convince the collector to part with something that was probably of no earthly good in terms of valuable Nazi propaganda posters or degenerate art, because it was really just some form of bookkeeping. Log, ledger, letter. The throwaway stuff. Which, I had to admit, might very well have already been thrown away. What interest would any document not directly related to a painting's provenance would the other stuff have? The original of the letter from Alfonsa to Leon would be great. But we did have the carbon copy she kept of it.

At the very least, I'd need to verify that the original had shown up as part of the hereditary obligation. What I found myself hoping for from the collector who had won the lot was something that could shed some light on Leon and Alfonsa's operation. I took a deep breath, then said, "Sylvette, would you be willing to call the specialist and ask for that name? As a Christie's client"—I didn't think I was troweling it on too thickly—"you'll have more influence. I wouldn't stand a chance."

"You mean they might find themselves wondering—" She slowed.

"What else you've got. Precisely!"

"We don't have to tell them I've got nothing."

"It need never come up."

"But the collector's name could be public information, for all we know."

"It could"—I nearly wheedled—"but you could save me a whole lot of time."

"Where are you in Tuscany?"

I told her. Then I introduced the carrot. "If you can get here, I can offer you one night's stay plus ziti alla Genovese prepared for you by Chef himself." I would damn well make him do it . . .

The amiable Sylvette laughed again. "You're on."

When I finished prowling around the Facebook food group, I closed the lid of my laptop and twiddled my fingers reflectively, debating whether to bring in reinforcements. Annamaria was the equivalent of any high school vice principal in creation. Left to her, Chef's posting a recipe on a food video Facebook group would get him a month of kitchen detentions, possibly at the St. Veronica convent, where he would be made to snap green beans and peel spuds. One Annamaria was the equivalent of a platoon of battle-ready soldiers. But I decided to take a kinder, gentler Nell Valenti approach and chew him out solo.

My phone sounded an incoming text. It was from Philip Copeland, and it included a photo of Muffy, Mimi, Annamaria, and himself lunching on ham salad sandwiches from Manny Manfredi's picnic hamper on the island in the middle of Lake Trasimeno. There the mist was inconsequential, the Tuscan sun was emerging, and they looked like they were having a good time.

Copeland's text was a whole lot more understandable than anything I had experienced in the last ten minutes. **Heard back from Femke at Met and exhibition will include Visentini and Rossi plans! She wants good shots of current site to verify changes.**

For a cynical nanosecond, I wondered how much more Copeland had to pledge to "make possible" the inclusion of our modest little material. But maybe Femke, whoever that was, thought the two architectural plans, spaced two hundred years apart, of an Italian privately owned villa (née convent) would round out the show. Still, my mind tumbled happily around what this coup would mean to the Villa Orlandini Cooking School. Could we afford to hire an actual PR person to run with it?

I remembered reading that over seven million people visit the Met every year. I bet we'll see a bump in reservations . . . two years from now. Not to the tune of seven million, of course, but it would keep the school going to run full-capacity workshops every weekend of every month. In fact, I didn't know how it had been able to keep the doors open even in the two months since it's been in business, what with the expense of the build-out. Maybe Rosa had a little nest egg the other Veronicans know nothing about and would frown upon if they did?

And when it occurred to me that, two years from now, I may not be the staff member handling the PR for the Villa Orlandini Cooking School, I stopped in my tracks. By then, for all I knew, I could be long gone. If Pete and I split up, if Chef went to the big *bocciodromo* in the sky, if I got a job offer back home that didn't originate from my parents, if the Villa Orlandini Cooking School just plain . . . failed, I'd be leaving Cortona. What they call a sobering thought.

I found Chef alone, whistling, in the kitchen, trying to match up springform pan sides and bottoms. I had caught him actually setting up for the afternoon's dessert ziti class. This preparedness was both heartwarming and out of character. The conversation went something like this, in Italian, English, and something in between:

"Hello, Chef, I see you're setting up."

"How's Pierfranco?"

"As of yesterday, he was—"

"We're making *torta contorta*."

"Have you ever—"

"Pierfranco didn't kill *quella strega*."

"I know that, Chef."

"Orange or rosé vinegar, you decide."

"Well, is there chocolate?"

"I think the old Americana birthday lady killed *quella strega*."

"Orange."

"I win Annamaria back when I do *Hot Chef*."

"Win back Annamaria?"

"Good, strong hands. That's what I see."

"What are you talking about? Winning back Annamaria?"

"Strangle hands."

I think my eyes crossed. "About the Facebook recipe post . . ."

"Yes, chocolate. But orange is better."

"Chef, about the Facebook group you—"

"Hands strong for the strangle. You'll see."

"Chef, you posted the ziti alla Genovese—"

"Do these match?"

"Yes."

"Turned out very well, if I—"

"—on a Facebook group with 89,000 members, Chef."

"With *panna cotta*, the rosé vinegar."

"We're charging people thousands of dollars to come here to—"

"Silent partner no let the olive grove go condo." At that, he went a little green. "Well, you know."

I didn't know what he was talking about. "Which silent partner? The one Pete owes?"

He shot me a furtive look. "Help with start-up is all."

I could tell he was casting about for a way to make the chewing-out go away. I'd keep him from finding one. "The villa cooking school is charging thousands of dollars for people to learn your world-famous recipes"—here I punctuated my remarks by poking him in the chest—"from you," I nearly shouted, "and you're giving it all away for free!"

"Is all the same."

"Chef!"

"How's Pierfranco?"

Bemused past the point of no return, I needed to clear my head, so I left him. To get some distance from the sort of conversational gaslighting that happens with Chef, I don't need strong coffee or a half-hour meditation in the lotus position. All I need to do is leave. It's like the blessed moment when the Tilt-A-Whirl slows to a stop. All you have to do is just get off the ride.

Out in the pinging November mist that felt like a luxury spa treatment, suddenly Rosa came running up to me with the news that the Copelands would be back in an hour because Mimi was upset.

"Who called?" I asked in Italian.

"Muffaletta," she said.

"Why is Mimi upset?" I hated to think of it on her eightieth birthday.

"She doesn't like the boat."

15

🌿

I've taken a tour on Lake Trasimeno, and although I'm not much of a fan of water sports—and believe me, being ferried by motorboat to the island at the center of the lake felt like a water sport: I was on the water and being a sport—it wasn't an occasion for alarm. Not for me. But it was a well-run operation with an experienced skipper. Poor Mimi. Something must have spooked her. "How is she now, did Muffy say?"

"Better," said Rosa emphatically, her cheeks rosy. "But Muffaletta wants to come back so Mimi can rest up for the afternoon in the kitchen."

Rosa and I parted at the cloister walk, patting each other's shoulders and heading off in our different directions. She was prepping Annamaria's evening meal of seafood stew with gremolata toast, and I was tracking the secretive Hera Neri, who had texted me an hour ago to say she was almost back from Milan and could start on the villa job. Her trusty orange Ape was empty, so I continued on down the path to the oil production space, an annex to Pete's cottage.

We villa residents call the space the "center," the oil production center, but it's a kind overstatement, since it isn't the center of anything—hardly any olives get pressed on any scale to make it a center—and Pete grudgingly lets it be used for storage. Until he can afford to build it out for commercial production, it reminds me more of a garage, where you stick bicycles, leaf blowers, picnic coolers, and badminton and croquet sets. Those kinds of things you can never quite use but never quite give away. Pete hated it that his beloved space—and his dream for it—was really just a holding tank for junk.

Still, it needed a paint job, and maybe a fresh look would bring a fresh point of view—for Pete or the rest of us who were torn between supporting him and wanting to make comments that sound utterly realistic. Inside the oil production center was Hera Neri up on a stepladder, running a paint roller with an extension handle over the ceiling. The unmistakable smell of fresh paint.

"Hera?"

A quick glance in my direction. "Hello, Nell. I assumed ceiling white."

"Looks good."

She considered the small patch and disagreed. "It hardly looks like anything," she said. "But that is the point of ceiling white," she added with repressed joy.

"Let's talk."

"What, now?"

"Yes, I think we should."

Setting her paint roller in the tray, Hera climbed down the ladder, a little more cautiously than I'd ever seen her. Was she stalling? Or just tired with the workday already half over? What could her future possibly bring? Today she wore a blue-and-white bandana over her short hair, and the

lines in her small face seemed a little deeper. She followed
me over to what there was in the oil production center in the
way of seating. I took the gray barrel-back armchair with
the cigarette burns, and Hera took the wooden bistro chair
missing one of its vertical slats. She waited with her hands
outstretched on her thighs.

Hera had told me she began her career in childcare, but
to me, that meant multiple kids all at once, like in a day
care setting. Had it only been one kid all that time, after
all? And if that kid was Renata Vitale, why would any
nanny stick around for thirteen years, which must have
seemed like the next best thing to the gallows. Was she the
swaggering Lodovico's mistress? From the little I knew of
the petite and competent Hera, the idea seemed kind of
grotesque. She packed her lunches and ate on the job. She
babied her old Ape into clinging serviceably to life. She
spent hours washing out paintbrushes so they last.

Once, I overheard her crying when she muffed *un
bordo*—an edge—in the woodwork she was painting. Was
this the kind of woman who sleeps with the employer in a
small and tight family unit, there in the unglamorous backwater, where gossip was as plentiful as cobblestones. The
Hera of seventeen years ago was unmistakable in the photo.
The tight press of the lips kept all the pain and smartass
retorts at bay. Clothing was a practical matter. Haircuts
were a practical matter. Saving money was the most practical matter of all.

So she was at the meeting the night of the murder. The
meeting at the Chamber of Commerce, where Renata laid
out her plans for demolition—"repurposing"—of the block
of shops inherited from her grandmother. Hera ran her
painting business out of the back of a hardware store off the
piazza. She had no retail operation, so it was a little more

than a storeroom for supplies, a wall calendar for gigs, a desk with possibly the last landline in Cortona, and a desk chair.

Whatever Renata schemed for that block on the piazza wouldn't affect Hera's shop. If anything, ironically, an enclave of luxury condos might mean painting jobs for Hera. So, why was she present at what was kind of a tenants meeting the night of the murder? Carlo hadn't mentioned her, but why would he? Had he even seen her? Could she have slipped into the Chamber of Commerce, hung at the back, contributed nothing during the emotional Q&A, and slipped back out?

From my tote, I pulled out *Celebrità di Cortona*, opened it to LODOVICO! and passed it to her. Her face slid through half a dozen expressions, including dismay and the kind of anger that—over the thirty-seven years of its existence—has dialed down but never completely turned off. Finally, she stared at the page, and just for a moment, I saw the same look Carlo had when he spied his *fantasma*.

"Where did you get this, Nell?" asked Hera, turning it over in her hand.

I kept my eyes on her. "They've got them at the Chamber of Commerce."

She let out a tiny laugh, one I know well, because I've used it myself when I can't quite bring myself to say what a thoroughly absurd matter life is. "If only I had known. All this time, two blocks away from me, this"—she appeared to weigh it in her palm—"this record."

"What are you saying? You would have burned them all?"

She brushed it off. "No, records like this, well, they're indestructible." From her painter's pants pocket she pulled an orange and concentrated on peeling it. "But I think I might have liked knowing. Wondering if anybody recognized me. Or"—she gave a violent shrug—"maybe not."

"You weren't named," I reminded her.

Now she genuinely laughed. "That's right." She pointed a finger at me as though I had just said something extremely clever. "I'm Unnamed Au Pair." She preened, offered me half of the orange, which I took, then knobbed her fist against her mouth. "Too funny."

"Unnamed Au Pair?"

Hera nodded in a slow reminiscence. "So long ago, Nell."

For a moment, we sat in silence. Then, I spoke. "I hear you were at the meeting at Benedetto's."

She raised her eyebrows and nodded.

"How did you know Renata was back in Cortona? And why did you go to that meeting? Your shop is two blocks away."

Hera stretched her back, then gave a segment of orange a thoughtful look. "Yes, my shop was safe from Renata's plans, but even if it wasn't . . . ?" She met my eyes. "I'd find space somewhere. Because I don't need much. So you are correct, Nell. I had no real business being there. I slipped in, sat at the back, blended. I went because I wanted to see what that terrible little girl had become." I let the words sink in, struck that of all the players in Cortona, where Renata had lived for five years as a teenager, nobody knew her better than Hera Neri, who, as the piece on Lodovico put it, had been with them from the beginning. "The first I saw Renata was at Sottovoce—you remember, you were there that day."

I did remember. Hera at the bar, Renata swinging by with poor miserable Carlo, stopping by our table to scatter some business cards and chat up the rich guy. "Did you reach out to Renata?"

"For old times' sake? With my fingers around her neck? You won't believe me, but no. Not there, not after the meeting, not ever. Believe me, if I didn't kill her as a public service all those years ago, I felt no urge to do it now. As a child, she lied, she stole, she blamed. Me, for one, and I was always afraid, but I needed to stay with the Vitales." At my look, she amended, "Or so I thought." Hera lowered her head. "It was almost a relief when she was old enough to turn her attention to breaking hearts." I pictured Carlo. Hera looked up at me and smiled. "My heart was broken long ago, really, so I was no good to her. I was finally free."

She went on to tell me that in addition to being the Unnamed Au Pair, she was also the Unnamed Other Woman, the Unnamed Culprit in what Bianca called marital interference, the Unnamed Idiot who believed the weak and smarmy celebrity Lodovico when he whispered time and time again that he was assigning her the copyrights of all his songs.

This, he promised.

This, he swore on the life of his mother—who was alive and well in Florida—was his bequest to his long-suffering mistress who stayed and stayed through the child's abuse of her, the wife's canny manipulation of Hera so she herself could live the celebrity lifestyle with the weak and smarmy Lodo, as she called him, whom she barely tolerated, and the whiny lies of the man himself. I thought of the picture on the LODOVICO! page of the brochure. Just one big happy family.

"In those days, I still believed him. It was my security, that bequest. My future."

"So what happened?" I felt we were getting close to the

heart of the story—not to mention a motive for murder. What she went on to describe pretty much started and ended with the terrible child. When the family, including Unnamed Au Pair, moved to Cortona, which, after Rome and Paris, felt like the country to the Vitales, Renata was thirteen. She had never been particularly, oh, governable— Hera smiled—but now the girl had a developing sense of deceit and manipulation she was honing. Hera stayed, but in an altered role. Now she became a kind of floater, working for Lodovico and the family wherever needed. She was travel agent, cleaning crew, appointment secretary, chauffeur. Whatever she had to do to stay with them.

"I had invested so much time already," explained Hera. "Years and years."

She was caught in a narrow idea of herself, one that couldn't see a life beyond the sick tangle of the Vitales. Renata became more willful and secretive, and Lodovico was busy being celebrity Lodovico, and Bianca was busy being celebrity wife Bianca, so nobody was paying much attention to Renata.

Except Hera, but even that, at a distance. One playful day in July, when Bianca and Renata went to Florence for a spa day, and Hera was so worn down from the absurdity of her own choices she hardly cared anymore, Lodovico wrote out a will, leaving the copyrights to all his songs to Hera Neri in recognition of her faithful service.

They sat at a café, Lodovico being effervescent, Hera being self-contained—she believed her conversation had dried up long ago—while he wrote. It was market day, and he got two itinerant fruit sellers to witness the will. "I will make my Renata the executor," he said. This was a man who could bellow and croon and charm and entertain, but he had no smarts about the people he loved. Hera happened to be in the room a few days later, when Lodovico explained to Renata what he called his sweet café will, which, he was careful to explain, only dealt with his copyrights.

"Of course, of course," Renata assured him.

Over the next two years, when Renata was eighteen, she took off. "I knew about Carlo, of course, because Carlo's lovely sleeves have hearts all over them"—she grinned—"but not about Pierfranco, in case you're wondering." Lodovico and Bianca also took off, for a recording stint in London, but they would be back, they enthused. Hera stayed on in Cortona, considering her options, and then Bianca died suddenly in London at a couturier's.

"Which," Hera added with a smile, "would have been her dream death."

Occasionally, she heard from Lodovico, who crowed about a sold-out performance in Manchester, or a great studio gig in Amsterdam, and yes, he'd be returning to Cortona, but still there was so much to do, to sing, to become, to savor. When Renata was twenty-one, he died of a stroke, and all the becoming was over. Hera waited to hear from Renata, waited to hear from a lawyer, but not very long.

It was in a follow-up piece in a music industry trade magazine that Hera learned that the fabulous Lodovico had died intestate and that his only child, Renata Vitale, inherited everything. The "everything" turned out to be, in addition to his valuable copyrights, some gold chains, a one-room cottage in Puglia, a five-year-old Lexus, and what was left in his checking account.

Hera Neri and I sat looking at each other in silence. "You never heard from Renata?"

She laughed. "She heard from me. I asked her about the bequest. Naturally, she said, 'What bequest?' I reminded her of the day Lodovico had told her about it, with me right there in the room. Renata couldn't recollect. 'The copyrights,' I insisted. She said I must be mistaken. I listened to her breathing hard on the other end, and then I heard my own slow, strange voice say what I knew to be the truth. 'When did you destroy the will, Renata?' And the terrible girl said hoarsely, 'Simply ages ago,' and just before she ended the call, she added, 'Bitch.'"

I lowered my eyes and had one of those moments when I'm pretty sure the other person is way ahead of me. "Quite a motive for murder, Hera." Then, "Cheated out of your inheritance. No financial security."

As she gazed overhead, I thought she was estimating how much more of the ceiling she could slather with paint today. "I would agree with you," she said, lifting an index finger slightly crooked from arthritis, *"tranne due cose."* Except for two things. When I gave her a short nod, she went on. "Killing the terrible child would have been more trouble than it's worth"—and then she held up a second finger—"and besides, I have a perfect alibi."

"Namely?"

"Ah, you want me to practice, eh? I will have to go see Joe Batta."

"I think it's a good idea."

"Very well, then, Nell." Straightening up in her bistro chair with the missing vertical slat, my painter pal announced, "Waiting for me just outside the meeting that night were five other women from my book club. We took right off for Siena to hear Paolo Giordano read from his latest book—do you know Paolo?—then had drinks at our favorite club, and finally shared an Airbnb for the night. Good?" She set a hand on my knee.

"Joe Batta will want names. But"—I inhaled thoughtfully—*"sta bene."* But Pete was still in jail.

"In the words of dear dead blighted Renata, 'Of course, of course.'" Hera stood up and stretched her arms over her head. "The difference being, I do what I say I'm going to do." She agonizes over straight lines and difficult edges. She never charges more than her estimate. She will take a painting job if everything about it meets her very high standards—she has to like the people, groove to the room, enjoy the colors, appreciate treats and tips.

It seemed to me as I looked at her that the single best thing Lodovico had ever done for her was to bring her to Cortona, a town where she could—considering how things unfolded—have enough work to pay her bills, have a little shop, a book club, and peace of mind.

"And as it turns out, Nell,"—with that, Hera Neri seemed to look in pleasure at a stored leaf blower as though it held a slideshow of her life—"I didn't need anything from the Vitales after all."

Reality everywhere I looked. My phone trilled. It was Pete. And I felt the pressure to help free him top all the other pressures—working to give the Copelands seventy-five thousand dollars' worth of a good time, working to bring the dead nun and artist Alfonsa Cambi out of the shadows, working to bring a shocking level of new visibility to the cooking school through the Met exhibition of architectural plans, and working to keep Chef out of my hair, which, at present, was beginning to crackle with flames.

"Pete."

"Nell, if you were thinking of coming, don't."

"Why not?"

"Pop's coming soon. We've got some things to discuss.

And later on, Annamaria's driving however many Bari sisters she can cram in her new car."

I felt stumped. "They won't all be able to get in to see you."

He sounded weary. "You and I know that. I've already had Joe Batta here today."

"There's a treat."

"He brings his own."

We laughed, but not for long. "What did he want?" It felt naive of me—Joe Batta could jolly well put any molecule of Pete's last forty years under a microscope anytime he liked—"He already arrested you. I assume he thinks he's got a case."

Pete snorted softly. "The coroner came back with the time of death."

He was about to save me a phone call later to Serafina. "Which was . . . ?"

"Between ten and midnight that night."

"Seems like a narrow window."

"It is. He asked me to be more specific about my alibi."

"And—?"

"Just about then, I was pulling into an Autogrill parking lot off the A35, in a full Renata Vitale daze. To get rid of a wife I didn't want, I'd have to sign over the olive grove I loved. I nearly fell out of the car and threw up. Finally, I fell asleep. And no, nobody saw me. Nobody can verify it. All I could think of doing was getting back to Rome, where my manager had a couple more meetings lined up." He trailed off.

We fell silent. It all felt like such a mess. "Pete," I said quietly, "I'd still like to come visit. What about after Chef?"

I heard him exhale. "Nell, I'd love to see you, but I need

you to figure out what happened to Renata, because I sure as hell know—"

I finished, "You didn't hurt her."

In the background, on Pete's end, came a male voice. "My time's up."

"Okay. Listen, Pete, I'll—"

He overrode me. "I always thought of Renata Vitale as a kind of scorpion. Even if you overlook her, you're just as dead."

"Is that how you felt at seventeen?"

A beat. His answer surprised even him. "It was. At seventeen"—he went on bitterly—"it felt sexy."

B y the time the Cucinavan pulled into the courtyard and decanted the Copelands, Muffy, and Annamaria, Mimi had recovered from whatever upset her about the motorboat on Lake Trasimeno. But she was tired and needed "a little lie-down," and the well-bred birthday girl seemed to float in the direction of the renovated barn room. Chef, surprisingly on hand to receive them all, cupped his hands around his mouth and blared after her, in Italian, that the afternoon class on dessert ziti commences at two p.m.

Without turning, Mimi Copeland waved her arms high in the air as though directing incoming planes on an aircraft carrier. Muffy said brightly, "She knows. She'll be there," and she half ran to catch up with her slightly wobbly old friend. When they were side by side, Mimi landed a loving arm on her friend's shoulder. Those two, I thought, most definitely got game.

Philip Copeland gazed after the two women with rather a stern look, like he was trying to understand something about life that was somehow eluding him. Since no one was paying Chef any attention, he muttered and headed toward the main building. And Annamaria was tapping the hood of the gleaming white Cucinavan, a farewell to Manny Manfredi, whose rubbery arm rippled a typical Manfredi *arrivederci* as he headed down the driveway. Copeland turned toward me then, slid his hands into the pockets of his designer coat, and said pleasantly, "What do you say we spend the time hunting?"

In the cold, quiet November noon hour at a Tuscan villa, it felt like a movie moment. His golden brown eyes were intense. So easy for someone to take him for the movie hero, lips hardly moving, putting the possibility of adventure out there. Like Mimi's "little lie-down," which left to her own devices could turn into a grand nap, Philip Copeland's suggestion we spend the time hunting felt bigger than the words it took to make it. I felt the thrill of a chase I couldn't even name.

I lifted my chin. "Go on," I said noncommittally.

"We leave the villa in twenty-four hours, Nell." He waited for that bit of common knowledge to sink in. When I raised my brows at him, he went on. "This is our chance to get the photos Femke wants for the exhibition."

At that, Copeland raised his phone, tapped in his password, and up popped two of the photos I had taken of the Rossi and Visentini architectural plans of the convent that became the Villa Orlandini three hundred years later. What Femke, the curator, was after were current pictures of the sites on the property where changes had occurred from the first set of plans to the second. "Do we know that no other major architectural changes have occurred since Visentini drew the plans mid-nineteenth century?"

"I checked with Chef." As if Chef Claudio Orlandini is an unimpeachable source on anything other than risotto or

garlic. Still, he was all I had, since no more recent plans
had turned up in the holdings I had thumbed through at the
Etruscan Museum.

"And?"

"He said no, and would I like some prosciutto."

The serious Philip Copeland laughed while his coat
flapped gently in one of those flash breezes I'd come to associate with Tuscany. With a quick rub to his interesting
face, Copeland told me he had identified three major architectural changes from the time Vincentio Rossi drew up his
plans for this first Veronican convent in 1571: the disap-
pearance of the calefactory—at my quizzical look, he
pointed to what was labeled "warming house" on the original Rossi plans—"where," Copeland explained, "the nuns
could go for some reliable heat"; the bombing destruction
of the infirmary on both sets of plans, repurposed as a library and storeroom by the Orlandinis, "which," he reminded me, "you and I puzzled over in the nighttime"; and
finally, the curious case of the "necessarium" and what
looks like a very lengthy drain. He smiled at the side-eye I
was shooting him. "The communal latrine."

We set off to photograph where the warming house, the
infirmary, and the latrine used to be, just—if I understood
what the curator meant—to authenticate the changes. First
up, because it was the closest—well, absence—was the
warming house, which would have been adjacent to the
dining room and the meeting room. Clutching my coat
more tightly against me, I started shivering, loping along
behind Philip Copeland.

As we rounded the corner of the chapel, which the Orlandinis now used as their dining room, he asked over his
shoulder, "Where do the Veronicans bury their dead?" He
slowed as we walked over a patch of ground that must at one

time have sported a warming house. "I've noticed there's no cemetery." He jiggled his phone in my direction.

We both then played paparazzi and started clicking off shots of what I started to think of as where the woozle wasn't. Copeland pointed out sunken areas in the cold turf, ridges here and there, stones that must have been construction materials, and areas where the soil had a timeworn, ashy look. I didn't know what he was talking about, but he kept taking photos.

"There's a crypt, I hear," I told him, adding that it had been sealed off about a hundred years ago to enlarge the wine cellar. "The Orlandinis are always more interested in the living than in the dead." Spots in the crypt were reserved for nuns of high standing, Annamaria had told me, so the lore went.

"And the others?"

"Buried in the graveyard they shared with a small monastery on an adjacent plot of land. When that order died out, the Veronicans took over the shared site and kept with the tradition."

Now it was Copeland's turn to look quizzical. "Odd for the graves to be off-site like that."

After a few more shots, I said, "Let's press on, if you don't mind. I'm cold." More than that, I was hungry. And more mist was whitening the air.

"Go get warm, Nell," he said, squeezing my arm. "I can finish this up alone."

I felt grateful. "Sounds good."

"Once I get the rest of the photos, I'm cooking all day," he said carefully, "so are you okay if I poke around these sites by myself this evening?"

I couldn't match his excitement. I couldn't even get close. Philip Copeland was a very hands-on kind of guy.

Maybe these were the kinds of details you obsess over when your foundation lays out the kind of money it takes to mount an exhibition at the Met.

"Be our guest." The man liked the night, that was for sure.

"By this time tomorrow, we'll be long gone." So he was just maximizing his last night at the Villa Orlandini before pulling out in the Rolls tomorrow after lunch.

Long gone.

So many miles behind them. So quickly.

It doesn't take long to be long gone.

The nuns in the crypt, the nuns in the graves, no difference between them now in the great democracy of goneness. Within just a few short hours, I would come very close to joining them.

16

An hour later, six of us were scattered around the largest worktable in our spanking new kitchen. Chef, as usual, commanded the long side closer to the sink, the fridge, and the counters holding two food processors. He looked unusually splendid that afternoon, wearing his tailored fit, single-breasted chef jacket in white with blue piping, crowned with his favorite white *douga* hat, typically worn in a West African ceremonial dance and now popular with the culinary crowd.

His face gleamed, and he was experimenting with a day's growth of beard. If there was a product that could whiten teeth overnight, he had found it. If I didn't know better, one of three possible things was going on in that labyrinth in his mind. Either he was impressing the hard-to-get Annamaria, or he was distracting the Copelands from pesky things like murder, or he was—

At that moment, Rosa swung over the threshold dressed in a cranberry-colored tunic over gray palazzo pants, announcing, *"Ciao, tutti."* I stared at her. From somewhere she had snagged a pair of pale pink Versace eyeglasses, and I believe her hair was a shade darker. All eyes were on my surprising and unflappable sidekick as she cast smiles all around the room and assured us the filming should *"non dovrebbe intralciarti."* That is, not get in our way. Just a video for *Hot Chef: Italian Style*, she will be needing them all to sign release forms, and have the time of your lives! The Copelands regarded each other wide-eyed, then appeared to get in the spirit of footage for *Hot Chef.*

With a look of regret on her face, now topped by pink glasses and dyed hair, Rosa motioned me out of the shot, and got busy. I took three steps back, eyeing Annamaria, who seemed to be controlling a grin. When Rosa moved the camera, Annamaria, who was allowed to stay, stuck out her tongue at me. I wrinkled my nose. Never had I been happier to be relieved of a job. From what I could tell, Chef picked up on my lack of enthusiasm for his *Hot Chef* dream and replaced me. Fine by me. On a cue from the barely recognizable Rosa, who crossed herself for good luck—I hope without having pressed the button for Video on her phone—Chef launched into an expansive Zorba moment, welcoming all to his very special class on dessert ziti.

Today's sweet ziti treat, in honor of the beautiful Mimi's birthday, is *torta contorta*, but first, a round of blood orange mimosas (cue Sofia, who entered with the drinks tray and served). The last glass standing was, apparently, mine, and I lifted if off Sofia's tray as she left. Chef went on to describe *torta contorta*'s origins, its nomadic culinary history, its colorful anecdotes involving vinegars and celebrities, and its ingredients. I don't know how he did it without a single note. Meanwhile, Rosa crouched sideways like a sand crab, filming *Hot Chef* applicant Chef Claudio Orlandini as though he was legging it down a runway, and the Copelands and Muffy were delighted.

For me, the healing properties of kitchen time are undeniable. The eyes, the hands, the tongue, and the nose all want to create beautiful food that rises above heartaches and aging flesh. Like Mimi Copeland, you may not be able to pull up the right son's name, or sometimes even the month you were born, but if you set your oven for 350 degrees, your *torta contorta* will come out perfect.

I sipped my Mimosa and let the class swirl around me, suddenly happy, despite Pete's fix, despite my gnawing sense that I was on the wrong track, missing something important. So it was calming to hear Chef notice that Philip Copeland's springform pan was just nine inches instead of ten inches. Unlike murder, such a solvable problem. Everyone fully appreciated that, as averted crises go, this one was light and easy. Annamaria swapped out the nine-incher for a bigger one from a baking pan drawer.

Chef's *torta contorta* was his own personal advancement in culinary boundary-busting. In his hands, pasta isn't just for dinner anymore. It gets rocketed into another zone altogether when it's found in the company of rum, chocolate, cinnamon, nuts, lemon, vanilla, and sugar, then baked in a stretchy pastry wrap and, before serving, topped with a berry mélange.

Two tortas were being made, blared the *Hot Chef* contender, with outstretched arms, one by Philip Copeland, the other by Mimi and Muffy. *"Una battaglia,"* blared Chef, trying to make an epic tale out of dough making, *"dei sessi."* A battle of the sexes.

Annamaria and I flashed crossed eyes at each other.

With that, Chef raised his rolling pin and explained why

the JK Adams nineteen-inch dowel-style maple rolling pin, weighing in at a perfect 1.6 pounds—here he slammed the hefty dowel into his palm and winced—was his favorite. How he found so very much to say about a rolling pin was beyond me, but it was as though an ace salesman at the Rolls dealership were pitching the Phantom.

With Rosa translating now, along with her filmmaking duties, he was regaling the poor Copelands with praise for everything from the pin's incomparable rollability to its state-of-the-art torque. At that point, Mimi and Muffy were regarding their own JK Adams nineteen-inch dowel-style maple rolling pin with reverence and alarm. Leaning into me, the beautiful birthday girl whispered, "I had no idea it mattered so much!"

Under Chef's beaming instruction, the Copelands mixed together the dry ingredients, measured out the wet ingredients, combined all, added water as needed, and blended until that ineffable moment Chef described as when "the dough come together." This mystical act, spoken in a hush as though he were referencing a maharishi's sex life, was designed to tug at the judges for the *Hot Chef: Italian Style* candidates. Mimi's fingers danced over the dough timidly, and I wondered how she had managed to diaper two babies. Philip, on the other hand, had a style I could only say reminded me of a one-handed squeeze with a stress ball. Giving the Copelands the side-eye, I was pretty sure dough making was not something that had ever crossed their golden thresholds—so, good for them for signing up.

It was the down-to-earth Muffy Onderdonk who got with the program, pressing so strenuously against the dough it was like she was pushing back the tide, once with Mimi's dough and then with Philip's.

And then Annamaria stepped in to demonstrate the fine

points of kneading. "These," she turned her palms toward the students, which cued Sofia to touch the fleshy parts of Annamaria's palms, "are the heels, the best workers for kneading your dough."

While I sipped and the others worked, my mind went back to the excellent point Philip Copeland had raised while we were outside together in the cold, taking photos of absent buildings. *Off-site burials seemed odd.* Why, five hundred years ago, was this new order of nuns burying its dead elsewhere? Was it some sort of advance planning—for what? against what?—that those of us coming centuries later couldn't readily see? Or had they buried their dead here on villa grounds after all, but had to move them at some later date and reinter them elsewhere? But what a job . . . and why?

While Chef, testing for readiness, was pressing his thumb into the Copeland's dough balls for their sweet ziti treat—"We want them soft but no sticky"—I slipped out of the kitchen and tiptoed noiselessly down the hall to the office, where I closed myself inside. Sitting down hastily at the desk, I pulled out my phone, checked my recents, and made my call.

It took the spry Sister Ippolita less than ten minutes to get to the nuns' shared phone in what could only be termed "the parlor." Forget the chapter houses of yore, this room had a sectional leather sofa with chaise, a sixty-inch wall-mounted TV over a console that was somehow also a gas fireplace, a bridge table, and a baby grand. There was also what looked suspiciously like a poker table, but Sister Ippolita assured me it was where their members of the Monthly Veil Club—I could get nothing out of her on that subject—gathered to eat sandwiches.

"Sister Ippolita? It's Nell Valenti."

"You said." She waited.

"Question."

"Go ahead."

"Annamaria tells me that, before the move to the new convent—"

"With the elevator."

"Yes, the elevator. Before that time, Veronicans of high standing were interred in the crypt. Here."

"That is so."

"Why aren't all the others buried on the grounds here, as well?"

She snapped, "The will of God." It wasn't unkind, just a rote response.

"Could you be more specific?"

"The story goes," said Sister Ippolita, her voice curling as though she was settling in to impart a choice bit of gossip, "that in the early times, the convent owned less land over there. Where you are. Barely more than what the buildings stood on."

"So," I said slowly, trying to work out the reasoning, "the Mother Superior had to find—"

"That woman," announced Sister Ippolita, "was a visionary. She could look all the way down the generations to come and know that the early sisters would lie in ground next to the chapel until the resurrection of the body, but the later sisters would have to be laid to rest elsewhere. No room! So"—she wheezed a breath bigger than her petite frame could hold—"all the Veronicans, earlier, later, would be laid to rest in the same place right from the start. A true visionary."

To me, Mother Superior was more like a quartermaster distributing the dead.

Sister Ippolita seemed to settle the question about the

nuns themselves, but I felt myself looking more narrowly at the problem. "So just during the war years, when Sister Alfonsa was the caretaker here, there were never any burials on the old convent grounds?" Something exceptional. I had it. "No deserters, for instance?"

Sister Ippolita got testy. "How do you think Sister Alfonsa spent her time? Out rounding up random bodies with a wheelbarrow? Eh?"

"Not routinely, no," I retorted, "but did she ever mention— or record in the convent log, say—an isolated incident? Something unusual that came her way?"

"Like what?"

I spun it for her. "A dead partisan, a stranger, a road accident victim, a stillbirth."

She made a *tscha* noise, like warding off bad luck. "Anyone," she insisted, "anyone would be buried here, signorina, in the blessed ground of our cemetery. Not there." It was a staunch reply, but not necessarily a true one.

So I had to make her consider it. "An unbaptized child?" I put it to her. When she inhaled noisily, I went on, "A victim of violence or disease, someone she felt it was better, less complicated, to keep to herself."

Silence. Then softly, "You have a strange mind, signorina. For that sort of thing, we would have no record, you understand."

"I understand," I said, but I felt stymied. "I'm wondering, Sister Ippolita, if Sister Alfonsa handled a death she wanted no one else to know about? Had Leon Eckhardt helped? Or was she entirely on her—"

"I will check the log, signorina," she announced, once again the staunch soldier. "Perhaps I am forgetting something. I will call you back."

No sooner had I gotten off the phone with her than it

rang again. This time, it was Serafina asking me to pass the word on to Chef that as next of kin to the next of kin, the *commissario*'s office has designated him as the cleaner-upper of Renata Vitale's belongings. To which I said something cogent, like "Huh?" In a single sentence, that woman had plunged me into a thicket of next of kins that I was failing to comprehend. I was even having some trouble with what she meant by cleaner-upper.

Serafina slowed down and tried to explain, and it turned out to be weird but simple.

As the dead woman's husband, Pierfranco is her next of kin. Serafina paused to let that sink in. It didn't. "However," she drawled, "his arrest means he's unavailable to clean out the dead woman's room at the Hotel Italia, so the little task passes to Pete's next of kin." She paused, and then uttered the fateful words: "Chef Claudio."

Any little task that involved Chef never stayed little for very long. "How much is there?"

"Clothing, toiletries, some devices."

I tried to remember. "You already have her phone, right?"

"Yes."

"And her day planner?"

"Correct. Can you come get the dead woman's room key? I've got to head out to the Chiesa di Santa Maria delle Grazie al Calcinaio on a vandalism call."

I suddenly remembered Jason Zale telling me that Renata Vitale recorded all the really important meetings on her phone. Instantly, I was interested. "Listen, Serafina"—I managed to keep her on the phone—"I'll tell Chef this is his task, but he's teaching right now."

"So?"

"Can he deputize me to collect Renata Vitale's things?"

"He can do whatever he likes."

"He does anyway."

"I figured."

One little probe. "Why can't Jason Zale collect her stuff?" The answer was immediate. "Not Zale," she barked. "No."

"Why not?" I pushed her. "He's heading back to the States, he can just—"

At that, the cop Serafina, infinitely preferable in my book to the detective Joe Batta, erupted in a string of Italian invective that lasted for a full minute and touched on points about "not cleared from suspicion," "in over your head," and "press your American luck." When that breath ran out, she ended reasonably. "It has to be Chef Claudio." When I had nothing to add, she did. "We're done with Vitale's things. I'll leave the room key at the front desk."

I started to feel jumpy. Italian invective always has that effect on me. "Which front desk?" Suddenly the world felt furnished in front desks designed to confuse me.

In the voice she must use to chide jaywalking six-year-olds, Serafina said slowly, "At Dardana Street. *Capisce?* Now I've really got to—"

"Of course. One more thing, Serafina. Just one. I want to see the dead woman's phone. I won't take it away. Can you do that for me?" Incoming low ball, "For Pierfranco?"

She sucked in air between her professionally whitened teeth. "It'll be with the key. Leave it when you're done. We're still following up on her phone calls."

"Passcode?"

"Disabled. *Ciao!*"

O n the back of an extra copy of the agenda for the four-day Ziti Variations course, I started to scribble a quick note to Chef when a light rap at the door signaled a visit from Annamaria. "Come on in," I called, and she entered but stayed just over the threshold, adorned with light blots of flour for the torta's pastry dough. Her face held a rare, placid expression, almost as if she had never uttered a *malocchio* in the range of ninety-five decibels.

In her default Italian, she asked, "Will you be visiting Pierfranco today?"

I twisted the pen. "No, he has business with Chef." The answer seemed rather thin to me, but I didn't have anything else to offer except, "Why?"

"I thought I could make a tiny *torta contorta* for him you could take."

I smiled at this beloved woman who—aside from rolling out pastry dough—was at work on a self-improvement project that included a healthy distance from Chef himself. "If it's ready soon, Annamaria, I have to pick something up at Dardana Street. I can leave the tiny torta with one of Joe Batta's people."

"Is not ready. Not even soon. Never mind."

I crumpled the note. "Could you please tell Chef the cops have designated him the next of kin of *quella strega*'s next of kin"—I still couldn't believe my boyfriend was, until two days ago, a married man; wouldn't my parents love that tidbit?—"which means it's now his job to pack up her belongings."

Until what I had just imparted registered with my friend on the threshold, I had never been able to picture a curling lip. Whenever I came across a line in a book like "his lip curled," I got flung straight out of the story, stuck on the elusive image. But now, looking at Annamaria's expression, I finally got it. The human face does indeed have those micro muscles. Her upper lip drew back over her top teeth in a look of complete disgust. When she recovered, the term *quella strega* found its way a few times into what she was saying, the substance of which fell out along the lines of cooties and bad, bad luck worse than what a lusty *malocchio* can deliver.

I got the impression that in some supernatural Italian worldview, handling the dead *strega*'s belongings was not a particularly welcome task. "Tell him I propose to save him the—" Instead of trouble, I upped it to "danger and do it myself." I folded my hands on the desk. Fixing me with a look like she hadn't eaten for a week, Annamaria fumbled around in her stylish pants pocket and withdrew a small object enclosed in her trembling hand.

She strode to the desk and set it down in front of me. It was a nail. "You borrow." She made the gesture that resembled the scattering of chicken feed in a barnyard. *"Tocca ferro,"* she whispered reverently. Touch iron. I knew she meant it seriously, more than seriously, so I bit the inside of my cheek to keep any unappreciative smiles at bay. "It will keep off the bad luck."

We nodded at each other for a while, and then I slid the nail toward me, held it up with what could only be called a demonic smile, and tucked it into a pocket. *"Grazie,* Annamaria," I said, hoping it passed for an appropriate response to the sharing of amulets. "Well," I said finally, pulling myself to my feet and patting my pocket, which was right at the level of where my holstered gun would lie, if I had one and was lost with it somewhere in the Old West. "I've got to push off, Missy," I finished, reminding her about telling Chef I was taking on his task. Swiping my jacket off a hook, I followed her out.

When I pulled onto Dardana Street, just down half a block from the HQ of the carabinieri, I parked and texted Pete. Just to let him know I was coming in, still on the case, if he'd changed his mind and wanted to see me. **Lawyer here now**, he texted back. **Then Pop. Try later?** The way my day had been going, I wasn't sure such a thing as "later" even existed, but I sent him a cheery **Sure!** All good, as good as could be, considering he was accused of murder, and then, just as I was letting myself into the HQ building, he texted something alarming. **I love you, Nell.**

Ah, nuts. I groaned and staggered back to the sidewalk. Now, why'd he have to go and complicate a perfectly rotten day? Women know very well indeed that the first time those words are uttered they have to be in person. Texting **I love you** is like being invited by a Facebook friend you've never met to like her ska band, antiaging face tape, or Macramé Is My Life page. Men really need to start carrying the rule book with them. So I texted him a thumb's-up emoji in response.

Inside the HQ, I stalked across the tiles to the front desk, where an inscrutable (must not be Italian) officer eyed my approach. As I started to introduce myself, he puffed out his lips and reached for a manila envelope stashed in a cubbyhole. *"Se chiama Nola Valenti?"* In the interest of saving two seconds, because on that day, I never knew when they'd come in handy, I answered, *"Sì,"* he turned over the envelope, and we bid each other tight-lipped farewells. But not before I gazed at the locked steel door leading down to the cells.

Back in the T-Bird, I ripped open the envelope and slid out the Hotel Italia room key to Renata Vitale's last bed on earth. For now, I left her phone in the gold metallic case untouched. First things first, and I felt Serafina was pushing back on department rules—like the heels of Muffy Onderdonk's hands kneading dough in impressive shoves—just to give me a shot at free rein over the dead woman's stuff.

I found a parking spot behind the hotel, sniffing around where, from Carlo's description, he had unloaded poor dead Renata in the cracked concrete berth between two parked cars. Nothing. But two days had passed, the mists had prevailed, and I wasn't expecting anything. After I let the gray-haired clerk at the reception desk know my mission, he thanked me, then gave me a mixed message about the poor dead American lady, and just when exactly would they be able to send in housekeeping for the next guest? I guessed an hour, then headed up to the third floor. Inside Renata's hotel room, I got to see Joe Batta's leftovers.

Renata Vitale had come to Italy with just a carry-on suit-case and a messenger bag that did double duty as both a purse and a briefcase. I swept the toiletries into a large zip-lock bag I had brought with me, emptied the few clothes from the closet and the dresser into the suitcase, and slipped odds and ends like reading glasses and hairbrush into the messenger bag. As a harbinger of doom, she certainly traveled light.

One final sweep around the pleasant room where—strange as it was to say—Pete's wife had slept her last, with visions of luxury condos capering in her head. *That terrible child,* Hera had called her familiarly. A terrible child who had grown up to steal an inheritance and then concoct a scheme for her own gain that depended on the eviction and disruption of unsuspecting others. Was that all she was? All she had ever been? Can anyone ever be quite that friendless?

Slinging the messenger bag over my shoulder and wheeling the carry-on, I left the room. I had done the task here, but the Orlandinis would have to take care of hiring help back in New York to close out the life and business of the murdered woman. Maybe some kindly colleague on the board of that arts organization she mentioned at our table in Sottovoce the night before her murder. Maybe Carlo would remember the name.

In the meantime, "All clear," I called in Italian to the clerk at the front desk as I passed. "Ready for housekeeping." And I fielded his thanks. In the very meantime, I'd off-load the clothing to Rosa and Sofia, who could take whatever they wanted, and the messenger bag to Chef, the next of kin to Renata's next of kin.

17

🌿

Back in the abbess's room, I untied the small stack of letters written by Leon Eckhardt to Alfonsa Cambi. Then I laid them out from left to right on the table in chronological order, according to the postmark. Just to get the big picture, if there even was a big picture, I read them all through, which took less than five minutes. A couple of things struck me.

They were short, and they were formal. Little more than a request for lodging for a couple of nights at the villa—"please find enclosed a check for a deposit, inclusive of meals." The usual good wishes for a satisfactory end to the war, her continued good health, and a time at some later date when he could serve as her guide to Berlin. Perhaps she will enjoy the enclosed list of the holdings at the Kaiser-Friedrich Museum, since she had expressed an interest?

I slipped this enclosure out of the second envelope. Letters one and three ran along the same lines: Eckhardt made reservations at the villa, sent best wishes, and enclosed a clipping from a local paper about something completely inoffensive—*"Wie man Flecken entfert,"* which, if the illustration of pouring salt on spilled wine was an indication, meant "how to remove stains"—or inoffensively interesting, like a travel trifold of Zurich, to which he had stapled a tiny note, *"Casa mia!"* My home.

I noticed how pointedly unpolitical his communications were, and how businesslike. Accommodations for a man on a business trip. Eckhardt carefully avoided calling her by name or revealing her circumstances—namely, that she was a nun. Too risky? Too easy, with some sleuthing, to identify her? Each of his letters opened with "Dear Lodge-keeper." But by far the most interesting angle was that, aside from the Berlin postmark, every envelope had no identifying marks. No return address. And most suggestive of all, just a carefully cut out space where Leon Eckhardt had written the address. These were both very careful people, Leon and Alfonsa. In the bloody chaos of those years, at every chance, they obliterated their tracks.

What was their dangerous game?

Setting aside the Zurich travel brochure and the useful information on how get out stains, I lifted the remaining enclosure. A two-page, double-sided, single-spaced typescript of the holdings of the Kaiser-Friedrich Museum, where Eckhardt worked. It looked to me like an internal document, the kind that was kept on file in the museum's administrative offices. Accurate, updated, used as a reference when staff needed the info. Nothing as colorful and attractive as anything produced for the public—or, better yet, potential donors.

The list Eckhardt had sent Sister Alfonsa, just because she was curious, he had said, had last been updated two months earlier. I scanned the pages. The broad categories were Paintings, Drawings, Sculpture, Miscellany. Within each category, the holdings were alphabetized by artist. The columns ran: Artist, Title, Date, Size, Medium, and Gallery.

My eye stayed glued to the Paintings category, since Alfonsa seemed to be a single-medium artist. The holdings of Berlin's Kaiser-Friedrich Museum during World War II were priceless. Had a Swiss German conservator and an Italian nun been in cahoots to commit art theft? Since that activity seemed to be a garden industry in the Third Reich, could the efforts by a twosome escape notice?

Staring at the listing, I decided to put my little idea to the test. Nights, Eckhardt labored down in the workshop on the museum's lower level. As risky as it would have been—more than risky, doomed to dangerous failure—to switch a painting on public view in one of the museum's galleries with a brilliant forgery by Alfonsa Cambi, could it have been done? Back to the question I had grappled with earlier. And I came to the same conclusion. Possibly, but not frequently, not with any sense of the urgency of the times.

As thieves, perhaps one great heist, followed by their own separate and well-timed disappearances, would have kept them in schnapps and villas for the rest of their natural-born days. But I couldn't see it. Not these two. "I am in it for the long game, Alfonsa. It is vital work. We both know that." And another: "Thank you, Maid Marian, for the copy of the Robin Hood tale." Reading between the lines of these cryptic letters, I believe they were in it for what he called the long game, and not in the way of a con. In the way of a sustained effort over however much time they could pull it off. Until caught or killed, or they lost their positions or their nerve.

They were stealing art in order to rescue it.

But from what fate?

Had Eckhardt gotten wind of the wholesale looting of art in countries now occupied by the Nazis? Although the Kaiser-Friedrich Museum was in Berlin, as the chaos and Allied bombings increased, wasn't art vulnerable to theft by German soldiers? Or, if not theft, actual destruction? Had Eckhardt believed Italy a safer place for however many masterpieces he could save? Did he have contacts we might never track down? Even so, I couldn't imagine that any place he chose to hide the rescued works came with an ironclad guarantee of safety. What happened, finally, to him and Alfonsa on October 22, 1944, could happen to the masterpieces themselves.

Aertsen, Bellotto, Botticelli, Botticelli, Botticelli, Cano, Caravaggio . . . down, down, down, my eye went. Ghirlandaio, Ghirlandaio, Hals . . . there had to be a couple hundred paintings cataloged, including their locations within the museum. Gallery 27, Gallery B-8, Gallery 105. And then there were the others, the ones with a chip or a discoloring or worse, taken down to the workshop for restoration, stored until the busy conservator could get to them. These were updated on the official listing of the museum's holdings: "Not on View." I clutched the typescript Eckardt had enclosed in his second letter to Alfonsa Cambi and counted.

There were seventeen paintings officially listed as "Not on View." I guessed the Conservation Department kept its own log of the art that had been consigned to its care. Once entered into the log—artist, title, date, size, medium, gallery—the painting was stored. Whatever else got noted on the workshop log, I would never know.

Maybe there was a triage system, in which the most vulnerable works got handled first. Here again, without a lot of research, I had no way of knowing. But I didn't need to know. I jumped up from my table and slipped the carbon copy of page two from Alfonsa's letter to Leon Eckhardt, scouring it for a clue. *So I favor a temporary outdoor cache for these valuables of MMC and VVG until you feel it is safe to go the rest of the way to the Vatican.* What I did want to figure out was, which two paintings had Eckhardt smuggled from the Kaiser-Friedrich Museum and replaced with the clever Alfonsa's forgeries? Which two?

She spoke of a cache and valuables and two sets of initials as though they were upper-class owners of priceless gems. It was really just veiled speech. Oh, Eckardt and Alfonsa needed a hiding place, that was for sure, but the valuables were masterpieces of art. Whose?

I scanned the list slowly, stopping at each entry for "Not on View."

One by one, I eliminated paintings. Only two had the exact combination of initials.

MMC. VVG.

Michelangelo Merisi da Caravaggio.

Vincent van Gogh.

I had to take several deep breaths.

Because it seemed to me, as I shoved aside half the drawn curtain and stared out into the early Tuscan nightfall, that Alfonsa and Leon Eckhardt had hidden two rescued paintings out there somewhere on the grounds of the Villa Orlandini.

Where they had remained for almost eighty years.

My phone trilled. It was Sister Ippolita.

The little ninety-six-year-old nun boomed at me in a way that made me tingle with hope. I didn't know her very well at all, but I could tell she had information to impart. Peering out the window, I regarded a courtyard scene that was normal and low-key, what with Philip Copeland brushing flour from his collar and heading into the dormitory, Rosa

and Sofia both chin-high with clean and folded sheets and
towels, and angling toward the barn room, and Chef stub-
bing out a cigarette with his foot, looking a bit smaller than
he usually does when he's "on."

After we lobbed our hellos and how-are-yous at each
other, Sister Ippolita announced in robust Italian that she
had found just one interesting item recorded by Alfonsa
Cambi in that old convent logbook from 1944.

My heart picked up the beat. "What is it?"

"A burial."

A burial after all. My breath caught in my throat. But if
nuns were buried at the new convent, whoever else Alfonsa
had buried on her own—a dead partisan, a stillbirth, a soldier on one side or the other—or with trusted assistance
from elsewhere, there seemed to be a problem. *Why had
she enter it formally into the logbook?* I put it to Sister
Ippolita. "Why would Alfonsa bury someone on the old
convent grounds, where burials weren't allowed, and then
record it?"

As soon as I heard her gleeful yelp, I knew Sister Ippolita had been waiting for it. "Because," she sang, "it
wasn't a person."

"Then what? A dog?" I was confused.

"Listen!" she told me. "Here is the entry." She cleared
her throat and read aloud. "14 September 1944. Burial of
Holy Objects. Annex. Suor AC."

Oh, Alfonsa, you clever woman. She managed to have it
both ways. Bury something she could legitimately record in
the convent log without arousing suspicion or triggering any
conflict. "Would the Mother Superior have to approve it?"

"Without a doubt."

I chuckled with a picture in my mind of how that bit of
communication might have gone. From Sister Alfonsa, ca-

sually: "Mother, I've come across some missals with torn pages, broken Rosaries, and cruets, and a stained thurible missing a lid . . ." From Mother Superior, concerned: "Oh, yes?" And again from Alfonsa: "Shall I just go ahead and bury them here? It's no trouble."

No trouble at all. Torn missals, beadless Rosaries, cruets missing handles or lips, thuribles . . . According to Sister Ippolita, burial was a way of disposing of ceremonial objects beyond repair. But just going by the information recorded in the log, there was no way of knowing where on all the acreage of the villa property that site could be.

"Sister Ippolita," I put it to her, "where would she have buried holy objects?"

"She didn't tell me," said the nun, "so how would I know?"

In truth, I thought, Alfonsa Cambi wouldn't have mentioned it to anybody. To her, it was a temporary measure, and she had no reason to fear for her life. She had found the outdoor cache she had wanted, and perhaps she banked a little too much on the safety of a religious order. I tried it another way with Sister Ippolita. "But you knew her. Think like her."

"Why is it so important, Signorina?" It's not that she suddenly distrusted me—I think she only wanted me to persuade her that any more effort on her part mattered somehow. But how could I tell her the scope of what I suspected? I couldn't. Not until I checked out the burial site myself.

"All I can tell you, Sister Ippolita, is that I'd like to find that site. Proof will just have to wait." Silence. "You saved her paints. You saved her paintings. All these years. I think you'll want to know what else she was doing with her time."

She sucked in air through her teeth. "Maybe some spot near the chapel. Yes, that would fit. I think she would want holy objects to be buried next to a holy place. Yes."

"Would she think the chapel was safe from bombing?"

Her voice was clipped. "Nothing was safe from bombing. And Sister Alfonsa," she added defensively, "was not a fool."

"All right, then. I'll look around the chapel grounds. Where else?"

A beat. Then, slowly remembering, she went on: "She had an herb garden. I remember her talking about it when she came for meals. In the old days, there would have been one, for medicinal purposes, you understand. But the Orlandinis must have let it go because when Sister Alfonsa took on the caretaker job, she wanted to bring it back."

"What would she have planted?"

"Oh, parsley, oregano, thyme, basil. What we need for sauce."

I frowned. What would be left of those plants after almost eighty years?

"Oh!" cried Sister Ippolita. "And maybe mint. Yes, I think mint."

"For sauce?" I couldn't picture it.

"No, no, no, silly woman. Not for sauce." Her voice was merry. "For everything else!"

"Well, I guess—"

A cry. "It's time for Vespers. I can't talk anymore. Goodbye, goodbye." Then, "Try the kitchen. Somewhere close to the kitchen. Look for a door. That's all."

And with that, she was gone.

*S*unset on the last day of the Copelands' Ziti Variations. I stood, turning slowly, in the empty courtyard, with just the little ocean blue Ape for company. Since the T-Bird was gone, I assumed Chef had gone into town for his meeting with Pete. Copeland Party of Three were all in their rooms resting. Annamaria and Rosa were in the kitchen prepping the final dinner for the Ziti Variations and eye-balling the baking of the *torta contorta* for Mimi's eighti-eth birthday.

When my eyes settled on the stately trees in Pete's Silver Wind Olive Grove, I stood still. Fluttering in the light breeze was the red-and-white Crime Scene tape, so distinct against the subdued landscape, and I headed down to the slope and into the grove. I recalled the scene with Renata and Jason the day before the murder, and then the moment when I found her body. What had once been—and legally still was—Pete's wife.

That terrible child.

Quella strega. That witch.

I drew up short against the place where she had been dumped. For the second time. A pathetic, strangled nomad. And I found myself wondering just how much of her "movements" that night the cops had tracked. I scuffed at the sparse grass where I had rolled right into the dead woman. The ground looked even more wintry than it had just three days ago. I could have been standing on a tree lawn back in Weehawken. In winter, one place looks so much like another. As I untied the tape and began to roll it up like a ball of yarn, I thought about Pete. My heart just plain hurt. Out of his financial troubles, he had mortgaged his beloved olive grove. I found myself wishing he had been franker with me—being what my mother, who has attacks of primness, would call "intimates"—but the fact was, he hadn't. And now he was charged with the murder of what he thought was his ex-wife. Again, not so good with the sharing of information.

I liked what I knew about Pete.

So what if he hid behind a text message to say, "I love you"?

In that moment, I knew myself well enough to say I might have done the same. Oh, yes. He just beat me to it. I crumpled the tape in my hand and held it as tightly as my determination to solve the crime. Once again, I let my mind play with the memory of Renata Vitale and Jason Zale standing at the edge of the grove, surveying the land, their fortunes, the possibilities. Luxury condos. *Revel in your little slice of the timeless beauty of Tuscany!* I could see the pitch, some glossy ad in magazines like *Bellissimo!*

She never had a chance to make her case legally, but I realized I was wrong in thinking they were trespassers. No wonder they looked so majestically comfortable standing there in their survey, like they owned the place. She probably did, either half or whole. If the two of them seemed unconnected to the villa itself, it's because they were. Zale had never been here, and Renata had left it behind twenty years ago. And if she was sneaking around with Pete under the nose of her actual boyfriend, the lovely baking Carlo, would she herself even have spent much time at the Orlandini homestead? No.

Grabbing my phone, I quickly scanned my recent calls and pressed the number. On the other end, a noisy fumble. In his pleasant Italian, Carlo said, "Nell? Are you there? How funny. I just pulled into the driveway . . ."

"The neighborly loaf?"

"You remembered."

"Chef's in town. At the jail."

"Aha, so, Pete, eh?"

"Right. Listen, Carlo"—I gazed at the sky that was losing its color in the dusk. "Who would have moved Renata's body from where you left her?"

"I don't know who."

"Not by name."

"What kind of person? Is that what you mean?"

I pressed on. "Somebody found her in that parking lot and moved her to Pete's olive grove."

"Go on."

"Is that something—and don't take this the wrong way—you would do?"

He took it the wrong way. Loudly. I should have made him promise. I let him rail away, and then told him to cut it out.

"I take it that's a no." Then, "Why wouldn't you?" I started up the hill. We caught sight of each other at the same time, and I watched as Carlo started hoofing it my way with one of his white bakery bags tucked under his arm. His old jacket was unzipped over his white apron.

"Why wouldn't I?" he yelled into the phone, although I could hear him reasonably well anyway. "Because it's the Orlandinis. I know and respect them all. I wouldn't bring that kind of shame on them. Not even Chef, who hurts my pride. He is a legend." What followed was a huffy spate of half-sentence tales about Gianninis and Orlandinis going back, back into the pinging, spritzing mists of Tuscan time to the point you'd think the families were crafting the traditional Etruscan red-colored vessels decorated with geometric designs together.

So, I pondered as I watched Carlo get closer, it was somebody else. Somebody who didn't know the Orlandinis since the days when the firmament pulled together out of the void. No personal connection. But why, then, did this disinterested bystander, who could have driven the dead woman clear out of town and dumped her body somewhere off the highway, bring it to the olive grove instead?

It took someone who didn't know the Orlandinis personally but knew enough on the spot in that awkward moment in the Hotel Italia parking lot to know at least that Renata Vitale had a connection. Dumping the body there pointed to someone who knew the olive grove existed, knew Renata had a claim to it, and knew just where to find it.

Because he had been standing there under Pete's olive trees just the day before.

Jason Zale.

Someone who knew dumping Renata there would divert suspicion from himself.

He was serving up a fine alternative murder suspect—the victim's husband.

"Ciao," said Carlo.

"Ciao."

He eyed the ground the way Stella narrows things down in the truffle zone. "Is this where you rolled into Renata?"

My lips went prim. "Where I discovered the body," I corrected him. "Yes." With an elegant sweep of my forearm, I indicated his former love's third posthumous campground.

At that, Carlo drew in a great breath, pressed his eyes shut, and tilted his head back. "Mm," was all he shared. I felt he was reviewing the little he knew about her life. It seemed respectful. So I forgave him for the cookie reviewer crack two days ago. "I brought the loaf of *pane rustica*," said Carlo without changing position.

"How did it turn out?"

"Good enough for Chef," he said ambiguously.

We smiled. Not so ambiguously.

Without a word, we started back up the hill. "It may interest you to know, Nell," said Carlo, flicking some flour off his apron, "that I met with Joe."

"Joe? You mean Joe Batta?" A first-name basis? How many loaves over how many years did that take? It seemed like a math problem.

"Yes, Joe Batta. And over some whiskey at Sottovoce, we made an exchange."

"Who was buying?"

"I bought one round; he bought one round."

Seemed aboveboard. "What got exchanged?"

At the top of the gentle slope, we stopped next to Carlo's car. "I was able to tell our *commissario* that I discovered Renata's body in the alley behind the bakery at exactly 10:17 p.m."

"Well, I'll bet he was pleased." Narrowing down the time of death, presenting the cops with the accurate crime scene. "What did you get in the exchange?"

With two hands and a stunning smile, Carlo Giannini passed me the bag holding the neighborly loaf. "In the exchange," he said quietly, "the *commissario* told me he wouldn't haul my tattooed ass to the station and charge me with any of two or three counts."

"Is that what he said? How would he know? About the tattoo, I mean." Was there more here than met the eye, so to speak? Unbelievably, I was more interested in this mystifying tidbit than in whether the carabinieri were truly letting him off the hook for his posthumous Renata removal.

Carlo widened his eyes and spread his hands in the world-famous Italian gesture that means, *Who can say?* Finally, as he opened the car door, he offered, "I suspect we have mutual friends." With a little pinch to my upper arm, the man slid quickly behind the wheel.

"*Grazie*, Carlo," was just about all I could say, lifting the loaf.

"*Prego*, Nell."

"What shall I tell Chef?"

He turned the ignition key and sat back, but not for long. "You decide."

"Me?"

Without the least bit of flirting, he said, in English, "It will be perfect."

18

❧

"It was you," I said into the phone in my best j'accuse voice. "Wasn't it?"

"What are you talking about? Who is this?"

"Nell Valenti." I squeezed every last syllable out of my name.

"For your information, I'm sitting on a chair outside Joe Batta's office right now. So I don't need any grief from you."

"You're the only one with a motive for killing Renata—"

He broke in, "I didn't kill her!"

"—who would dump her body on the Orlandinis. None of the Orlandinis would have come across her corpse and put it literally on their own doorstep. It was you." I remembered how he had slipped in his supposed alibi when I ran into him that morning. "Sure you got into your rental car and headed out of town toward the Florence airport, but"— emphasis on the *but*—"you turned around." Brilliance of the third magnitude.

"Plenty of people saw me at the airport," he cried.

"No, Jason, I don't think so. Not until much later." When

he got very quiet, I saw my chance to paint the picture. "How far did you get," I asked him, "before something—passion, anger, or despair—made you turn around and head back to Cortona?" One more chance, was that it? A final, persuasive argument the lawyer in him had to try on Renata. "Did it include hands tightening around her neck?"

"I told you—" He sounded choked up.

"Jason, your alibi is crap. Your only hope of getting Joe Batta to fix you with any kind of a warm Italian eye is for you to make a strong case for your own stupidity. Or haplessness. Give him something he can use." Get specific, Nell. "You say you didn't kill her." In this evening's performance, the parts of both good and bad cop will be played by Nell Valenti. "Then how did it make you feel when you found her?" The test, then, at that precise moment was more a check on Carlo's truthiness than in anything Jason Zale had to offer.

"How did it make me feel? Finding her dead in a heap next to my rental car? All the chances gone to set things straight between us?"

Was he playing for sympathy? I didn't think so. Still . . . "All that may have been your first reaction, Jason—no help from Renata with Rosenberg and Estis, no check from Renata for outstanding wages, no understanding looks, no warm handshake, no hot kisses—"

"Okay, okay," he said through gritted teeth. "I thought there was a chance we could make it up."

"But there she was, strangled and dumped. You two had had a pretty public fight just hours earlier. I heard you. Chances are I wasn't the only one."

His voice rose. "Don't you get it? Someone was making the murder my problem."

It was interesting to me how he assumed the killer knew

one of the two cars in the bookends of Renata's corpse in that hotel parking lot was Jason Zale's rental. Not really likely, but he was shocked enough to see it that way. "How was I supposed to explain our relationship to the cops if they were the ones who found her there? Renata hadn't been in this godforsaken town for twenty years. Who here had any sort of a motive that would boil for that long? It was all on me, me. I was current. I was fresh. I traveled with her. Slept with her. Took care of her business." I heard the shudder in his voice. "Christ," he muttered, "I had to move her."

"So you implicated the Orlandinis."

"It was the only place outside of downtown I could think of."

"And it held the charm of a husband whose motives might outnumber even yours."

"Yes, yes, all of that. Understand I don't have any bad feeling about them. It was more like"—he grasped at the idea—"more like a game of hot potato."

"Hot potato."

"Just get rid of it, get rid of it fast."

I felt an unexpected pang on Renata Vitale's behalf. "You know she wasn't murdered next to your car." I couldn't help adding, "Just to give you a hard time."

A beat. "What?"

"No," I managed, tired to the bone, and I still had a couple of long-buried masterpieces to dig up. "Yours was the second unloading of the inconvenient Renata that night." *Quella strega.* For a dead woman, she really got around.

"Where," he stammered, "where was she killed?"

"Ask Joe Batta. Maybe he'll tell you. But you have to come clean about leaving her in the olive grove." Driving

Miss Deadly, was how I wanted to put it. "I'm out of time, which means you're out of time, too, Jason." I pulled up my sleeve to check my watch. "You're on the clock. I'm giving you fifteen minutes to tell Joe Batta and have him call me back. Otherwise I'm calling him. And I don't think that would be his first choice. You will have to watch him chew candy for a very long time." I took a shot. "Say four to five years."

As Jason Zale started to whine, I ended the call without so much as an *arrivederci*.

And I set the timer on my phone for fifteen minutes.

D usk. Not my favorite time of day. Too early for head-lamps, too late for UV therapy, bugs. To the good, it doesn't last very long, that slide into nightfall, so I picked up the pace in my search along the far side of *la cappella* that had been transformed into the Orlandinis' dining room. Suddenly the interior sprang into light, and on tip-toes, I could see Sofia preparing the room for the Cope-lands' final meal with us—with the crescendo of the *torta contorta* they had learned and prepared that afternoon.

From the interior, the light from the chandeliers and sconces hit the stained glass windows, throwing reds and blues and golds in my grassy path. These were the moments I loved at the Villa Orlandini, these surprising flashes of beauty, that I believed I would never ever find again, else-where. When it came to my soul's baseline on the subject of elsewhere, there were days when I yearned for it and days when I yearned to stop yearning.

Watching Sofia light the ecclesiastical-looking standing candelabras, I tapped on the window. Why should I feel so delighted when she heard me, found me, waved enthusiastically at me like I was the headliner at a rock concert? Then she turned back to work, and I scuffed along more slowly, passing staggered plantings of Russian sage and fire thorn bushes, with their red winter berries. But these plantings looked younger than anything that would have been around back when Sister Alfonsa was caretaking the villa.

Then I came to the angle in the main building where the chapel connects to the kitchen corridor. In an inconspicuous recess was an arched doorway that five hundred years ago was a narrow entrance to the interior of the main building. Over the centuries, nuns had let in providers of produce, cooking supplies, firewood, and help. Here was Sister Alfonsa's nearest exit to what would be a kitchen garden, if she had one.

I came to a stop close to this dogleg, just a dozen feet past the benefit of the chapel lights, and clicked on the flashlight on my phone. It seemed set apart from the rest of the grounds along this far side of the chapel. No window was set into the wall on the kitchen corridor side of the angle. No windows on this long side of the chapel extended this far. Behind me, no paths, no buildings in daily use, no benches for private time, no labyrinths, not much of anything.

The effect right there was one of a funny coincidental kind of total privacy. Here, the more recent plantings stopped. Here, the afternoon sun would give the oregano, parsley, basil, and thyme Sister Ippolita mentioned the four hours they needed. And here, right now, was a plush spread of indestructible mint, because mint is a hardy invader that loves to spread out under the right conditions. I got excited. Now it was dying back from the nights of November frost.

I picked a leaf, pinched it between my fingernails, and tasted. Still flavorful. Eighty years ago, what would this patch look like?

At that moment, my phone trilled. Serafina, telling me Jason Zale had come clean.

I cleared my timer, wondering where Joe Batta stood in the investigation.

Then, crouching, I ran my fingers over the ground covered by mint, wondering just what I was hoping to find. Systematically, I crab-walked across the patch that used to be the kitchen garden of the clever Sister Alfonsa, feeling the ground as though it was some kind of botanical braille. It wasn't until I was just a couple of feet from the stone wall of the main building's angle that my hands touched something . . . different. I spun my phone flash on the spot, pushing aside what was left of the season's mint crop. What I saw made my heart pound.

I put a hand on a naturally flat stone that measured maybe nine by twelve inches and set into the ground just enough to secure its place, but not at all deep otherwise. Affixed to this stone was something remarkable. I turned the flash on it from many directions. It was a "repurposed" piece of silver that had been hammered flat with no small effort, but—here I inspected it closely—which had once been a dome-shaped lid with a pattern of rectangular apertures encircling it. Although metal eyelets remained at its peak, and in two places still visible after the hammering, the chains were missing. It looked unmistakably like the lid of a thurible, an incense burner used during Mass.

Crudely engraved into the flattened silver was a crucifix, and below that, in what had to be Sister Alfonsa Cambi's hand, were the words *Oggetti Sacri*. Holy Objects. Nothing more. No embellishments like, "Here Lie Holy Objects," no justifications like, "Damaged Holy Objects." For a few moments, I stared, falling forward onto my knees, taking it in. What lay below, in a grave meant to be the temporary outdoor cache she trusted for those masterpieces, was just a couple of feet beneath me. I could hardly catch my breath. I needed a shovel. Tonight, at the very least, I could start—

"Nell?" came a quiet voice. I whirled. In the near darkness, I could see it was Muffy Onderdonk, standing a few feet off. Almost imperceptibly, I shifted just enough to block her line of vision. "What are you doing?"

"Picking the last of the mint. For tea later." To make it true, I pinched off a couple of twigs.

She nodded, then brightened, her small face lively under her signature purple hat. "Rosa sent me to get you. There's antipasto set out in the common room."

"How's Mimi?" I stood up, brushing off my pants legs.

"Good. Every inch the birthday girl."

"Class will out."

We started walking. "In her case," said Mimi, "it's already out." As we approached the line of stained glass windows in the long wall of the chapel, Mimi, Philip, and Annamaria were inside chatting, looking reasonably happy and rested. They watched us make our way along, possibly wondering what I was doing outside alone in a deserted spot on the grounds, waiting for Muffy and me so the birthday party could start.

Later, I'd return with a shovel and a headlamp.

Or I could get a good night's sleep and tackle the Holy Objects grave in the morning. Cold light of day, a good breakfast, and two cups of dark roast onboard, that's what made sense.

No, later I'd return with a shovel and a headlamp.

* * *

*A*nnamaria had prepared a dinner that I'll always remember became an occasion.

It wasn't so much her scallop carpaccio appetizer, served with Pete's Moraiolo olive sorbet, although the scallops alone—for me—would have been enough. But it was followed up by her chicken skewers with peanut sauce, a bold dash into new Italian cuisine that Chef would have tried very hard to talk her out of had he been around and not conferring with Pete down at the jail.

The fact that he savored everything she set in front of him showed me—and not the Copeland Party of Three, I hoped—just how tired he was of Ziti Fest. If you whip up anything in the kitchen that includes black-and-white sesame seeds, sesame oil, sake, and soy sauce, Chef flings stricken looks like he's just taken a nap and woken up in— Jesus, Mary, and Joseph—Tokyo. The single *contorno*— side dish—Annamaria served was her fresh fig salad seasoned with unlikely plate fellows: fresh marjoram and red chili peppers.

Annamaria had kept her menu light for this final dinner together before the Copelands left tomorrow after lunch, easing on down the road in their Rolls Phantom. I would miss them. A Duke Ellington playlist colored the air around the table in a delicious loop of his signature bounce and muscularity. As I sipped my white wine—Rosa had presented the table with five bottles of Le Macchiole's Paleo from the villa wine cellar—I glanced around the table.

That dinner, that evening, that company, those bursts of lights, every part of the scene drew all of us into a common experience. Each face shone. Each voice held a funny story. Eighty-year-old eyes sparkled. Seventy-year-old hands worked to keep wineglasses topped off. My own thirty-year-old heart—what could I contribute?

Finally, out came the *torta contorta* the Copelands had made that afternoon, served on a thin slab of genuine agate stone, which Sofia set in front of Mimi Copeland.

"My ziti cake!" she cried, delighted. She added, "You remembered!"

A few of us exchanged glances. She herself had rolled out dough, boiled the ziti, grated the chocolate, and had a joyful time doing it, from what I could tell. And now, for Mimi, this special birthday dessert Sofia had expertly set in front of her was something totally new.

The torta had been sprung from its springform, and the pastry dough that contained the ziti sweetened with grated chocolate and nuts made the *torta contorta* look like an edible gift. The confectioner's sugar dusting across the top was white and even, but instead of a smattering of unruly berries, the class had chosen slices of kiwi and dragon fruit laid out in concentric circles. Arranged at the very center were silver, block-letter candles LXXX. At a quizzical look from Mimi, Annamaria lighted them and explained, "Your birthday candles, signora. In Roman numerals."

Mimi roared, grabbed Muffy, and then quipped to the group, "Good use of limited space." As we laughed, Mimi blew out her two candles, then drove the cake knife into the torta. The singing of "Happy Birthday" was robust, some in Italian, some in English. Philip and Muffy kept their eyes on her as Rosa leaned in to catch each slice wherever it might fall. When I reached for the dessert plate she was handing me, my phone vibrated against my thigh.

I set down my slice of birthday ziti cake, pushed my chair back, and glanced down at my phone. A New York exchange. *"Scusi,"* I murmured to the others—no one appeared to care—and slipped out into the hall and answered the call.

"Hello," said the woman's voice. "Is this Nell?"

"It is. Sylvette?" I felt a little frisson of expectation.

"I got that name for you"—she went on happily—"from the Christie's assistant who handled the sale of Uncle Leon's collection."

Despite the wonderful dinner, I suddenly felt hungry, so close to knowing how one important part of Leon Eckhardt and Alfonsa Cambi's story ends. Where paintings, posters—and the original of Alfonsa's page two—landed. "I'm listening," I said.

"The buyer of that lot," she said, turning off a shrill tea kettle in the background, "was a Philip Copeland."

I didn't know what any of it meant. My first move was to walk on shaky legs to the end of the corridor and—hoping to clear the brain fog—step outside into the cold air. No jacket, no slice of *torta contorta*, no clarity. What good is winter if it doesn't power-wash your brain? For one shivering minute, all I could conclude was that it's a weird coincidence. Philip Copeland showed up here for a four-day ziti workshop, mom and bestie in tow. Not all that long ago, Philip Copeland bought Christie's Lot #37, the posters and paintings collection—and relevant miscellany—of Leon Eckhardt.

Strange coincidence! Weird stuff! Part of me wanted to charge back into the dining room, brightly lit with wine, cake, and "I'm Beginning to See the Light," and slap Copeland on the back and say, "You wanna hear a crazy coincidence?" Everyone will listen, make spooky noises, and have more wine. Or I could not say a thing. Let sleeping coincidences lie. The joys of brain fog. Drink up.

I slipped back inside to the main corridor, where I leaned against the wall. If I switched the order of things, I saw them in a way that led to a dull thudding in my chest. I let everything extraneous in the events fall away, like torta crumbs to the floor. Philip Copeland bought Leon Eckhardt's art collection, and now he'd come to the Villa Orlandini, where Leon Eckhardt and his coconspirator in Robin Hood art theft died. What, I asked myself with my eyes pressed shut, was the first thing I wanted to know? In three seconds flat, I had my answer: Is there a connection? A cause and effect?

In all fairness, and weak knees aside, I couldn't say. But one thing I did know for sure: if there was a connection, Philip Copeland was keeping it entirely to himself. The man had paid $75,000 to the Villa Orlandini Cooking School for the exclusive rights to a workshop chosen to please his ziti-loving mother. Was it all a blind? What else—without our even knowing it—did that kind of cash outlay guarantee him? Were all three of them in it together, whatever "it" was? I didn't like it. I didn't like any of it. Suddenly everyone seemed suspect to me. Of what, I had no idea, but my fallback is always to get more information. A quick glance at my watch—8:14. If I could get rid of the Copelands for an hour or two, I could put in some productive time on my laptop—but in the abbess's room, where I could get more privacy.

When I returned to the table, everyone was warbling about the *torta contorta*. Talk about blinds, it came at just the right time. Instead of giving everyone the fisheye—*All right, Mimi, if that's your real name, who was the Grand National champion horse in 1987?*—I was able to dig into the chocolate, almond, vanilla, walnut, sweet pasta treat and keep my disorganized thoughts to myself. I made good time to the espresso, smacked my lips only just a little, and addressed the Copeland Party of Three. "And this evening?" I widened my eyes at Mimi, Muffy, and Philip, as all ten of my fingers held my demitasse cup poised at my lips.

"As yet undecided," said Philip. "Possibly a return to Arlecchino . . . ?" He shot his mother and Muffy a look.

Mimi mused. "Arlecchino."

"Dance club." Muffy tipped her off. "But it's karaoke night at the Globe."

"Oh, I'll do 'Dancing Queen,'" breathed Mimi. It must be her signature song.

"Will you come, Nell?"

"I'll try," I said, "but no promises. I've got some work to do."

Philip turned. "Chef? Annamaria?"

In effusive Italian, Chef said something along the lines of "Only if I can join Mimi in 'Dancing Queen.'" Even Annamaria found it funny, and the non-Italian speakers thought it must be something funny because it was Chef who said it. With a nearly imperceptible look at me, Annamaria was measuring just how desperately I wanted to be alone. I gave her a smile and tipped my head in the direction of the others. With that, Annamaria accepted the invitation to join the little party. I was grateful to her for going and for taking Chef with her. The issue of Rosa and Sofia sprang up. Could they come? But who would stay back and clean up?

"Go, go, go!" sang out Rosa.

"We come if we finish, *sta bene*?" explained Sofia, beaming. "And we bring Nella!"

For some odd reason, that seemed to persuade everyone that the plan was sound.

I poured myself a large glass of seltzer water, tugged on

my jacket, and hotfooted it down the path to my room. All I really wanted to do with the night was play grave robber, but I wanted some fast answers about Philip Copeland and whatever he had in mind that he was keeping very much to himself. I locked my door, drew the shades, and booted up my Mac.

But holding back the shades with the backs of my fingers, I kept a stealthy watch for fifteen minutes on what I could see of the courtyard, counting heads as the merrymakers sorted themselves out for the evening's romp. Some piled into the Rolls, some into the T-Bird. One car would have held the five of them, but they were taking two—more flexibility, I guessed, more room to spread out. Maybe they were splitting up—if either Chef or Mimi Copeland was having second thoughts about "Dancing Queen," my money was on Mimi. Slammed doors, low-pitched rumbles, swinging headlights, gone.

I sat at the laptop and googled Philip Copeland. The first few hits were for the Philip B. Copeland Foundation. Going back to 2002, grants to community health organizations in Africa, grants to environmental organizations in Indonesia, grants to educational institutions for women in Afghanistan. Then, two years ago, came a piece in the *Wall Street Journal*, noting:

> In an unusual move, the Philip B. Copeland Foundation
> has departed from its traditional focus on environment,
> health, and social justice, to fund an exhibition at
> the Met. Reached by phone, the notoriously reclusive
> PBC, as he's called in nonprofit circles, explains
> that he views the new focus on arts organizations as
> really still about environment, community health, and
> social justice.

Talk about a *torta contorta*. I snorted. His explanation was a twisted cake if ever I heard one. Aside from that piece, nothing was jumping out at me.

I chugged some seltzer water.

I didn't have far to scan when I hit upon what had to be the big tragedy in Mimi Copeland's life. The accidental death of her son William. First came a piece from the August 21 issue of the *Southampton News*.

> Rough Seas Claim Life of Yachtsman. Coast Guard investigators said the eight-foot waves caused the capsize that knocked a man into the Long Island Sound. William Copeland, expert yachtsman, was thrown into the turbulent water during the storm. Copeland, forty-seven, was an international businessman.

There wasn't much more, just a squib about particular caution necessary during the summer storm season, speculation that William Copeland wasn't wearing a flotation device, and shock from fellow members at the Southampton Yacht Club. "And poor Bill had just moved back to the States after a dozen years!" said one club member.

In the next issue of the *Southampton News* came the obituary for the dead William. The picture chosen by the family was nearly a decade old, a black-and-white pretty photo of what looked like the landscape of one of the Greek islands, the whitewashed houses climbing the hills, away from the Aegean, which I could only guess was shockingly blue. In a three-quarter shot, William was turned toward the tranquil sea, with what looked like light brown hair, average build, average height, left hand apparently shading his eyes as he gazed. He had a compact grace that must have been appealing.

The obituary was brief, as though whoever put it together had used a template. Five minutes on the phone with a family member would have furnished the few facts. Age, cause, date of death, date and place of birth, parents' names, schools, major, hobbies, career, private burial.

William Atwill Copeland, forty-seven, of New York City, died August 21, 2019, in a boating accident in Long Island Sound.

Mr. Copeland was born July 24, 1972, in Chappaqua, New York, to Simon Astor and Mimi (Atwill) Copeland.

He attended the Taft School in Watertown, Connecticut. He continued his education at Lafayette College in Easton, Pennsylvania, graduating in 1993 with a bachelor's degree in cultural studies.

He enjoyed boating, traveling, horse racing, and high-stakes poker. An entrepreneur, at the time of his death, he was CEO of Imago Ltd., an international import firm of photographic equipment.

He is survived by his mother, Mimi Copeland, and brother Philip Copeland of Manhattan.

He was preceded in death by his father, Simon Astor Copeland.

No service will be held. Arrangements are private.

I felt a swift sweep of disbelief, even sadness, for the expert yachtsman who had gazed so familiarly at that raw blue Aegean Sea with only a decade left to his life. In the obit, where there was a chance to elaborate on the dead William Copeland, there was just a pathetic lack of specifics. Did nobody really know him? Was he not at all close to Mimi or Philip? Or was his work "history" a blind, really, for the younger Copeland, and was he a trust fund baby, or a globe-trotting bum?

I wondered suddenly if Mimi Copeland's trouble that day on the boat tour of Lake Trasimeno was because the sight of her son Philip on a boat brought back all the pain of the day the brothers capsized on Long Island Sound. Two went out; one came back. And maybe even without being able to articulate her fears, Mimi couldn't risk the one son she had left. The boat tour was cut short, and the Copeland Party of Three—still three—headed back to the Villa Orlandini.

Finishing my seltzer, I heaved a sigh and checked my watch. I had spent almost an hour on a Google hunt and didn't feel any further along. Philip Copeland bought Leon Eckhardt's collection at auction, and three days ago, he showed up at the villa. Why here, why now? I still didn't have the connection. On an impulse, I dragged out Sister Alfonsa's paint box from under the bed, set it quickly on the table, opened it, and lifted out the false bottom. My eyes settled on the carbon of page two of her letter to Leon Eckhardt.

Very likely what I was reading had also been read by Philip Copeland in the original.

I didn't have to look far.

19

There, in the very first line was a clue: "2/ place, I favor beneath the statue of Veronica, but it is likely to undergo repairs in the next few years, and so we take a risk." The crumbling statue of St. Veronica was a kind of landmark. Something that narrowed down the whereabouts of masterpieces rescued by Eckhardt and Alfonsa. If this letter had put Philip Copeland wise about their two-person operation in the last year of the war, he was on the same hunt that I was.

Wherever the Caravaggio and Van Gogh had been hidden, there was a statue of St. Veronica. That's all he could know for sure. From Eckhardt's things in the Berlin collection, Copeland could put together facts about the Swiss conservator's work life and periodic trips to Tuscany. He could draw the same conclusions I did about the bold plan to substitute forgeries for authentic priceless paintings hidden for their protection. But—here I was struck by what now seemed powerfully obvious—he couldn't pinpoint exactly where those treasures were.

Somewhere in Italy, somewhere with a statue of Veronica, but where? All he or anyone would be able to infer was that it was somewhere north of the Vatican, because nothing else made sense. From the correspondence between Alfonsa and Leon, no mention had even been made of her being a member of a religious order, so there was no way to narrow down the possibilities.

Philip Copeland could undertake some time-consuming and massive research plan to locate a Veronica statue anywhere at all—scouring the Italian landscape across villas, public parks, government buildings, universities, museum grounds, funky little forests and preserves—but even then he couldn't be guaranteed success. For it seemed entirely possible that whatever was crumbling in 1944 was downright unidentifiable rubble in 2019. Worse yet, if unwanted or irreparable, gone altogether. Cleaned up, toted away, its shards worked into patio pots around the neighborhood.

There was, I could see, nothing he could do.

Until now. When something had made the difference.

But, what?

Carefully, I set the false bottom of the paint box back into place, secured the lid, and gently shoved the box back under the bed. For some reason, that Nell Valenti urge to indulge in a reality check, never particularly welcome, made me sit back on my heels. Was I wantonly flinging myself at conclusions that I couldn't really support? I thought about the Philip Copeland, who had—at great trouble and expense—arranged to treat his aging, ailing mother and her bestie to four days of cooking at a villa in Tuscany.

The man had serious chops. An impressive history of philanthropy. Business success at a stratospheric level, even for New York, that spoke to his talents. A known, true attachment to his mother. The Yale Club and a well-ordered life in which he either harbored no vices or had enough respect for himself and others that he worked hard to keep them from public view.

From the little I knew of him, the man had no responsibilities he was shirking. No wife, either present or ex, no kids. If anything, as odd as it was to say, there was something a little odd in its downright clean-and-tidiness. Maybe designer Rolls and clothes pointed to a controlled taste for luxury. All that dropping at least a hundred grand, when he paid for three first-class tickets on Alitalia, plus our fees, proved was that he could. Secret drinker? Not that I could see. Philip B. Copeland's drink was single malt scotch, he could indulge himself in the best wherever he sat down, but whenever I was with him, it was a hobby of taste, not a habit.

Why would a man with stature, seemingly endless means, and no demons worth a damn, be on a kind of treasure hunt here, now?

Very slowly, I pushed back my Mac and finished drinking my seltzer. All the time in the world. No time to lose. Which was true? I couldn't tell. *Don't I know you?* was all I could hear, cascading over and over, making the inside of my head an echo chamber. Those drinks at Sottovoce, the day the Copelands arrived for Ziti Variations, when Renata had stopped at our table on her way out, with Carlo in tow. I think we had all thought it was a pickup cliché, more a conversation starter than a truth. *Don't I know you?* Not quite it, because Renata Vitale would have prettied it up, but close.

Suddenly I realized I was so wrapped up in the mysteries around the Holy Objects grave that I hadn't exhausted the envelope the munificent Serafina—I couldn't quite tell whether she was after Pete or me—had made available to

me. Whatever trance I had fallen into was gone. Grabbing
the envelope, I shook out Renata's phone, passcode generously disabled by Joe Batta's crew. It was the craven Jason
(Bodies Moved While-U-Wait) Zale who had told me that
Renata kept her really important dates in her phone. Anything more public, more likely to become more public, she
wrote down in the day planner. Or had Jason do it.

I stared at it, which didn't get me far, and then I swiped.
Clicked on her Notes app—quick recipes, words to look up,
inspirational quotes (she could have used more of them).
Back to the Home screen, and down to the dock, where I
clicked on her Calendar. It opened up into November, and
I tapped the day the Copelands arrived at the villa and Renata Vitale had oozed up to our table at Sottovoce. She had
noted appointments tersely:

> **11 a.m.**—City Hall, deed.
> **12 noon**—Ernando Coletti, Intesa Sanp. [A quick
> search—the bank]
> **1–3**—JZ, strat sess [Strategy session? Could take at
> least two hours.]
> **5**—CG, try. [What? Carlo's patience? Feel him out?
> Feel him up? See if he can be a new shark in her
> tank?]

Nothing specifically on drinks at Sottovoce, where she
said to Philip Copeland, *Haven't we met?* That was it exactly. And as pleasant as she came across, there was something a lot more pointed about those precise words than if
she'd just asked, *Don't I know you?* Nothing was down in
her phone's calendar for later the same night. I clicked on
the next day, and there it was. Bright and early:

7 a.m.—Re PC, check A4HS last By the Sea guest list.

Below the 7 a.m. reminder about the guest list, but without a specific time, Renata had typed, **Obit obit obit!** Underlined three times, in red ink, not the blue of the previous entry. Then: **News story same week, maybe two, either side.** Either side of what? Renata's notes were her own shorthand, but from her 7 a.m. entry about checking the gala's guest list and the red ink entry, I could tell she'd moved on to a new and separate reminder, hastily scribbled, to herself.

Scanning the files in her Finder, I hit paydirt: By the Sea gala guest list, dated a year ago. Centered at the top of the first page was the logo of Art for Heart's Sake, and underneath ran **By the Sea gala, The Pavilion at Port Jefferson, Long Island.** Now, why did Port Jefferson sound familiar? When Renata seemed to recall meeting him at the gala, Philip Copeland told her he hadn't been there. Scanning the guest list, which ran three pages, he was right.

But Renata Vitale narrowed her golden brown eyes at him. And looked thoughtful.

What had she seen in those last couple of minutes before she dropped off a couple of business cards, collected Carlo, and departed?

I needed fresh air.

Plus a headlamp.

Plus a shovel. And I'd have to work fast, before the Copelands returned. Before I'd even pressed the spade into the soil, my hands had begun to shake. I was digging up two paintings that had been "Not on View" for nearly eighty years. And all I felt was fear. Slipping Renata's phone back into Serafina's envelope, I slipped it into Alfonsa's paint box under the bed. Then, from the nightstand, I grabbed my Petzl headlamp, crowned myself with it, and flicked the On switch. Off went the table lamps, on went the front door lock, and out I went into the strange vast stillness of the November night.

Trotting to the part of the barn that had been preserved as a tool shed, I slid off the lock that was never locked and stepped inside. From the rack of shovels built into the old barn wall, I chose one that looked light enough that I could use it, yet big enough for grave robbing detail. Back in the courtyard, I stood motionless for a moment, just listening. No car sounds out on the roadway, no wintering night birds in bare branches. If Rosa and Sofia were still cleaning up in the kitchen, I couldn't hear them. Maybe they had finished up and left.

One of them had left a couple of dim sconce lights on in the chapel, and the low light reaching through the stained glass window scenes felt friendly. Gripping the shovel in my hand, I tramped around to the far side of the chapel, wondering still about Renata Vitale's calendar memo and whether I should have replaced the battery in my headlamp.

At the dogleg between the chapel and the kitchen corridor, I sniffed the air in the darkness that felt like the first darkness of all time. Full of shape and mass. Like solid geometry. Mint. Faint, faint, but still there, like a memory. I eyeballed the stone marker with Alfonsa's engraving of Holy Objects on it and broke ground about a foot away from it.

The soil felt hard but not frozen, making my job easier. I worked quickly, spading the burial site, wishing I could save some of the mint that had screened it from view over all these years. From a quick glance in Wikipedia, I learned that the Caravaggio painting—if my guess was correct—

was his *St. Matthew and the Angel*, and it measured six by nine feet. Not a miniature. The Van Gogh, *The Painter on His Way to Work*, was much smaller, measuring seventeen by eighteen inches.

From her page two carbon, I was convinced Sister Alfonsa had made a temporary—which I was hoping meant shallow—grave. But in the nearly eighty Tuscan winters that had passed, I could only hope she had buried these masterpieces below the frost line. After half an hour of spade work, I had pretty much staked out the dimensions of the Caravaggio, starting to sweat in the cold, in fear that with the very next spadeful, I could damage the beautiful painting. If these paintings had survived the elements after all these years only to be done in by Nell Valenti, I think I'd just have to step into the grave and pull the dirt in over me.

How would Alfonsa have wrapped these treasures? As I dug, picturing the parading images of coffins, footlockers, oilcloth sacks, the night seemed to enclose me in a box of my own fear. When it seemed like a good idea to dig deep in one small area, just to be able to determine how far down I had to go before making contact with something other than small roots, rocks, and clumps of earth, I focused the grave robbing on an area that measured maybe two square feet. My knees were shaking, my headlamp was dimming, and pretty soon, I couldn't tell the difference between the body heat from hard work and the cold from November in Tuscany.

Finally, two things happened nearly at once. Sinking a little over a foot into the hole I was making, my spade hit something that felt like cloth. Oh, not cloth, Alfonsa, not *cloth*. What kind of protection is that? I pulled up on the spade. My fear for the paintings, then, was so acute I pressed my eyes shut. Which may explain why I didn't hear the voice when it came to me out of the dark.

"I really have to thank you."

With a quick gasp, I opened my eyes. Philip Copeland stood just a few feet away from me. I don't think in all of my thirty years I had ever found myself in what anyone would call a movie moment, until then, that night, and there, out of the range of the friendly dim lights of the chapel. It was a scene from every movie I never wanted to see, no matter how tasty the popcorn, because why let myself in for that kind of terror? As I tried to say something, and the only thing that got barely uttered was, "Why—why aren't you with the rest of the ziti lovers?" I understood something, at last, about terror. In real life, it's never something we do to ourselves.

He went on, waving his gloved hand, which was when I realized it held a revolver. I refused to stare at it. It took all my might—what was left of it after an hour of digging. "I was beginning to think," he said, coming one step closer, "you weren't going to prove useful after all. That I'd have to send all of you"—his golden brown eyes widened in disbelief—"on a thank-you cruise just to get the place to myself." He stretched his back, his unbuttoned coat falling open, the white shirt like a flash of truth.

"That," he said softly, "would have been better for you, obviously." He waited for us both to enjoy the joke, but it didn't happen. Then, "But this way, with your industry and determination, Nell, you can see it's better for me. After all"—his voice dropped, his shaved and gleaming head tilted—"I've waited for quite some time." This he spoke in a way that little boys whine to their parents—*Well, why can't I have a puppy?* For one moment, his gaze drifted, but the revolver moved higher. "All I had to go on from Eckhardt's stuff was a statue of St. Veronica." His shoulders shook with weary laughter. "Somewhere in Italy."

"No way of knowing," I put in, just to hold up my end of things.

"No way of knowing, indeed." He sighed and moved his head in a large swing from left to right. "I see you understand." Then he came back to the moment, poised to spring, to fire, to dig—I couldn't say what. He grinned. "Until one day, showing up in the stack of mail at the office, was . . . *Bellissimo!*"

I felt breathless. "The cover photo." Pete, handsome and strong by his olive trees, and in the background . . . the tumbledown fountain and a statue of St. Veronica.

His expression changed. As he raised his gun hand, he said through lips that barely moved, "I can take it from here."

I had to stall, but I had nothing to say. My paltry thirty years of life had rolled into that minute, and all I wanted was to spring Pete from jail, have Annamaria fix me some toast, and learn to tango. I was angry. "You can't keep killing us all," I yelled, realizing I would now never know why Renata Vitale was strangled.

"I would have thought so, too, Nell, but it's really been working out so well."

Just as I held my breath, all out of backchat, another voice came out of the dark, sharp and clear. "Philip!"

As Philip Copeland turned and fired, I stepped into a forehand I had never achieved on a tennis court, swung the shovel swift and sure, hardly slowing when I struck the back of his wretched skull, and he fell forward—either out cold or dead, and I didn't care which.

20

In the eight hours that followed, I made peace with surprise.

First, Muffy Onderdonk slapped handcuffs on the unconscious Philip Copeland. When I fixed her with disbelieving eyes, she turned modest. "I may wear purple hats," she said, "but"—she gave a sweet little yank to the handcuffs—"I know a real fashion accessory when I see one."

Next, Annamaria made me toast. Topped with pistachio-rose butter. At midnight.

Joe Batta carted off his new best murder suspect. A German tourist could place Copeland in the alley behind the bakery at the right time, and the Slovenian clerk at the *tabacchi* shop sold him the burner phone. A dim-witted thug in Arezzo, happy to be of help to the illustrious Commissario Batta, sold the Americano the revolver *"quel giorno stesso!"* That very day.

A team from the Uffizi Gallery was on its way to recover the paintings.

A team from the Vatican Museums was on its way to recover the paintings.

A team from the Bode Museum, formerly the Kaiser-Friedrich, was on its way to recover the paintings.

As the husband of Renata Vitale, Pete was the heir to the block of shops on Piazza della Repubblica that housed Carlo's bakery. No one expected a rent increase.

Mimi Copeland, back from karaoke night, witnessed her son being manhandled into the black Fiat of the carabinieri. "What did that poor fellow do?" She turned sad, anxious eyes to Muffy, who could only squeeze her arm.

Nell Valenti left them all, walked silently back to her room, and fell asleep in her clothes. But I was up early, and staring at myself in the bathroom mirror as I brushed my teeth, I suddenly made a connection. I knew where I had seen "Port Jefferson" before. Without so much as rinsing my mouth, I dashed to Renata's phone, and went to work.

*A*n hour later, when the Tuscan sun was edging its way above the horizon, Muffy Onderdonk left Mimi asleep in their barn room and joined the rest of us on high stools that Rosa had set around the worktable where, just yesterday, the Copeland Party of Three had rolled out their dough for *torta contorta*, the closest Chef Claudio Orlandini could get to a sweet ziti cake. Sofia set out fresh plum cakes, Chef set out his famous *panini con l'uva*, raisin buns, which only ever make a rare appearance in his kitchen. Annamaria kept refreshing my coffee and patting my arm, and Rosa, who apparently believed we needed more culinary distance from the present macabre awfulness, went clear back to the days of the Etruscans and served up a porridge of milk and farro.

The floor was Muffy's. In flawless Italian, she described

how her office in the Department of Commerce—the Artifacts Authentication Agency—had been on the trail of Copeland for a few years. A few shady deals in the secondary art market seemed to point to him—those frequent trips to Europe—but in his public life, he seemed generous and above reproach, as though he could never be involved in anything shady, that the agency just kept a watchful eye.

"Mimi Copeland and I *had* lost touch for many years," said Muffy, plucking the raisins from her bun and setting them in a half ring on her plate.

Chef went very still.

"But when I learned she had been diagnosed with dementia, and within a year William died in the boating accident, I felt sick with nerves for her. It smelled like a setup. William, a gambler and spendthrift extraordinaire, was due to inherit half the Copeland estate. The second-best child, Philip, must have found it particularly galling that golden boy William, who did nothing to deserve the love of Mimi, who wasn't able to see him for what he was, would inherit and no doubt squander a fortune."

So Muffy Onderdonk came out of retirement, reentered Mimi Copeland's life, and moved into 350 West End, where she could keep an eye on her old friend. "The drowning death was ruled an accident."

Everyone nodded. More coffee. Quartered pomegranates. Plum cakes.

Muffy pressed her lips together. "And then, after William's death, Philip came across a lot his brother had bought at auction from Christie's."

"Leon Eckhardt's personal art collection."

"Propaganda posters from World War II, a few small paintings he saved from Nazi fires, art-related letters, logs, documents."

I saw it. "He figured out the secret rescue of paintings from Berlin."

Muffy nodded. "And finally"—she breathed—"Philip Copeland had found something worth killing for."

Into the short silence that followed, while her terrible point sank in, Chef asked whether he had been too stingy with the sugar.

"No, no," muttered Annamaria with a wave of her hand, knowing he was easily reassured.

Then Muffy explained to Chef and the Bari sisters how Copeland had narrowed his search to the villa grounds.

A thought struck me. "The architectural plans exhibition at the Met."

Muffy smiled. "Real enough."

"He seemed so keen."

She snorted. "He was. Get you interested, and you wouldn't give it a second thought if he was prowling around the grounds all day long."

"To take pictures, he said. But really—"

"To try to locate the hiding place of the Caravaggio and the Van Gogh."

"But the villa plans really got accepted into the exhibition?"

"I believe so. Up to you if you want to stay."

I scanned the table for a consensus. "We're in."

Muffy nodded once. "A nice opportunity for the cooking school."

I moved on. Taking a big breath, I asked, "Last night?"

"So easy, really. He must have known how close you were. All the rest of us went to the Globe, but Philip, who said he was going back to Arlecchino, really came back here." We caught each other's eye. In her expression, I could tell she knew how close I had come to dying. "I left

Mimi at the Globe singing 'Dancing Queen,' in Chef and Annamaria's good hands, parked up the road, and waited."

While she talked, all six of us dug hungrily into our milk and farro, spoons clicking against the bowls. Annamaria gently pushed a nutmeg grinder toward me, and I cranked it over my porridge.

Dabbing my lips, I had to ask. *"Quella strega?"*

Muffy took in a big breath. "Renata Vitale. Just her bad luck to be a New Yorker. I believe she recognized him"—she raised a cautionary finger—"partly. Do you remember the cocktails at Sottovoce, when she came up to our table and asked Philip Copeland if they'd met?"

I nodded. "She thought it was at the By the Sea gala on Long Island."

"I got the address of the cottage Renata was renting on Pirate's Cove."

I knew where she was headed. "In Port Jefferson." It was Renata's red-inked note to herself, after all, that steered me in the right direction. I checked newspapers from a couple of weeks on either side of the By the Sea gala, and there it was: the story on the drowning death of expert yachtsman William Copeland. Off Pirate's Cove in Port Jefferson, Long Island.

"Oh"—Muffy went on airily—"she recognized him, all right. It was Port Jefferson, but not the gala. Renata Vitale didn't put it together until later."

Annamaria piped up. "Then what? What did *la strega* see?"

Muffy folded her hands, which she then studied for a long moment. "I believe she saw Philip Copeland on the beach." She looked up at us. "Where he had just come from killing his brother, William."

"How do you know?"

She let out a sharp laugh. "I'm guessing he was wet." She reached for a plum cake. "Having just swum away from the boat." After a nibble, Muffy went on. "Google street view puts the cottage close to the water. He never knew anyone was there."

I put it together slowly. "So, at Sottovoce, when she tried to figure out where she knew him from, and she mentioned the gala in Port Jefferson—"

"He had to kill her. He couldn't take the chance. Either she'd expose him or blackmail him, and neither option appealed."

Chef narrowed his eyes. "Maybe cops get it out of him, eh?"

The ever-practical Rosa folded her arms. In her direct way, she even tried some English. "What happen Mimi now?" Rosa bit her lip, then went on. "She lose both her sons."

Sniffing, Chef leaped away from the table to scrounge around for a tissue.

Sofia looked like a guest had just complained of bedbugs.

Annamaria was listening hard.

Muffy deflated a little bit. "Very tough. I don't know what to expect. Will she lose ground? Will she absorb it?" Then, with a bright smile, Muffy Onderdonk looked around the table in the warm, safe kitchen of the Villa Orlandini Cooking School, and said, "But she'll have me."

Rosa pointed. "You not move?"

"From 305 West End?" She shook her gray head. "Oh, no, it's a fine place for a retiree from the DOC. And besides," she added with a catch in her voice, "my best friend lives there."

Although Chef, Rosa, Sofia, and even Annamaria each

offered to drive Muffy and Mimi in the Rolls Phantom to the Florence airport, Muffy declined sweetly. I could tell she wanted the return trip—to the airport, to JFK, to the Upper West Side—to begin here in the villa courtyard with just the two of them. There were important conversations in store for Mimi Copeland. And when we tried to persuade them to stay an extra day, although maybe now with no more ziti, Muffy thought it was best to stick to the original plan. Mimi would expect it.

Two hours later, after Rosa had opened the doors to the Rolls, we hugged Muffy and Mimi. Annamaria fussed with Muffy's purple hat, trying a jauntier angle, and I gently pushed back a springy white lock of Mimi's wavy hair, and Chef loaded their suitcases into the trunk. Muffy stepped back from the passenger side door and waited for Mimi to say her goodbyes.

"Grazie, grazie, tutti!" she exclaimed, shifting gracefully on her feet as she blew us all kisses. Then, as an aside to her best friend: "Where's my William?" She caught herself. "I mean Philip?"

A beat. The rest of us held our breath. "He's staying behind. There are some things he has to take care of."

"So like him," she murmured proudly. "So responsible." She began to slide onto the luxurious leather seat. "Will he be a while?"

Muffy shot me a stunned look, then nodded fondly at her friend. "Yes, Meems, Philip will be a while."

Say, the rest of his natural-born days.

With a catch in her voice, Mimi stiff-armed the door Muffy was trying to close and commented, "Then we'd best not wait." In the face she turned to her best friend, I saw Mimi Atwill, Wellesley grad, debutante, one of the

New York 400, better in every way than the world that went on to trap her. Very clearly, she asked, "Who's left?"

Muffy straightened up. "I am."

"Muffaletta," said her friend softly.

They looked at each other with understanding. Then Muffy shut the door and walked around to the driver's side. It was a small nod she gave me, and as they set off down the driveway, our lineup of Chef, Baris aplenty, and one Nell Valenti broke up, moving aimlessly apart. I found myself longing to hear her do "Dancing Queen" while feeling pretty sure that last night at the Globe in Cortona, Italy, would have been my only chance.

Once the Rolls was out of sight, I squared my shoulders, noticed there was an absence of mist, let myself into the T-Bird, and went to pick up Pete at the carabinieri HQ in town—where they had dropped the murder charges against him in the death of the wife he didn't know he still had, Renata Vitale.

*W*ithin hours after I clobbered the killer senseless, the Holy Objects burial site yielded up a crudely sewn made-to-order oilskin bag big enough to protect the paintings for nearly eighty years. The excited chatter among the rival conservators and three reporters stopped as they carefully slipped out the treasures, shrouded in parachutes. Thinking of Alfonsa, I started to cry. She had known about the frost line and had taken care to hide the paintings below it. Gloved fingers opened up the parachute coverings, and our little crowd pushed closer to see.

I had brought Sister Ippolita. When we alighted from the T-Bird and the Bari sisters were shocked at the thin black cape she was wearing, Annamaria wrestled her into a down coat from the villa lost and found, Rosa plunked her plaid bomber hat with fake fur ear flaps down on the little nun's head, and Sofia insisted on a wool muffler and down mittens. Then we gently pushed Sister Ippolita to the front of the gathering, a ringside seat. By me, she represented the interests of the extraordinary Alfonsa Cambi.

Ippolita grunted at me. In Italian, she said, "You remember Alfonsa's bread?"

It took me a second. "The loaves she recorded in the log?"

Ippolita looked straight ahead, inscrutable. "It was people."

"What?"

"It was code for people. *Brioche*," said Sister Ippolita, lifting one hand oratorically, "was French Jews. *Pane toscano* was local partisans. It was a"—here she made a classic alms-begging gesture with her uplifted palm—"a subway." When she lifted her chin, the whole muffler rose.

I was astonished. "You mean an underground railroad?"

"Is that not a subway?"

I remembered how secretive Alfonsa had seemed. "How do you know?"

"I helped."

I sucked in cold Tuscan air. "You're just telling me this now?"

In the heavy down coat, she shrugged. "I'm a busy woman."

We watched while the teams exposed and separated the Van Gogh and the Caravaggio. When we all held our breath in the cool, bright daylight, we gazed in wonder at *The Painter on His Way to Work* and *St. Matthew and the Angel*. Leon and Alfonsa had saved these two masterpieces just half a year before a blaze swept the Berlin fire tower, where hundreds of paintings, drawings, and sculptures from the Kaiser-Friedrich Museum had been stored for safekeeping, and instead, destroyed them. More to themselves than the rest of us, the conservators pointed out damaged areas in the works, some crackling, some fading. Years of work ahead, however long it would take, cautious optimism.

Over the next two days, Pete and I pretty much lived together in his cottage. Nobody seemed to expect much from us. I showed up in the office just to update the cooking school's website. Pete showed up in the kitchen to raid the *frigorifero* for shrimp, scallops, eggplant, whatever he couldn't find in the cottage fridge. He declared he would not be pursuing a television career, after all. Best, he decided, to let his fifteen minutes of *Bellissimo!* fame be a heady little one-off in his life. I was content. We slept in a happy tangle, listening to rain on the roof. He frowned whenever his peculiar inheritance from the dead Renata struck him.

Over wine the second night, he told me he wanted to give the building in the piazza to Carlo and the other shopkeepers in that block, and they could run it as a co-op. Anything was fine by me. We tried new red wines, liked a couple of them. Benny Goodman felt about right. On day three, he seemed distracted, and if he was wondering about a life together, Pete and Nell, he didn't speak about it, and neither did I. A whole expanse of time unrolled before us, and we were happy.

"I have to go into town," he said, tucking in a white shirt after lunch. "The bank."

I looked up from the *Nero Wolfe Cookbook* I had found on Pete's shelves. "Ah."

He checked his watch, kissed me lightly, and was off.

Suddenly, he turned. "Nell, when I get back—" He seemed stuck.

"What?"

"We need to talk."

Coming from anyone else, those words are doom, uncorked. "Sure," I said, smiling.

Half an hour later, I ambled over to the main building, through the pinging mist that had returned—I shook my fist at it—and found Chef scrambling in a pointless, barnyard way in the kitchen. In tongue-tied Italian, he slid his phone across one of the counters and said something to Annamaria about the silent partner.

Handing me a bowl of fresh fruit to put out on the coffee table in the common room, she shot him a quizzical look. *"Che dici?"* What are you saying?

Chef was decked out in a black collarless shirt and jeans that actually fit him reasonably well. Both hands splayed out over his head, like he was going for a hold that would lift it clear off his neck. *"Troppo presto,"* he said in some kind of agitation. Too soon. What I usually thought of as his Al Pacino peepers now fixed first me with a look of wild-eyed desperation and then Annamaria. She gave up trying to make sense of him and turned away. "Pierfranco is on his way, but—but—"

I watched Chef Claudio Orlandini as he tried to find words and struggled to move his limbs in ways familiar to a bocce champ but failed, and I wondered if he was having a stroke. Maybe this was not the time to mention I had just fielded an email from the *Hot Chef* show, letting Chef Claudio Orlandini know they are in receipt of his video submission and will be letting him know in a time frame that sounded to me like before the next ice age and that he should have a nice day. I regarded the other person in the room. Since Annamaria was placidly rinsing vegetables in the sink, I decided she knew Chef's garden variety fits better than anyone, and she was unconcerned.

So I headed toward the common room with the fruit bowl, where I stood serenely in front of the expanse of wall that would hold a tribute to the wartime work of Sister Alfonsa Cambi. Then I looked around, considering other possibilities for fruit. When I heard a car door slam in the courtyard, and it didn't have the heavy, rusty creak of the T-Bird, I knew it wasn't Pete back from town.

Chef came howling at a run, yelling something again about a silent partner, damn it all to hellfire, with Sofia right at his heels, her arms laden with clean, fluffy towels. She gave Chef a quick, disapproving look up and down, like he had forgotten to zip his fly—always a possibility—and at the sound of feet on the gravel just outside, started to push open the door.

Just then I heard the T-Bird squeal into the courtyard, followed by the heavy thud of the door, and Pete, yelling. "Nell, wait! Wait! Nell, I can explain—"

As I turned slowly to the door Sofia was holding open with a smile, I took in the man who stepped over the threshold into the villa. With a gasp, I set the bowl down on nothing at all, where it broke, and stared at the newcomer.

It was Dr. Val Valenti.

My father.

Gorgonzola con Salsa di Fichi
(Gorgonzola with Fig Sauce)

SERVES 4

*In memory of my chef cousin, Lisa Fein Lang,
who gave me this easy and delicious recipe*

1 c. dried figs
1 c. water
¼ c. sugar
1 two-inch strip of lemon peel
1 two-inch strip of orange peel
4 thin slices of Gorgonzola piccante

Trim off hard stems from the figs. Chop the figs finely.

In a small saucepan, combine the figs, water, sugar, lemon zest, and orange zest. Bring to a simmer and cook, stirring occasionally, until the liquid is reduced and thickened, about 15–20 minutes. Let cool. Discard lemon and orange zest.

Place the Gorgonzola on serving plates. Serve fig sauce on the side.

ACKNOWLEDGMENTS

Thanks first and always to Emilie Richards, Casey Daniels, and Serena B. Miller—great brainstormers and friends. Thanks, too, to editor Miranda Hill, agent John Talbot, and Dean Yoder, Cleveland Museum of Art conservator of paintings.

Ready to find
your next great read?

Let us help.

Visit prh.com/nextread

Penguin
Random
House